ALMA CLASSICS LTD
Hogarth House
32–34 Paradise Road
Richmond
Surrey TW9 1SE
United Kingdom
www.almaclassics.com

This collection first published by Alma Classics Ltd in 2015

Extra Material © Richard Parker

Printed and bound by CPI Group (UK) Ltd, Croydon, CR0 4YY

ISBN: 978-1-84749-565-5

Contents

Other books by F. SCOTT FITZGERALD
published by Alma Classics

All the Sad Young Men

Babylon Revisited and Other Stories

Basil and Josephine

The Beautiful and Damned

Flappers and Philosophers

The Great Gatsby

The Intimate Strangers and Other Stories

The Last Tycoon

The Last of the Belles and Other Stories

The Love Boat and Other Stories

The Pat Hobby Stories

Tales of the Jazz Age

Tender Is the Night

This Side of Paradise

F. Scott Fitzgerald (1896–1940)

Edward Fitzgerald,
Fitzgerald's father

Mary McQuillan Fitzgerald,
Fitzgerald's mother

Ginevra King

Zelda Fitzgerald

The Fitzgeralds' house in Montgomery, Alabama

The Fitzgeralds' grave in Rockville, Maryland,
inscribed with the closing line from *The Great Gatsby*

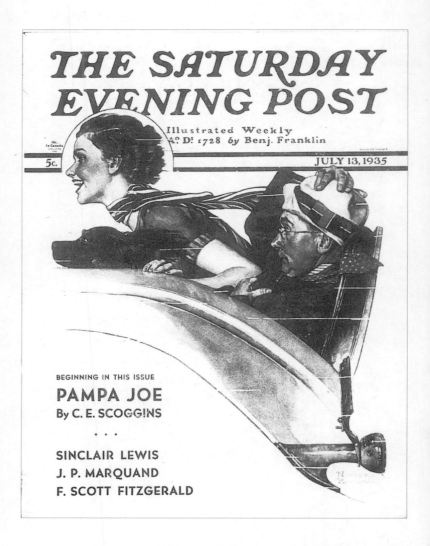

Cover of the 13th July 1935 issue of the *Saturday Evening Post*,
which included Fitzgerald's story 'Zone of Accident'

Image on the Heart
and Other Stories

Zone of Accident

1

B ILL MISSED THE USUAL FEELING of leaving her house. Usually there was a wrench as the door closed upon the hall light and he found himself alone again in the dark street. Usually there was a series of light-headed emotions that sometimes sent him galloping half a block or made him walk very slow, frowning and content. He wouldn't have recognized the houses nearby going away from them; he only knew what they looked like when he came towards them, before hers was in sight.

Tonight there was this talk of California, the intensity of this talk about California. Half-familiar, suddenly menacing names – Santa Barbara, Carmel, Coronado – Hollywood. She'd try to get a screen test – more fun! Meanwhile he would be completing his second year as an intern here in the city.

"But mother and I would go to the shore anyhow," Amy said.

"California's so far away."

When he reached the hospital, he ran into George Schoatze under the murky yellow lamps of the long corridor.

"What's doing?" he asked.

"Nothing. I'm looking for somebody else's stethoscope – that's how busy I am."

"How's everything out in Roland Park?"

"Bill, it's all settled."

"What?" Hilariously, Bill slapped George's shoulder. "Well, congratulations! Let me be the first—"

"She was the first."

"—let me be the second to congratulate you."

"Don't say anything, will you – not yet?"

"All right." He whistled. "Ink scarcely dry on your medical certificate and you let some girl write 'meal ticket' on it."

"How about you?" countered George. "How about that love life of yours?"

"Obstacles are developing," said Bill gloomily. "Matter of climate."

His heart winced as he heard his own words. Walking along in the direction of the accident room, he had a foretaste of the summer's loneliness. Last year he had taken his love where he found it. But Thea Singleton, the demon anaesthetist, was now at the new Medical Centre in New York; and gone also was the young lady in the pathology department who sliced human ears thinner than carnation sandwiches, and the other attractive ghoul on the brain-surgery staff who spent her time rushing into people's brains with a sketch pad and pencil. They had been properly aware that, seriously speaking, Bill was nobody's business – that he was in the safety zone. And now, in a fortnight, there was a girl who didn't know centigrade from Fahrenheit, but who looked like a rose inside a bubble and had promised to trade exclusive personal rights with him in another June.

The accident room was in a dull humour. Holidays are the feasts of glory there, when the speed merchants send in their victims and the dusky brand of Marylander exhibits his Saturday-night specimens of razor sculpture. Tonight the tiled floor and walls, the rolling tables packed with splints and bandages were all for the benefit of a single client, just being unstrapped from the examination table.

"It's been wonderful," he said, humbly drunk. "I'm going to send you doctors a barrel of oysters." Barber by trade, he stood swaying gently in his worn coat. "My father's the biggest fish dealer in Carsontown."

"That'll be fine," the intern said. The patient regarded his bandaged hand proudly.

"I can take it," he boasted, "can't I?"

"You certainly can. But don't push your hand through any more windows."

His friend was summoned from without and, wobbling a little, the injured barber strutted out. The same swing of the door admitted a stout man of fifty who blurted incoherent words to Doctor Moore, intern on duty; Bill turned meanwhile to Miss Wales, who for a decade had been priestess of this battlefield. "Any high comedy?" he asked.

"Mostly regulars," she answered. "Minnie the Moocher turned up again, carrying her head under her arm and wanting it sewed on again. She was cut this morning. Why is it niggers never know they're sick till after dark?"

"Terror by night; let's see – *a negotio perambulante in tenebris.*"*

"Whatever that means," agreed Miss Wales. "And there's another coloured number with a hundred-and-three-point-two waiting for the medical man."

"I'll take a look at him."

Doctor Moore had meanwhile backed away from his exigent vis-à-vis; he turned to Bill.

"Here's a mystery for you. This man—"

"You don't understand!" cried the stout man. "We can't let anybody know! She made me promise!"

"Who did?"

"This lady outside in the car. She's bleeding from her whole back. I live only two blocks away, so I brought her here."

Simultaneously the interns started for the door and the man followed, insisting: "It's got to be no publicity. We only came because we couldn't get a doctor to the house."

In a small sedan in the dark, deserted street slumped a bundled form that emitted a faint moan as Moore opened the door. It took but an instant for Doctor Moore to feel the blood-soaked dress.

"Get the stretcher out quick!"

The middle-aged man followed Bill to the door.

"It must be kept quiet," he persisted.

"You want her to bleed to death?" Bill answered sharply.

A few minutes later, the patient was wheeled into the white light of the accident room. A curtain was flung aside from a cubicle which contained an operating table, and the two interns began untangling the ravel of dish towels, torn sheeting and broadcloth in which she was swathed. It was a young girl, the pale colour of her own ashen hair. Pearls lay along her gasping throat, and her back was slit from waist to shoulder.

"Lost a lot of blood," Moore said. He was looking at the blood-pressure gauge. "Say, it's low – eighty over fifty! We'll pack the wound right away. Tell Miss Wales."

Miss Wales faced the father, as he admitted himself to be, and spoke impatiently, pad in hand: "You've got to tell the name. We can't take care of your daughter if you won't tell the name."

"Doctor Moore wants to pack the wound right away," said Bill. To the father he added, "Wait outside. Your daughter's badly hurt. What did it?"

"It was an accident."

"What did it – a knife?"

At his peremptory voice, the man nodded.

"You didn't do it?

"No! I can't tell you about it except that it was an accident."

He was talking at Bill's vanishing back; presently, bumped by a hurrying nurse and orderly, he was pushed out the door.

Back in the cubicle, Bill whispered, "How's the pulse?"

"It's thready – I can hardly get it."

He was sponging the wound, exposing the lovely young lines of the back. "This is going to leave a beautiful scar."

He spoke low, but the patient heard him and murmured: "No scar."

Bill called Moore's attention to the pearls, and whispered, "This girl's well off; maybe she cares about her back. You ought to send for a good surgeon."

"And let her bleed to death while we wait?"

"I was thinking of the resident."

"You medical guys!" said Moore disgustedly.

"All right," said Bill. "Anyhow, I'm going to get the father's consent and protect you that much."

"He's not John D. Rockefeller.* Or why did he come to the accident room?" Moore dried his hands thoroughly. "How do you know these are real pearls – five-and-ten, maybe."

6

"I know this woman's well dressed – or was till half an hour ago."
Bill went out in the hall again.

"I want this woman's name," he said to the father. "If you won't tell me, I'll trace it through the car licence."

"Labroo!" he breathed, incomprehensibly.

"Who?"

This time Bill heard the name, Loretta Brooke, but it meant nothing to him until the man added: "in the movies". Then Bill remembered it vaguely.

"Our name's Bach – that's German for Brooke. Loretta stopped off here to see me on her way out to Hollywood…" He gulped and swallowed the rest. "I can't say any more. They throw them right out of the movies for any trouble. First thing she said was, 'Papa, keep it a secret.' But she kept bleeding and I couldn't get hold of our doctor."

The accident room grew suddenly crowded – there was a boy with a twisted knee; a Jamaica Negro badly cut about the head, but refusing treatment with the surly manners of his island. The usual number of second-year medical students had drifted in and stood about in the way. Pushing through them to the cubicle, Bill closed the curtain behind him; Moore had begun to sew the wound.

"The blood pressure is down to sixty over thirty-five," he muttered. "We'll have to do a transfusion. Better be getting a donor."

Bill went to the telephone; in a few minutes Moore came out, saying anxiously:

"I don't like waiting any longer. I can hardly feel the pulse now." He raised his voice. "Isn't there somebody here that sells blood – a Group Four?"

The second-year medical students moved about uncomfortably.

"I'm Group Three myself," Moore continued, "and I know Boone and Jacoby are Group Three."

Bill hesitated; his own blood was Group Four – the kind it is safe to transfuse to anyone – but he had never given any blood, never had the economic necessity of selling any, as did some interns.

"All right," he said, "I'm your man."

"Let's get them matched up then."

7

As he arranged matters for his little operation, Bill felt a broad amusement. He felt that part of himself was "going into the movies". Wouldn't the future blushes rising to the cheeks of Loretta Brooke be, in a sense, his blushes? When she cried, "My blood boils with rage," would it not be his blood that was boiling for the excitement of the public? When she announced that the bluest blood in America flowed in her veins, would that not be a subtle tribute to the honourable line of Dr William Tullivers, of which he was the fourth?

He remembered suddenly that Intern George Schoatze was also Group Four, and thought fantastically of sending for him instead and determining the effect of the placid content of George's veins upon the theatrical temperament.

By the time he had been bled, refreshed himself with a drink and got up feeling curiously well, Doctor Moore's suture was finished and Bill waited around with more than personal interest to see the case through; elated that, before the transfusion was finished, Miss Loretta Brooke's blood pressure had risen and the pulse was stronger. He took the news to the man waiting in the hall. His chief concern was still the concealment of the scandal.

"She'll have to stay here," Bill said. "The hospital authorities must know who she is, but we'll protect her from the newspapers. She'll want a room in a private ward, won't she? And a private nurse?"

"Anything she would need."

The valuable person of Loretta Brooke, strapped face downward to a rolling stretcher, was pushed by an orderly into an elevator and disappeared into the quiet anonymity of the corridors above, and Mr Bach was persuaded to go home and sleep. By midnight the great hospital was asleep too: the night porter sat in a small-hour daze under the great stone figure of Christ in the entrance chamber, and the night nurses walked lightly along the silent distances of the halls; only in a few corners people stayed awake to suffer silently or noisily, to die or to return to life; and in the accident room, still brightly gleaming at two, at three, at four, all the processes of life went on repeating themselves to the swing of Miss Wales's starched dress, as the beaten and the broken, the drunken and the terrified trickled in the door.

Bill dreamt about being in Hollywood, parading up and down in a one-piece bathing suit before a stand full of judges; across his breast he wore a sash with red letters on it which spelt "Mr Baltimore".

2

DOCTOR TULLIVER CAME into the room at the same moment that a blowing shutter let in a burst of sunshine. The sunshine sought out Miss Brooke, enclosing her still-pale face in a frame and lighting one cheek to a faint geranium. Her eyes were half closed, but as he came in they opened – and opened – until he could scarcely believe there were such eyes, and simultaneously a small tongue tip passed momentarily over her upper lip, changing it to a brighter shade.

She looked him over from his fine, serious face to the white suit, unwrinkled by a new day.

"If it isn't Doctor Tulliver!" she said calmly. "Where've you been these last three days?"

"How do you feel?"

"All right. When can I really lie on my back?"

"Why, you're practically lying on it. A person can *see* you now; you've really got a third dimension."

"I keep worrying about the scar," she said.

"You needn't worry about it," Bill assured her. "In the first place, a better spot couldn't have been chosen if anyone wanted to avoid marking you up."

"Will it show in a low-backed dress?"

"Hardly at all. Moore did a good job and the plastic surgeon improved it. Why, I've seen bigger scars from a chest tap."

She sighed.

"I never thought I'd see the inside of this hospital, though I was born two blocks away from here and I used to go by it on roller skates."

"Very different from me. I always knew I'd see the inside of it. My father was an intern here."

"What do you interns have to do – just stay around here for ever, like a monk or something?"

"Until they're no longer afraid to let us practise outside."

"I suppose you make love to the trained nurses. That's what the doctors did in a picture I was in."

"All day long," he assured her. "Every intern has certain nurses assigned to him."

"You look it, Doctor Tulliver."

"What?"

"You look as if you were very good at it."

"Thanks," Bill was pleased. "I certainly will have to grow a pointed beard and get down to business."

"My back itches. Shall I scratch it?"

"And make the scar worse? No, we'll get them to change the dressings oftener."

She shifted restlessly.

"What a thing to happen! How did that halfwit find where my father lived?"

Bill busied himself with a gadget on the blood-pressure machine, but he was listening eagerly. It was the first time she had mentioned the origin of the accident in the three weeks she had been there.

"What do you think he wanted?" Miss Brooke demanded suddenly.

"Who?"

"You might as well know. I like you better than anybody here, and I feel like telling somebody. It was my old dancing partner – a man I danced with at a hotel in New York two years ago. He wanted me to marry him and take him back to Hollywood and get him a job."

"So he took a whack at you?"

"I promised I'd see him in New York when I came east. And when I came to visit my father, he followed me down here. It was terrible; I hate to think about it. He got threatening and I took up a fork and told him he'd better look out, and then he picked up a paring knife." She shivered. "After he cut me, he went right on out and passed my father on the porch without even bothering to tell him what had happened. Can you imagine? I didn't realize what had happened myself for about five minutes."

"Have you heard about him since?"

"There was a crazy note from New York – sorry and all that. Sorry! Can you imagine? But nobody knows and you mustn't tell."

"I won't."

It was, indeed, the doctors who protected her from herself in the matter of undesirable publicity, taking a gossipy night nurse off the case and discouraging the visits of hairdressers and manicurists. But the doctors came themselves; there was usually a small visiting gallery of interns, assistant residents and even greying medical men of mark, yielding to the glamour of a calling which the people had pronounced to be of infinitely greater prestige than their own.

"I'm getting started out there for the second time," she told Bill. "I was a sort of Shirley Temple* of ten years ago – that's why you all remember my name. Now they're trying to make me a real actress, and the question is: can they?"

"It's done. We – I mean a girl and I – found one of your pictures at a second-run theatre and we thought you were great."

"A girl – you mean your girl? Have you got a girl?"

He admitted it.

"Oh."

"In fact, her one ambition is to meet you. She's going to California this summer and she wants to hear about Hollywood."

"She wants to go into pictures?"

"I hope not. No, she just talks about it – like every other American girl – about how wonderful it'd be."

"I don't think it's so wonderful," Loretta said.

"You've been in it all your life." He hesitated. "I wish you'd tell her why you don't think it's wonderful. I hate to have her going away with some crazy notion."

"I'd like to meet her."

"To tell you the *ab*solute truth, she's downstairs now. She'd like nothing better than to come up for just a minute."

"Tell her to come up."

"That's mighty kind of you. She's been begging me—"

"It seems a very little thing to do for the man who saved my life."

"What?" He laughed. "Oh, we don't think of that as—"

"Never mind. It's made me feel sometimes as if we were – oh, blood brothers, like Indians, you know. Now that I know you're engaged, I can confess that. You think I'm silly."

Admitting hastily that he did, Bill went to get Amy.

When he introduced them they exchanged an appraising look, and it struck Bill that Amy was the more vivid of the two. It took a moment of looking at Loretta Brooke to realize that there was a constant activity in her face. There was always something going on – some little story, grave or gay, that took a moment to catch up with before it could be followed. After that it was a face that could be looked at almost permanently, with a fear of missing something if one looked away. Amy, on the contrary, was there all at once, darkly and breathlessly pictorial.

They talked of being in pictures.

"I can't imagine not liking it," Amy said.

"It's not liking or disliking. It's just plain work to me; when I was a child, it was play that I didn't quite understand. When I was fifteen, it was worry about whether I'd be pretty. Now it's fighting to catch on or hang on, and there's so little that you can do about it."

"But it's such a wonderful game," Amy said. "And if you do win—"

"There are games where the price isn't so high."

"Like what?"

Bill said lightly:

"Love and marriage, darling."

"Don't be absurd," said Amy. "There's nothing especially distinguished about love." She laughed and turned to Loretta. "Unless it's very good love in a very good picture."

"You've got to have a model somewhere," said Bill.

"We've got to die, too, but why bring it up?"

Loretta drew the onus of the exchange upon herself: "It's a very artificial life. All the time after I was – hurt, I kept thinking of the impression I was making on the doctors."

"And ever since then," Bill said, "the doctors have been thinking about the impression they make on you. I don't know what we'll do when you leave."

Driving home, Amy said:

"She's wonderful, but she just doesn't know how lucky she was to be born in the movies." After a moment's hesitation she added suddenly, "Bill, I've decided to go in the contest after all. You think it's silly—"

He groaned.

"—but it's really a big thing – girls from cities all over the East. I didn't go in the preliminary because you objected so, but Willard Hubbel thinks he can slip me in anyhow. In fact he knows he can, because he's handling the newspaper end."

"Of all the—"

"Wait till I tell you everything. It isn't so much to go in the movies, but I'd get a free trip to California. Oh, Bill, don't look so gloomy."

They rode along in silence for a moment.

"I'm glad I met Loretta Brooke. It'll be something to talk about to this other man."

"What other man?"

"This man who's coming from Hollywood to run the thing. Willard Hubbel's bringing him to see me tonight."

"Oh, he is?"

"You said you had to go to the hospital early, Bill."

"All right, darling," he said grimly, "all right. Have your fun, but just don't expect me to go into a dance about it."

They stopped in front of her house, and as he pulled her lovely head close to his for a moment, it didn't seem to matter what she did as long as he possessed her heart.

Life in a hospital is a long war on many fronts – vigorous offensives are followed by dreary sieges, by inexplicable lulls, by excursions and alarms. An alarm sounded suddenly that week – the dreaded tocsin of influenza. The disease settled like a snowfall on the hospital; members of the staff came down with it and all the wards, public and private, were full. On double duty, then triple duty, Bill had little time for Amy and less for Loretta Brooke, who lingered in bed running a very slight intermittent fever.

He talked for her, though – that is, he answered her long-distance calls from California from her agent and her producer. He affected the tone of a very haughty old doctor, but the producer's questions revealed a persistent suspiciousness:

"We'd like to know when we can expect Miss Brooke."

"We can't exactly say."

"If you tell us what the trouble is, we can figure out ourselves how long it'll be."

"I've told you it was an accident – no more serious than a broken arm. We don't give out medical details except to the patient's family. Miss Brooke ought to be starting west in a week or so, as soon as her temperature is normal."

"Sounds a little phoney to me," the voice growled over three thousand miles of wire. "It isn't a broken nose or anything like that?"

"It is not."

When the man concluded, with a vague hint that the hospital might be detaining Miss Brooke for profit, Bill rang off.

Five minutes later, as a sort of postscript, a mild-mannered secretary called to apologize – Mr Minska, she said, had gone to lunch.

"You mean supper," said Bill irritably.

"Out here it's one o'clock," explained the secretary.

Bill found time to drop in and tell Loretta Brooke.

"They owe me a vacation," she said. "Anyhow, I like the atmosphere here, now that I can sit up. You've all been so good to me."

"We'll get rid of you as soon as that fever disappears."

"Please sit down for a minute. Lately you've been acting as if I was rather repulsive."

He sat tentatively on the side of the bed.

"Half the men in our service are down with flu," he said. "That is the first time I've had a minute."

He had had no supper, but as her face brightened, he felt a sudden pity for all this youth and loveliness penned up here because of an idiot with a paring knife.

She snuggled into the lace of her negligee.

"Why don't you come out to Hollywood?" she demanded. "I could get you a test. What do they pay you here?"

He laughed.

"Nothing."

"What?" She sat up in bed. "Nothing?"

"We get our board."

"Don't they pay any doctors in hospitals?"

"No. Only the nurses. And the patients are paid after the first three years."

"Why, I never heard of any such thing in my life." Loretta's idea began to grip her really: "Why don't you come to Hollywood? Honestly, you've got more It than Clark Gable."*

He winced with embarrassment.

"We make lots of money later," he said lightly.

She considered.

"Now that I think, I never did hear of anybody marrying a doctor."

"I never did either. I don't know a single doctor who got himself a wife."

"But you're getting married."

"That's different. I'm lucky enough to have a little money of my own."

"I suppose I'll end marrying somebody in pictures," she said. "Somebody with a steady future, like a cameraman."

The arrested rhythm of the hospital, the flow of quiet along the corridors, the disparity of their two destinies always made what they said seem more intimate than it was. When he moved to get up from the bed, something happened so swiftly that he was not conscious of any transition – she leant forward into the circle of his arms and he was kissing her lips.

He was not thinking, too fatigued even to be stirred by her nearness, too fatigued to worry about a position that might compromise his assistant residency. It was only his muscles that held her for a moment, then lowered her gently to the pillows.

She welled over in a little sighing sob.

"Oh, what's the use? You don't care. You saved my life, but you don't—"

The prospect of a long night of work unrolled itself before him.

"I like you enormously," he said, "but after all, we *are* in a hospital."

There were other objections, but for the moment he couldn't think what they were. He knew the attraction of the well for the sick, and such things had happened before, sometimes ludicrously and unpleasantly. But during the next few days, as he moved like a ghost through a maze of cases, he remembered this as having been fun.

He had been forty-nine consecutive hours on his feet, and the nurses coming on duty had begun to feel a sort of crazy awe for his fatigue; they had begun babying him a little, allowing him extra time to leave orders as his mind fumbled with the transition from one case to another. He began to be a little proud of his power of survival. On rounds he found time to ask news of Loretta from the nurse at the desk.

"Is she still running that fever? I don't understand it. It can't be from the wound."

The matter had bothered him as he watched over many graver fevers. He wanted the business of her illness to be cleared up.

"I just this moment gave her the thermometer, Doctor Tulliver. I'm going in now."

"Never mind – I'll see."

He went towards her room quietly, and with a step taken from the rhythm of the dying, half-asleep, he paused in the doorway; this is what he saw:

Loretta held the thermometer in her mouth, but simply between tongue and lips, moving her mouth over it and then taking it out and looking at it, returning it, rubbing it, looking at it, frowning – shaking it once very gently. Then, with the air of having achieved her object, she removed it permanently.

At that moment she saw Bill, and simultaneously he grasped the whole matter – the business of faking the temperature by which she had lengthened her stay for two weeks. A current of resentment flowed through his fatigue as her egotism stood out ugly green against the sombre blacks and whites of the past fifty hours. He was angry at having spent worry on her in this environment of serious illness and frantic haste, and professionally he felt a disgust at having been fooled. He thought of the phone calls from Hollywood and his answers from the authority of his profession – answers now made into lies.

"I'm afraid that's a pretty delicate instrument to fool with," he said.

She broke into real tears as the thermometer broke into glass ones and Bill left the room.

He drove to Amy's house, forgoing his turn to sleep; he had a sudden need for a world where people were "brought up" so that they could not do certain things. The young doctor, having abandoned more than a fair share of illusions, subscribes instead to a code of ethics more rigid than that of a West Point cadet – subscribes so firmly that he can joke about it, mock at it, blaspheme it and profane it, and do it no more harm that if it were earth itself. That is why a doctor who has lost this thing is nearly the most sinister character of which one can conceive.

He walked into Amy's house without knocking. At the door of the drawing room he stopped, stared... then he sat down, feeling more tired than he had ever been in his life.

"…Why Bill," Amy said, "don't let's make a scene of it."

When the gentleman from Hollywood had taken his departure, Amy cried:

"He asked me to kiss him once, Bill. He's been so good about this, and it didn't mean anything: he's got a real girl in California and he was lonely."

"Aren't you a real girl?"

She came close to him, frightened.

"Bill, I could kill myself right this minute for letting it happen."

She pressed against him and he found himself patting her shoulder absently.

"So we won't make a fuss about one kiss, will we?" she pleaded.

He shook his head.

"That was a hundred kisses; you don't belong to me any more."

"You mean you don't want me?"

"Yes, yes, I guess I want you too much – that's just the trouble."

He drove back to the hospital and, to avoid meeting anyone, went in through the accident-room entrance; from behind the screen door came the murmur of a drunken Negro and, as he passed on, Miss Wales came out into the corridor.

"Doctor Tulliver."

"How do you happen to be on day duty?

"There isn't anybody else. And believe me, I'm glad. Look what Santa Claus brought."

She displayed a ring set with three small emeralds.

"Getting married?"

"Not I. This is from our little patient, the actress – Loretta herself. She stopped by on her way out."

"What?"

"Just ten minutes ago. And was she pretty in her clothes? I hardly knew her."

But Bill was gone, walking fast and feeling very afraid.

At the desk he found that Miss Brooke had gone for good and left no address behind.

3

A MY PHONED HIM THREE TIMES that night; the third time he answered.

"You've got to know the whole truth," she said. "It may sound commercial and calculating, but at least you'll see it wasn't that I wanted to kiss him, Bill."

"Skip it," he said wearily.

"But I can't skip it," she wailed. "I tried to be attractive to this man, because if I don't get this free trip, then Mother and I can't go at all. Mother went over her accounts at the bank yesterday and we have literally nothing to spare."

"And the kiss fixed it all up," he said ironically. "Now you're sure to be elected?"

"Not at all. It's much more difficult than that," she said with unconscious humour. "But now I'm in the running, even though I wasn't in the preliminaries. These are the finals; he's slipped me in instead of a girl who won in Washington."

"And now I suppose all you have to do is neck Will Hays,* Laurel and Hardy and Mickey Mouse."

"If that's how you feel—"

"I go on duty at twelve," he said. "I'm going to rest now, so I maybe won't fall down in the corridors."

"But, Bill, can't you tell me one sweet thing, so I can sleep? I'll just fret and worry all night long and look terrible the day after tomorrow. Say one sweet thing."

"Kisses," he said obligingly. "Fifty-foot kisses."

The contest was sponsored by Films Par Excellence, a string of newspapers, and the ABC chain stores. The main contest – there was also a contest for children – had been narrowed down to thirty girls from as many cities in the North Central States. Each was on hand, her expenses having been paid to the city.

For several weeks all this had been in a newspaper, and each day Bill had gazed unsympathetically at the faces of the three judges: Willard Hubbel, local dramatic critic; Augustus Vogel, a local painter; and E.P. Poole, a chain-store magnate who understood what the public liked. But tonight the paper screamed something new at Bill which caused him to jump and pace his room. The magnate had suffered a collapse, but luckily Miss Loretta Brooke, local product and Wampas Baby Star of a year ago, had consented to take his place.

She was still in town. The city seemed to enlarge, take on colour, take on sound, take on life; it stood suddenly erect on its corner-stones, when, twenty-four hours before, it had been flat as a city of cards. He was shocked to find how much her presence mattered. Women were liars and cheats – Loretta's deliberate malingering to remain in the hospital in a time of stress was less defensible than what Amy had done. Nevertheless, Bill got thoughtfully into his dinner coat. He would look over the contest, after all.

When he arrived at the hotel, the lobby was already full of curi-ous ones cloistering the stately passage of slender stately figures. At his first sight of these latter, each one seemed unbelievably beautiful; but by the time he had mounted in the elevator with six of them and squirmed through a crush of a dozen getting out, he decided that Amy might very well hold her own.

He thought so again when he saw Amy, unfailingly lovely and picturesque; she stood in a group watching the preliminary con-test for children, which had already started; and when she saw him, the wild excitement in her face made way momentarily for a look of sad wistfulness. She beckoned but, pretending not to see the gesture, he made his way to one of the chairs that lined the sides of the hall. On a dais at the end sat the judges, Loretta in the middle. At the sight of her, he wondered that the girls down-stairs had caught his eye for an instant, wondered that Willard Hubbel and Augustus Vogel, the painter, who flanked her, could concentrate on the mincing brat who danced and mimed before them. The face that, in the accident room, had been tragically drained of blood, the wan face on the hospital pillow, with its just slightly doubtful smile, was framed now by bright clothes, lighted by converging shafts of attention and admiration. This personage, poised and momentous, was not the girl who had broken the thermometer, and to whom he had spoken bitterly – and suddenly Bill wanted her back there on the quiet ward, away from these terribly inquisitive eyes.

The children's contest progressed slowly. Difficult as it was to nag and coax the candidate into animation, it was harder still to extinguish the flame when time was up. One mother had caught his attention from the first – a thwarted mother, a determined mother with fanatical eyes. While the child spoke, the mother's teeth were set as if she were holding her offspring in her mouth; and as she withdrew reluctantly to wait for the verdict, her gaze searched the judges savagely for any hint of prejudice or collusion. Ten minutes later, when the verdict was announced, Bill did not associate her with the word that slipped down the row of chairs: "Is there a doctor in the audience?" But slipping quietly out into the ante-room, he saw her writhing in the arms of two strong men.

"Let me at them!" she shrieked. "I'll kill them! My baby won! It was fixed! They paid them! That woman! Oh, how could they?"

"Are you a doctor?"

Bill sized up the situation and ducked it.

"You need a psychiatrist," he said.

"Are you one?"

He shook his head and walked back to his seat. He remembered once there had been a string of patients admitted to the nerve clinic of the hospital who were haunted by a horror film.

"Dementia Hollywoodensis. Manifestation X."

The real contest had begun. Singly the girls advanced, making the circuit of a table, then sitting at it, taking something from a pocketbook. Then they answered the questions of the judges:

"I'm a student at the Musical Institute…"

"Of course I'd like to go to Hollywood…"

"I've had Little Theatre experience…"

"I went to Wellesley for a year…"

There was a dying-swan girl, who denied that she admired Lillian Gish,* and a wedding-cake girl, and a full-lipped waitress, and a superior art student. There were three Garbos and a Little Black

Hat; there was a girl with overwhelming pep; a young girl with an old complexion; a professional dancer; a neat little Napoleon.

The judges noted on their lists, and in lulls talked among themselves. Bill had the impression that although she did not look in his direction, Loretta knew he was there.

When Amy was nearing the head of the waiting line, it became evident that this part of the contest was to be turbulent also. By the door, the representative of Films Par Excellence was involved in a lively argument with a hard, bright blonde and her escort, a neat, sinister man in a neat, sinister dinner coat, and Bill realized that the argument seemed to concern Amy. Once more he edged his way to the back of the room; the moving-picture man was urging his noisy vis-à-vis towards the door.

"Oh, Bill, this is terrible," Amy whispered. "That's the girl who won in Washington. You see, I lived in Washington once, so they slipped me in instead. And that gunman with her is perfectly furious."

"I don't blame him."

"But she's too tough for pictures."

"She could play tough parts."

For the second time that evening a cry came through the crowd that a doctor was needed immediately.

"Lord!" Bill exclaimed. "Why didn't they hold this in the accident room?"

As he went outside, Amy's name was called; he saw her pull herself together and start towards the judges' dais.

"Goodbye to all that," he thought morosely.

The new casualty was stretched on a carpet in the hall. It was the moving-picture man. He had been struck with some weapon which might have been a blackjack or even a railroad tie. His temple was torn open and a curtain of blood was seeping down his face. The neat, sinister young man and his girl were not to be found.

"Needs stitches, and I've got nothing here," Bill said. "I'll put on a temporary bandage and someone better rush him to the hospital."

When the victim had been wheeled into the elevator, Bill phoned the accident room at the hospital.

"I'm shipping over another movie case, Miss Wales... No, you needn't bother how the stitches look this time. And you might send over a fleet of ambulances to the hotel, because now they're going to pick the winner and things may get really rough."

When he re-entered the ballroom, the judges had retired to make their decision; the contestants stood about with families and admirers, some insouciant, some obviously jumpy, some pale with the fatiguing wait, some still fresh and lovely. Among these latter was Amy, who ran over to Bill.

"I was terrible," she said. "Oh, Bill, I know you don't want me to win, but please pray for me."

"I do want you to win," he said.

"Do you think I have a chance? I think Willard'll vote for me; it depends on the other two."

"Your Hollywood boyfriend has gone to the hospital," he said.

"Oh, has he?" In her excitement she didn't know what she was saying. "He said he always wanted to be a doctor..."

A newspaperman spoke to Bill in a low voice:

"Miss Brooke would like to see you for a moment, doctor."

"God! She's not hurt, is she?"

"No, she just asked me to find you."

Loretta stood outside the judgement chamber.

"I'm glad you're still speaking to me," she said.

"Of course I am."

"Well, listen. Do you want your girl to go to Hollywood?"

Her eyes, looking into his, were full of the question, as if she had considered a long time before asking it.

"Do I? Why, how can I—"

"Because it's up to me. The vote is one and one. Your girl is more of a stage type. All that colouring won't count out there. But – it's up to you." And now he could not deny there was a question behind the question in her voice. In a turmoil, he tried to think.

"Why... why, I don't seem to care any more," he said. And then suddenly, "Hell, yes, let her go."

She made a mark on the paper she held in her hand.

"Of course, if she makes good she may not come back."

"She doesn't belong to me any more," he said simply.

"Then I'll go tell them." She lingered a moment. "I hope I'll be able to will her my luck. You see, I'm not very keen to stay in pictures – if I can find something else."

He stared after her; then, after what seemed a long time, he was listening to her voice speaking from the dais, and as far as her voice reached her beauty seemed to flow into the intervening space, dominating it:

"...so it seems to us... these beautiful girls... Miss Amy... represent this section of the country... others not feel disappointed... You were the most beautiful candidates for screen honours I have ever seen."

To his surprise, no one fainted, no one wailed aloud; there was suddenly a loud boom, like a cannon shot across the room, and Bill jumped, but it was only the flashlight photographers going to work. Loretta and Amy were photographed over and over, singly and together. They looked very lovely together, and it didn't seem to matter which one Hollywood had – that is, it didn't matter except to Bill. And in the sudden ecstatic joy of meeting Loretta's eye, all his rancour at Amy disappeared, and he wished her well.

"The movies give and the movies take away," he mused, "and it's all right with me."

Fate in Her Hands

W HEN CAROL WAS NINETEEN years old she went into a little tent set in a corner of a ballroom. There was music playing – a tune called 'The Breakaway'.* All the evening many people, mostly girls, had been going into that tent, where they faced a fiery little blonde woman whose business was the private affairs of everyone else.

"You don't really believe in any of this, do you?" she asked Carol surprisingly. "I don't want to worry people about things that they can't help."

"I'm not the worrying sort," Carol said. "Whatever you tell me about my hand, I won't be able to remember it straight in half an hour."

"That's good." The woman smiled reassuringly, not at all offended. "Especially because I wouldn't want to worry such a lovely girl – one with so much consideration – such a gift for people…"

"I won't be worried." Carol repeated, embarrassed at this last. "Go ahead."

The fortune-teller looked once more into the outheld palms and sat back in her camp chair.

"For a beginning: you'll be married this year."

Carol laughed noncommittally.

"Are you engaged?"

"Not exactly. But anyhow, we hadn't planned to do anything about it till spring."

The woman looked into her hand again quickly.

"I'm sure it's this year, and I'm seldom wrong about such things. And that means this month, doesn't it? It's already December."

Carol thought that if the question of such early nuptials should possibly arise, this cool prophecy would somehow weigh against her consent. She wasn't taking any brusque commands from fate – not this year.

"All right: go on."

"The second thing I see is great fame, great publicity. Not as if you were the heroine of some amateur play here in the city. Great notoriety all over the country. Headlines!"

"Mercy! I wouldn't like that. We're very... I've grown up in a very conservative family."

The palmist sighed.

"Well, I tell you only what I see. So don't be surprised if you marry Mahatma Gandhi about – let's see – three years from now."

"But if I'm to be married within a month!" Carol laughed... Then she frowned suddenly. "You know, somebody else told me that I'd be notorious that way – with cards or tea leaves, I think—"

The woman interrupted drily:

"That must have been very interesting... Well – so we come to the third thing." Her eyes had grown very bright – she was restless in her chair.

"This is what I felt at the moment I saw you, even before I'd really studied your hand – but you're going to be a wise girl and laugh at me. Your hand is very oddly marked, very sharply marked – with events, and their time too. About six years from now, in May, I think, something very dark threatens you and yours. If I'm right you can't beat it – black accident – six years from now – in May..."

She broke off, and her voice rose with sudden passion:

"Let me tell you, I hate fate, young woman. I..."

Suddenly Carol was outside the tent, uttering a strange crying sound. "Not on account of what she said. But because she jumped up as if she had frightened herself!" Carol thought.

Outside the tent she found Harry Dickey waiting for her.

"But what did she tell you?" he demanded. "Why do you look like that?"

"She told me some things I've heard before: early marriage – fame or notoriety – and then something that sounds simply terrible."

"That's probably the early marriage."

"No."

"What was it? Come on – tell Papa."

"No, I won't."

"Then don't tell Papa. Marry him instead. Marry him tonight."

A few months ago she might almost have considered such a suggestion from Harry Dickey. He was not the man to whom she had confessed being almost engaged, but he had been in and out of her mind for several years, and quite welcome there until Billy Riggs made his first flashing visit to the city several months before. Now she only said:

"She was a spook, that woman. I felt that any minute she was going to vanish."

"She has."

Carol looked around. Where the tent had been there was suddenly nothing.

"Am I crazy – or has it disappeared?"

"It has. She's got it folded up under her arm, and she's just this minute gone out the door."

Billy Riggs and his friend, Professor Benjamin Kastler, swooped down upon the city two days later. When the long yellow car stopped in front of her house Carol's heart bumped and her blood pressure increased.

"And if that isn't love, what is?" she asked herself. "At any rate, life will be exciting with milord."

Billy Riggs was one of those who carry his own world with him. He always seemed less to arrive than to land, less to visit than to take possession, less to see than to conquer. Carol found it difficult to calculate her own position in the scene after they were married. She approved of his arrogance; she managed him by a good-humoured non-resistance.

For a few minutes Carol did not connect his sudden change of plans about their marriage with the fortune-teller's prophecy: he wanted them to be married before Christmas. There was nothing seriously against it: she was of an age to know her mind, both of her parents were dead and only the wishes of the parties concerned need be consulted. Yet...

"I won't do it, Bill," she said.

He had reasons, but to Carol her wedding seemed one matter in which her own slightest whim was of more importance than anyone else's logic.

"You talk to her, Ben," Bill said finally.

By this time they had been arguing for most of twenty-four hours and it was almost necessary to have a third party present as a sort of buffer. The victim was Ben Kastler, the prematurely grey young pedagogue whom Bill had brought with him as a weekend entourage. Now Ben tried:

"If you two love each other, why, then..."

They glared at him.

"Of course we love each other!"

"Then why not each set a date and then flip a coin?" he suggested ironically.

"You're a great help," Bill complained. "This isn't a joke. I've explained to Carol that Grandfather can't live a month. Well. I won't go and get married just after he dies – as if I were waiting for it. So it's either right now or else wait till June."

"We can get quietly married any time," said Carol. "I've always wanted just to drive out to my uncle's, in Chester County, and have him marry me."

"I don't like an elopement."

"It's not an elopement – he's my uncle and he's a minister."

After the next half-hour it scarcely looked as if they would be even engaged much longer. Just before the irrevocable things could be said, Ben dragged his friend from the house. Upstairs, Carol walked her room, weeping angrily – this was not going to be the first of a series of submissions which would constitute her life. Of course, it had started with the fortune-teller – if Carol spoilt the first prophecy, that would break the charm. But now the struggle against Bill's will had assumed even greater importance. She had reconciled herself to ending her engagement when the phone rang that night. Bill capitulated.

She made it hard for him. When he came next day, bringing Ben along in case hostilities should break out, she laid down her terms. He must agree to put off the wedding until after the first of the year, and also to be married informally by her uncle. Then, sorry for his wounded vanity, she suddenly agreed that he could decide everything else.

"Then it's understood that you'll marry me any time next year?"

"Anytime."

"How about New Year's morning?"

"Why – sure, Bill; that'll be fine."

"You give me your word of honour?

"I do – if Uncle Jim is willing to marry us."

"That ought to be easy to fix." His confidence drained back into him moment by moment. "Ben, you're a witness to the contract – now and next month too. And as you're a professor of law—"

"Economics."

"—whatever it is, you know what a contract is."

After Christmas, Bill and Professor Kastler arrived. With each day the marriage grew more inevitable – her uncle had no objection to performing the ceremony at five minutes after twelve on New Year's morning. It was to be as small and informal an affair as she could have wished – Bill's best man, the aunt with whom Carol lived, her two closest friends and two cousins of Bill's.

And on New Year's Eve she felt trapped and frightened. She had given her word and she would go through with it, but at nine o'clock, when Bill went to meet his cousins at the station, it was this feeling that made her say:

"We'll start on – we five. Bill will be there almost as soon as we are – he knows the way."

They started off through the crisp darkness, with Ben at the wheel and Carol beside him. She heard the home of her youth crunch away into the past on the hard snow and she looked at Ben.

"It's sad, isn't it?"

When he did not answer she looked again, finding him as always too silent and too old for his youth, but liking a curious form and set to him, something that came from inside, as if he had constructed it himself, and that made a sharp contrast to Bill's natural buoyancy.

"What's the matter?" she demanded.

Still he did not give her any answer.

"Maybe I should have married *you*," Carol said, talking on faster and faster, "or somebody else. That's the sort of thing that worries me—"

He was speaking, and she was utterly startled at the intensity of his voice:

"Yes. You should have married me, Carol."

She looked at him quickly in the glow of a street lamp, to be sure it was just Ben Kastler... But it wasn't. It wasn't Ben at all. He wasn't plain; he was handsome. The straight-ahead glitter of his dark eyes sent a sharp sword through her – her own voice was different, too, when she whispered:

"I didn't know you cared about me. I didn't have any idea, I feel terribly—"

"Let's not talk," he said. "It's almost over now. I wouldn't have told you, except..."

"Except what – tell me! I have to know. There's something in all this I have to know. Oh, I feel as if things had been kept back from me – and I've got nobody to ask."

"I'll tell you," he said grimly. "I should have spoken the day you had that quarrel. He lost you then, but neither of you knew it."

She sat silent, heavy, and frightened. They were out of town, and he drove faster, through a long suburb and out on to the state road. Desperately she counted the little townships they passed – till only one remained. Then she said:

"You're right. It was over then, if there was ever anything. But what does it matter?"

"You're going to go through with it?"

"I promised."

"That's right. Your words is your bond – Portia."*

He was silent so long now that the last village before her uncle's house rushed up and went by before he spoke:

"But do you happen to remember the exact words?"

Five minutes later the group were blinking under the lights of her uncle's parlour. Ceremoniously arrayed, he greeted them, but there was no time to lose and Carol took her uncle into another room.

"You've got to listen very carefully," she said.

He listened to the storm of old words, new intentions.

"...It'll be terrible for Bill, but marriage is for life... and better now than later... my promise was – now, listen – 'if Uncle Jim is willing to marry me'."

"But I *am* willing."

"But you *wouldn't* be willing if I was already married to somebody else."

Carol was very beautiful and convincing, and she had always been a pet of her uncle's. At ten minutes to twelve o'clock, she and Ben Kastler were made man and wife.

Waiting for her husband, Carol Kastler bought the baby daughter a new toothbrush, and then stepped on scales that politely refused to accept her nickel. On one side of the scales was an automatic pin game; she didn't want to play that by herself – the drugstore was just across from the crowded city campus and she was a dean's wife. But the nickel wanted to be spent, and next to the gambling board was a slot machine. Into this she put the coin, receiving in return a small white card:

> You're the kind who cuts lots of capers;
> Look out you don't get your name in the papers.

She read it and smiled. Then she put in another nickel and pressed a lever:

Don't you worry. Some fine day
Lots of fame will come your way.

This time she did not smile.

"Why, I do believe it's the old curse," she thought. "I wonder what would be the mathematical probabilities of these two cards turning up one after the other."

She was about to put in a third coin when her husband came in.

"Gaze at these, darling. Fate's creeping up on me. Remember, about three years ago that fortune-teller told me I'd be notorious?"

"Oh, you mean that fortune-teller," he said, as they got into their car. "I'm sorry – I was thinking of something else."

"You ought to be grateful to that fortune-teller," Carol reproached him. "If it wasn't for her we wouldn't be us."

"Oh, I'm grateful – but I don't think you've ever gotten over it, the second-sight business, I mean. It was just as accidental as these penny cards."

"Nickel cards... But, Ben, it's due now – three years, she said. And, lo and behold, these funny little cards!"

"It's good I don't believe in signs, then," he said placidly, "because notoriety is the last thing we want right now."

"Have you heard anything?" Carol asked eagerly.

"Too much – I have to pretend to be deaf."

"If it *did* happen – at your age – oh, Ben..."

He slowed down suddenly. "You see the effect on me – I'm excited, I step on it, I get arrested for speeding, the regent sees it in the papers – there's your notoriety for you – and I'm disqualified."

Discouraged from mentioning fate, either in its larger aspects or in the possibility that Ben might be the new president of the university, Carol nevertheless thought a moment longer about the cards. They were a warning – but she couldn't think how any unpleasant notoriety could spring out of the quiet happiness that so far was the story of her marriage.

But the cards had somehow disturbed her, and her last thought that night was that if there were a University of Fortune-Tellers she might have a talk with the president. She decided to enquire around among her friends at a Junior League committee meeting next day. But in the morning it seemed silly, and going into town she put it out of mind.

The league was sponsoring an infants' health show, and Carol took her child along to see the champion babies. Just as she entered the hall of the civic building an almost theatrically dirty and ragged woman, carrying a child, spoke to her:

"You belong to this Junior League?"

"Yes," said Carol.

"Well, how about this show for healthy babies? I'd like to let them see this one that I can't get enough to feed her."

"Go to Room 312. That's the Welfare Bureau."

"You got something to do with this baby show?"

"A little, but that's another matter—"

Two men had drawn near and were listening with unusual interest to the conversation. The woman was insistent:

"Well, if you're so interested in babies, you might look at this baby of mine…"

Impatient at the importunity, Carol peered hastily into her bag, found only a nickel and a ten-dollar bill. Simultaneously one of the men touched his hat.

"Excuse me, lady, but if you're on the baby-show committee I'd like to have your name."

Instinctively her lips froze upon her name; to the woman she said, "I'm sorry. I only have a nickel…"

"Hold it, lady."

At that instant she saw the camera, and in a split second more she had whirled away from it – just as the corridor flashed full of light. She grabbed up Jean and darted into an elevator as the gate clanged. A woman she knew spoke to her.

"Were they after you, Mrs Kastler?"

"I guess so," Carol panted. "What on earth is it?"

"It's a tabloid newspaper stunt – you know: 'Rich Boast Babes While…' That sort of thing. Did they photograph you?"

"They tried to..." Carol paused.

They *had* photographed her – though her back had been to the camera at the flashlight – and she had nearly given her name. They wanted a victim from the Junior League, and she had almost played into their hands. They might have pictured her handing a nickel – a nickel – to a wretched mother with exaggerated reports of her social activities. The headline danced in her brain:

Dean's Wife Spares Nickel.

And she saw the regents of the university in conclave, each with the impression that Dean Kastler was married to a particularly callous and penurious social light.

Notoriety, indeed! She decided to go home without attending the meeting; she went downstairs by another elevator and slipped through a drugstore into the street. Only when the apartment door closed upon her did she draw a breath of relief.

It was a short breath – in a moment the phone rang and a man's voice asked for Mrs Kastler.

"I don't think she's in." Carol was on guard again. "Who is this, please?"

"This is for a newspaper society column. Can you tell us if Mrs Kastler has a hat with a bow of ribbon on it?"

"No, I haven't," said Carol – and immediately could have bitten off her tongue.

"So *this* is Mrs Kastler. We'd like to get a story about you and that kid of yours. We'll have a man out there—"

"I won't see him!" she cried, and hung up.

After a moment she called the university, but Ben could not be located. Stories and movies that told of tabloid persecutions rushed through her mind – if they were after you they sent reporters down chimneys. Not since the sins of childhood had she so passionately wanted to be far, far away.

With the thought came a quiet inspiration – Mary Kenyon. This was a friend who had many times invited her to spend a week in her boasted Arcady – a cabin not three hours from the city, but totally isolated; without neighbours, newspapers, radios or telephones.

In a hasty letter Carol explained to Ben what had happened. She gave the envelope to the maid, with instructions about carrying on in her absence.

"I haven't sealed this letter," she added, "because if Mr Kastler calls on the phone you'd better read it over the phone to him right away." The maid was rather flashy but intelligent enough. "If anyone else calls, just say I won't be home for a week and you don't know where I am."

At the moment of leaving Carol took a final precaution: she went all over the apartment gathering up every picture she could find of her baby and herself, and locked them into a closet. Then she ordered a taxi to come to the service door.

That night Carol told Mary every detail, from the palmist to the hat with the ribbon bow on it, and she added:

"I brought that along and I'm presenting it to you."

The four days she had allowed passed tranquilly. There was no fear when Mary started with her and the baby for the station; there was only eagerness to see Ben.

A few miles down the road a farmer neighbour hailed them from beside a stalled automobile.

"Sure hate to bother you, Miss Kenyon, but my car burnt out a bearing – these two gentlemen—"

One of the two men with him spoke up briskly, and in a momentary resurgence of panic Carol wondered if the newspapers had caught up with her.

"We want your car for half an hour. We're from the police department, and we want to make a few inquiries near by."

"Up to Marky's shack, Miss Kenyon. They think—"

"Never mind," said the detective.

Mary drove as she was directed, off the main road and down what was little more than a wagon track, until told to stop.

"You wait here in the car," one of the men said.

When they were out of sight the farmer laughed. "Ain't had the law down here since white-mule days."

"Well, we don't want excitement," Mary said. "What are they after?"

He lowered his voice: "I think it's about the kidnapping of this woman and—"

"Heavens! We haven't seen a paper for four days."

"No? Well, there's nothin' else in the papers – the kidnappers are askin' twenty thousand dollars. Kidnapped the wife and child of the president of the university – name of Kastler."

The idea had been the maid's – with the help of an ambitious boyfriend. The maid had a police record herself, and when Mrs Kastler was so kind as to disappear of her own accord, leaving no trace save a letter which need not be delivered – well, what better opportunity for extortion?

But they bungled the job and were in course of being captured about the time when Carol reached her husband by telephone. Their conversation was long and shaky. It was days before they could talk logically about the matter to each other.

What confused Carol most was the reiterated question of how much it had been predestined. Once again she wondered if the future really was engraved in her hand – or if the prophecy itself, by frightening her, had been responsible for the event. Irresistibly her thoughts swung to the third and most sinister of the predictions, and she tried to remember the exact wording the woman had used: "Six years from now… a black accident threatening you and yours… look out for the month of May…"

Several years after the "kidnapping", when Carol went home for a visit, she determined to locate the woman and ask for another reading. When, after some difficulty, Carol located the woman, she was startled to find herself remembered.

"It was at a dance – nearly six years ago," said the palmist. She looked briefly into Carol's hands.

"I remember – everything. Tell me, do things go well?"

"Very well. That's why I'm frightened. You told me—"

"It's all still in your hands. Do you want me to repeat it?"

"Just the part about the accident – about May. Is it still—"

"Let me look again."

For a long time she stared into Carol's right palm, then she asked the date of her birth and wrote some figures below it.

"Go along with you," she cried. "I've nothing to tell you."

"You mean it's still there – it's so awful you won't tell me?"

"Just remember this – if I was infallible I'd now be travelling the world in splendour."

"Don't send me away like this," Carol begged. "Would it make any difference if I took very good care of things, of myself, of those I love?"

"Not if it's *really* written there. Oh, best forget it, Mrs Kastler, and wake up one day and find it's June, and say, 'That old fool didn't know what she was talking about.'"

The experience of being sentenced is commoner than is generally supposed – it must have been remarked that at the moment of birth one is sentenced to death. But the terror of the dentist's waiting room, the terror of the death house depend on clock and calendar. And thus it was with Carol – she was afraid of time.

"After the first of June," she promised herself, "I'll put this out of my head."

At the beginning of May she had erected, to the best of her abilities, a Chinese wall around herself and her two children. There was little she could do without Ben's knowledge, but what she could do she did. Privately she gave his chauffeur ten dollars to drive him always at a moderate rate, even when he objected, and twice she followed in a taxicab to be sure.

Her daughter was five, her son was two. There was a nurse, but, during May, Carol went out only when necessary. Several times during the month she took both children to the doctor for examination.

For herself, her precautions were mostly of a general order, but she crossed streets at intersections only, she cautioned drivers, she did not run downstairs nor undertake labours involving struggles with inanimate objects. And all during the month her restlessness grew till she would have welcomed the prospect of some lion-hunting at the month's end.

Ben sensed an increased timidity in her. It was because of this that he told her only a part of the Holland House matter.

Holland House was a frame structure about eighty years old, long used as an administration building, and housing, among other bureaux, the president's office. It was of the Federal Period* and, as far as could be ascertained, it was the first extant college building west of the Ohio. Ben had a special affection for this landmark, and now the question had arisen of sacrificing it to progress. For the city was putting in a subway branch which would run within fifty feet of it. Would the building survive the blasting? A substantial number of regents wanted it condemned to the woodpile. Ben wanted to preserve it at almost any cost.

This much Carol knew. What she did not know was that, after getting expert advice to back his contentions, Ben had announced his intention of sitting in his office on the afternoon of May thirty-first, when the blasting would occur on a street nearby. Mrs Wheelock, the dean's wife, rang the Kastlers' doorbell early that afternoon.

"You'll think this is an odd time to call, Mrs Kastler – and I admit I'm on a presumptuous errand."

"Not at all," said Carol ambiguously. "But I was wondering if you see what I see. My daughter is in the act of climbing up that pine."

"Let her climb," said Mrs Wheelock. "She might be startled and fall down – now I *am* being intrusive."

"Jean, come down!"

A face looked reproachfully from a ten-foot branch of the ladder-like pine.

"Oh, can't I?" it protested.

"I'm sorry; not till you're six. We'll have to call it a 'big crime'."

She sat down again, apologizing and explaining to Mrs Wheelock about big and little crimes.

"I was saying," resumed Mrs Wheelock, "that I've come about the Holland House matter. It is a matter between…"

For a moment, watching Jean's descent, Carol only half heard. But suddenly she was listening with her whole body.

"—of course, if these termites haven't eaten out the insides of the lumber, your husband can sit in his office till doomsday. But if they *have*, then this blasting—"

Carol was on her feet.

"Why didn't I know this?"

"Your husband's been argued with but, as you know, he's a most determined man—"

Carol was already in action, seizing a hat, summoning the maid.

"I won't be gone an hour… let the baby sleep – don't disturb him… Jean is not to climb trees…"

As they hurried down the walk to Mrs Wheelock's car, Carol took a quick last look at Jean and her three little friends from next door, with their collie.

"They're all right," she thought, and then aloud: "I hope I can get to him in time."

She saw the excavation as they turned in at the university gate – that part of the street was marked off with red flags. In front of Holland House she stared at a placard on the door:

NOTICE
THIS BUILDING TEMPORARILY CLOSED
BECAUSE OF BLASTING
OFFICES MOVED TO MCKAY BUILDING

Ben was alone in his office, leaning back thoughtfully in his swivel chair.

"Good Heavens, Carol!" he exclaimed. "What do you want?"

"I want you to come out of here."

He groaned disgustedly. "There isn't a bit of real evidence that termites—"

"Come with me now – right away, Ben, before they begin. You've got to – there's a reason you don't know—"

"Darling – I can't believe you've been listening to soothsayers again."

"Ben, what if I have – couldn't you do this one thing for me? I'm not a coward, you know that, but after the other two things how can you laugh at me? I'm trying in every way I know to fight against it – and here, with danger in the air, you run deliberately into it."

"Hush!" he said, and then, after a moment. "I wish you'd get out, Carol."

Darkly she hated him for his obtuseness.

"I won't go without you. If you cared you wouldn't sit there."

"I sit here because I do not believe this building will be damaged. I have given in to the extent of ordering out the personnel and removing valuable records. But it's a point of honour that I remain here myself to vindicate my judgement."

She had never hated him so much, admired him so much; but, as an undertone to his words, other words thundered in her head, mingling with the music of a forgotten dance:

"—black accident… May… you and yours—"

"But I do wish you'd go, Carol," he said. "The ceiling is wood, but a little moulding may fall."

He broke off suddenly as the air was split as by a cannon outside. Simultaneously there was a mutter of the windows, a mutter that became a rattle; the frames themselves became faintly blurred and a chandelier was swaying.

Br-rr-rr-rr CLAP! Clipclip WA-A-A-A CLAP!

In a sudden stillness she heard Ben's voice:

"That was the first blast. There'll be three, half a minute apart."

At the second boom the windows took on so hearty a vibration as to compete in sound with the timbers – this time the whole fanfare in joist and moulding, the shaking and snapping, endured so long that the third *boom* came before it had ceased. Presently through this, like a new, high motif, they heard the tap of plaster falling in a few rooms above. Then a sound went through the house like a long sigh, a last eerie whistle that ended somewhere in the eaves – the quake was over.

Ben got up and walked quickly about the room. His eyes were flashing with delight.

"Is it over?" asked Carol, dazed.

"All over. The next blasting will be half a mile away."

Only now for the first time did he seem to become truly aware of her presence – he put his arm about her.

"How do things go at home?" he said. "Carol, what is the matter lately? Tell me all about it – you can't go on being afraid of bogies."

"I know, Ben. I'm glad this happened. I'm glad I was here this afternoon."

"You're making the children jumpy, too – you scarcely let them exercise."

"I know. I've been a nut." Impulsively she picked up his phone, called the house and spoke to the servant:

"This is Mrs Kastler... I just wanted you to tell Jean she *can* climb that tree."

Carol hung up and turned to her husband. "You see, I've changed. I won't be such a ninny – honest."

And now she confessed everything – the last interview with the fortune-teller, the bribing of Ben's chauffeur – "But not any more. Take me home in the car now, and we'll have him just tear along."

"I had some work—"

"Not today. I feel released – all that sort of thing."

He was rather silent and thoughtful on the way home.

"People who figure on chance and fate and luck – you know about Napoleon and his star – how he used to figure out whether his generals were 'lucky' generals?"

"I don't know about Napoleon," Carol said, "I never knew the man. I just know about you and me. We're lucky."

"No, we're not – we're logical from now on."

There was an unusual silence about their house as they reached the door. Yet Carol, usually sensitive to such things, did not notice that anything was wrong until the maid rushed at them in the hall.

"Now, don't worry, Mrs Kastler. The chillen's upstairs and all right."

"What is it, Emma? Now, what is it?" Carol shook her by the shoulders.

"No cause to worry *now* – but we had plenty roun' here the last hour. I tried to call you when that mad dog—"

"What?"

"That collie dog next door. He been actin' funny lately, an' he began actin' funny this afternoon, goin' roun' snappin' at them chillen, and he nipped at that little George an' they took George to the hospital – say don't you look so funny, Mrs Kastler; you sit down there."

"Did he nip Jean – where was Jean?"

"I tell you Jean was all right – I told Jean what you said on the phone – so when it all began to happen she was sittin' way up high in that tree."

When she had taken the spirits of ammonia, Carol did not follow Ben upstairs but sat very quiet in the dining room.

If she had not telephoned home about the tree Jean would probably have been bitten like the other children. On the other hand – if the dean's wife hadn't called...

She gave it up. Ben was right. You could regard the future only in the most general way. She sighed wearily as the phone rang and she lifted the receiver.

"Oh, Mrs Kastler, I recognize your voice. This is Spillman."

That was his secretary – couldn't Ben be left alone after a day like this?

"Can I take the message?"

"Well, I thought he'd want to know. It's about Holland House. It – why, it collapsed like a house of cards about ten minutes ago. Nobody was in it—"

"Oh, my Heavens!" she said. Then, after a long pause: "I'll tell him, Mr Spillman."

She sat quiet in her chair. Faintly from above she heard Ben saying good night to the baby. And Jean's voice: "Daddy, he snapped so quick you wouldn't know, and the man that took him away said they'd keep him under obligation…"

Carol sat still. She felt no sense of triumph, no desire at all to tell Ben about the house; she would rather that the news be deferred as long as possible.

She looked at the clock: the hands stood at six. It would be the first day of June in exactly six more hours.

Six more hours.

Image on the Heart

1

THE TRAIN ROLLED INTO THE LITTLE FRENCH TOWN as if it were entering a dusty garden. As the floor of the railroad carriage trembled and shifted with the brakes, the stationary human figures outside the window became suddenly mobile as the train itself, and began running along beside it. The passengers seemed to blend right into the countryside as soon as the porters on the platform were running as fast as the train.

She was waiting for him – eight months was a long time and they were shy with each other for a moment. She had fair hair – delicate, shiny, essentially private hair – it was not arranged as blondes preferred at the moment, but rather as if it were to be let down for someone alone sometime, somewhere. There was no direct challenge in it, and in her face there were the sort of small misproportions that kept her from being smooth and immediately pretty. But in her nineteen years she had managed to be a standard of beauty to two or three men – Tudy was lovely to those to whom she wanted to be lovely.

They got into one of those old-fashioned victorias that have a last refuge in the south of France; as the horse started off down the cobblestoned street, the man turned to the girl beside him and asked simply:

"Do you still want to marry me?"

"Yes, Tom."

"Thank God."

They interlaced hands and arms. Even though the cab was moving so slowly up a hill of the old town that pedestrians kept pace with them, it didn't seem necessary to let go. Everything seemed all right in this mellow Provençal sunshine.

"It seemed for ever till you'd come," Tudy murmured. "For ever and for ever. The university closes in another week – and that's the end of my education."

"You finish as a freshman."

"Just a freshman. But I'd rather have had this than any finishing school – especially because you gave it to me."

"I had to bring you up to my standard," he said lightly. "Do you feel improved?"

"Do I! Maybe you think these French universities haven't got standards. It's…" She broke off to say suddenly: "There's you, Tom – don't you see? That French officer coming out of the *magasin de tabac** across the street – he's your double."

Tom looked over towards the sleepy sidewalk, picked out the man and agreed. "He does look like me, at least like I looked ten years ago. We'll have to look him up if he lives here."

"I know him, he's been here a week on leave. He's a naval aviator from Toulon. I wanted to meet him because he looked so much like you."

Like Tom, the man was darkly blond and handsome with a flickering in his face, a firelight over high cheekbones. Not having thought much of the matter for years, he stared curiously at the naval officer – who recognized Tudy and waved at her – and said meditatively:

"So that's what I look like."

A minute later the carriage clattered into a green cove under a roof of poplars; beneath the soft roof slept the Hôtel des Thermes, tranquil as when it had been a Roman bath two thousand years before.

"Of course, you'll stay on at your *pension* until Mother comes," he said.

"I have to, Tom, I'm still a student. Isn't that absurd – when you think that I'm a widow?"

The carriage had drawn up at the door. The concierge was bowing.

"Mother will be here in ten days – then the wedding – then we're off for Sicily."

She pressed his hand.

"In half an hour at the Pension Duval," she said. "I'll be in the front garden waiting."

"As soon as I snatch a bath," he said.

As the cab started off without him, Tudy squeezed back in the corner. She was trying not to think too much, but irresistibly she kept saying to herself:

"I'm a lost soul maybe – I don't feel at all like I ought to feel. Oh, if he'd only come a week ago."

They had known each other for many years before this rendez-vous in France. Or rather, Tom had known her people, for he had thought of her as a little girl until one day at Rehoboth Beach a year before. Then word had gone around the hotel that there was a bride of a week whose husband had been tragically drowned that morning. Tom took charge of the immediate situation – it developed that she had no one to turn to and that she was left penniless. He fell in love with her and with her helplessness, and after a few months he persuaded her to let him lend her the money to go abroad and study for a year – and put something between herself and the past. There were no strings attached – indeed, nothing had been said – but he knew that she responded to him in so far as her grief permitted, and there was correspondence more and more intimate and in a few months he wrote asking her to marry him.

She wrote him a glowing answer – and thus it was that he was here. Thus it was that she sat opposite him in an outdoor restaurant on the Rue de Provence that night. The electric lights behind the leaves swayed into sight sometimes in a faint wind, making her head into a ball of white gold.

"Oh, you've been so good to me," she said. "And I really have worked hard, and I've loved it here."

"That's why I want to be married here, because I've so often thought of you in this old town – my heart's been here for eight months."

"And I've pictured you stopping here when you were a boy, and loving it so much you wanted to send me here."

"Did you really think of me – like your letters said?"

"Every day," she answered quickly. "Every letter was true. Sometimes I couldn't get home fast enough to write you."

If only he had come a week ago!

Tom talked on:

"And you like the idea of Sicily? I have two months. If you have any other place—"

"No, Sicily's all right – I mean, Sicily's wonderful."

Four men, two of them naval officers, and a girl had come into the little café. One face among them emerged in the hundred little flashlights and dark patches of leaves – it was that of Lieutenant de Marine Riccard, the man Tudy had pointed out that afternoon. The party settled themselves at a table opposite, grouping and regrouping with laughter.

"Let's go," Tudy said suddenly. "We'll ride up to the university."

"But isn't that my double? I'm curious to meet him."

"Oh, he's very – young. He's just here on leave and he's going back soon, I think – he probably wants to talk to his friends. Do let's go."

Obediently he signalled for the check, but it was too late. Riccard has risen from the table, with him two of the other men.

"—'Sieu Croirier."

"—'Sieu Silvé."

"—soir."

"—chantée."*

"Why, we *do* look alike," Tom said to Riccard.

Riccard smiled politely.

"Excuse me? Oh, yes – I see – a little bit of a bit." Then he conceded rather haughtily, "I am the English type: I had a Scotswoman for a grandmother."

"You speak English well."

"I have known English and American people." Fragmentarily his eyes strayed towards Tudy. "You speak French well – I wish I could speak so good English. Tell me," he said intently, "do you know any tricks?"

"Tricks?" Tom asked in surprise.

"Americans all know tricks and I am like an American that way. We have been doing tricks this evening before we came here. Do you know the trick with the fork where you hit it so" – he illustrated with graphic gesturing – "and it lands here in the glass?"

"I've seen it. I can't do it."

"Neither can I mostly, but sometimes though. *Garçon*, bring a fork. Also, there are some tricks with matches – very interesting. They make you think, these tricks."

Suddenly Tom remembered that though tricks were no hobby of his, he did happen to have with him something of the sort bought for a nephew and undelivered. It was in his trunk in the hotel, and it was plain that Riccard would consider it a prince among jests. Pleased by the thought, he watched the French people bring their ready concentration, their delight in simple things made complex, to bear upon the forks and matches and handkerchiefs that presently came into play. He liked watching them; he felt young with them; he laughed in tune to Tudy's laughter – it was fine to be sitting beside her in the soft balm of a Provençal night watching French people make nonsense at the day's end…

He was an astute man, but he was so wrapped up in his dream of Tudy that it was not until two nights later that he realized something was not as it should be. They had invited several of her friends from the university and Lieutenant Riccard to dine with them in the same little café. Tom did the trick that he had recovered from his trunk, a familiar old teaser that depended on two little rubber bulbs connected by a thin cord two yards long.

One of the bulbs was planted under the tablecloth beneath Riccard's plate, and by squeezing the other bulb from across the table, Tom was able to make the Frenchman's plate rise and fall inexplicably, jiggle, bump, tilt and conduct itself in a generally supernatural manner. It was not Tom's notion of the cream of human wit, but Riccard had asked for it and so far as practical jokes go it was a decided success.

"I don't know what can be the matter with my fork tonight," Riccard said mournfully. "You Americans will think I am barbarian. There! I have done it again! Can it be that my hand is trembling?" He looked anxiously at his hands. "No – yet there it is – I am destined to spill things tonight. It is one of those matters in life that can never be explained…"

He started as the knife on his plate gave a little sympathetic clink.

"*Mon Dieu!*" Once again he attempted a logical treatment of the situation, but he was obviously disturbed and he kept a watchful eye on the plate. "It is because I haven't flown in ten days," he decided. "You see, I am used to currents of air, to adjustments very sudden, and when it does not come I imagine it…"

It was a warm night, but there was extra dew on his young forehead, and then Tudy's voice, very dear and piercing, cut through the tranquil air.

"Stop it, Tom, *Stop* it!"

He looked at her with an amazement as great as Riccard's. In fear of a contagious mirth he had been avoiding her eyes, but he saw suddenly that there was no mirth in her face at all – only an engrossed compassion.

His world tilted like the plate for a moment, righted itself; he explained to Riccard the mechanics of the joke, and then, as a sort of atonement, presented him with the apparatus. Riccard, trying to get back at someone, tried immediately to put it into action, inveigling the proprietor of the restaurant to sit down on it, but for the time Tom only remembered the expression on Tudy's face when she had cried out. What did it mean when she could be so sorry for another man? Perhaps it was a general tenderness, perhaps her maternal instinct was so strong that he would be glad later when she felt that way about their children. Oh, she was good, but there was something in him unreconciled to the poignancy, the spontaneity of that cry – and on the way home in the cab he asked her:

"Are you by any chance interested in this French boy? If you are, it's all right with me. We've been apart for a long time and if you've changed—"

She took his face between her hands and looked into his eyes.

"How can you say that to me?"

"Well, I thought that maybe gratitude was influencing you—"

"Gratitude has nothing to do with it. You're the best man I ever knew."

"The point is, do I happen to be attractive to you?"

"Of course you are – other men seem unimportant when you're around. That's why I don't like to see them. Oh, Tom, I wish your mother would hurry so we can get married and leave here…"

As he caught her into his arms, she gave a sob that went through him like a knife. But as the minutes passed and she half lay in his arms in the shadow of the cab's awning, he loved her so much and felt so close to her that he couldn't believe anything could really have gone wrong.

Tudy took her examinations. "Not that they matter, because of course I'm not going on. But that's what you sent me for. I'm now 'finished'. Darling, do I *look* finished?"

He regarded her appraisingly.

"You've probably learnt enough French to get you in trouble," he said. "You're a little sweeter, perhaps, but not much – there wasn't very much room for improvement."

"Oh, but French wasn't all I learnt. How about Siamese? I sat next to the cutest little Siamese all during one lecture course, and he tried so desperately to make up to me. I learnt to say 'No, I will not climb out the window of the *pension* tonight' in Siamese. Do you want to hear me say it?"

It was a bright morning – he had called for her at eight to walk to the university. Arm in arm they strolled.

"What are you going to do while I'm being examined?" she asked.

"I'm going to get the car—"

"Our car – I'm wild to see it."

"It's a funny little thing, but it'll take us all over Italy…"

"Then what will you do the rest of the time, after you get the car?"

"Why, I'll try it out and then I'll probably stop in front of the café about noon and have a bock, and maybe run into Riccard or one of your French friends…"

"What do you talk about with Riccard?" she asked.

"Oh, we do tricks. We don't talk – not exactly, at least it doesn't seem like talk."

She hesitated. "I don't see why you like to talk to Riccard," she said at last.

"He's a very nice type, very impetuous and fiery—"

"I know," she said suddenly. "He once told me he'd resign his commission if I'd fly to China with him and fight in the war."

When she said this, they had come to a halt engulfed by a crowd of students pouring into the buildings. She joined them as if she had said nothing at all:

"Goodbye, darling. I'll be on this corner at one o'clock."

He walked thoughtfully down to the garage. She had told him a great deal. He wasn't asking her to fly to China; he was asking her to go for a quiet honeymoon in Sicily. He promised her security, not adventure.

"Well, it's absurd to be jealous of this man," he thought. "I'm just getting a little old before my time."

So in the week of waiting for his mother, he organized picnics and swimming parties and trips to Arles and Nîmes, inviting Tudy's friends from the university, and they danced and sang and were very gay in little restaurant gardens and bistros all over that part of Provence – and behaved in such a harmless, lazy, wasteful summer manner that Tom, who wanted only to be alone with Tudy, almost managed to convince himself that he was having a good time…

…until the night on the steps of Tudy's *pension* when he broke the silence and told her he wasn't.

"Perhaps you'd better think it over," he said.

"Think what over, Tom?"

"Whether you love me enough to marry me."

Alarmed, she cried: "Why, Tom, of course I do."

"I'm not so sure. I like to see you have a good time, but I'm not the sort of man who could ever play – well, call it 'background'."

"But you're not background. I'm trying to please you, Tom; I thought you wanted to see a lot of young people and be very Provençal and 'dance the Carmagnole'* and all that."

"But it seems to be Riccard who's dancing it with you. You didn't actually have to kiss him tonight."

"You were there – you saw. There was nothing secret about it. It was in front of a lot of people."

"I didn't like it."

"Oh, I'm sorry if it hurt you, Tom. It was all playing, Sometimes with a man it's difficult to avoid those things. You feel like a fool if you do. It was just Provence, just the lovely night – and I'll never see him again after three or four days."

He shook his head slowly.

"No, I've changed ideas. I don't think we'll see him any more at all."

"What?" Was it alarm or relief in her voice? "Oh, then all right, Tom – that's all right. You know best."

"Is that agreed then?"

"You're absolutely right," she repeated after a minute. "But I think we could see him once more, just before he goes."

"I'll see him tomorrow," he said almost gruffly. "You're not a child and neither is he. It isn't as if you were a debutante tapering off some heartsick swain."

"Then why can't you and I go away until he leaves?"

"That's running away – that'd be a fine way to start a marriage."

"Well, do what you want," she said, and he saw by the starlight that her face was strained. "You know that more than anything in the world I want to marry you, Tom."

Next day on the Rue de Provence he encountered Riccard; by mutual instinct they turned to a table of the nearest café.

"I must talk to you," said Riccard.

"I wanted to talk to you," Tom said, but he waited.

Riccard tapped his breast pocket.

"I have a letter here from Tudy delivered by hand this morning."

"Yes?"

"You must understand that I am fond of you too, Tom – that I am very sad about the whole thing."

"Well, what?" Tom demanded impatiently. "If Tudy wrote that she was in love with you—"

Riccard tapped his pocket again.

"She did not *say* that. I could show you this letter—"

"I don't want to see it."

Their tempers were rising.

"You're upsetting Tudy," Tom said. "Your business is to keep out."

Riccard's answer was humble but his eyes were proud.

"I have no money," he said.

And, of all things, Tom was sorry for him.

"A girl must make her choice," he said kindly. "You're in the way now."

"I understand that too. I shall perhaps shorten my leave. I shall borrow a friend's plane and fly down, and if I crash so much the better."

"That's nonsense."

They shook hands and Tom duplicated the other's formal little bow, succinct as a salute...

He picked up Tudy at her *pension* an hour later. She was lovely in an inky-blue muslin dress, above which her hair shone like a silver angel. As they drove away from the house he said:

"I feel like a brute. But you can't have two men, can you – like a young girl at a dance?"

"Oh, I know it – don't talk about it, darling. He did it all. I haven't done anything I couldn't tell you about."

Riccard had said much the same thing. What bothered Tom was the image on the heart.

They drove southward past cliffs that might have had Roman lookouts posted on them, or that might have concealed barbarians waiting to drop boulders upon the Roman legions if they defiled through some pass.

Tom kept thinking: "Between Riccard and me, which is the Roman, and which is the barbarian?"

...Over a crest of a cliff a singing dot came into sight – a dark bee, a hawk – an aeroplane. They looked up idly, then they were suddenly thinking the same thing, wondering if it were Riccard on his way back to the naval base in Toulon.

"It probably is." Her voice sounded dry and uninterested.

"It looks like an old-fashioned monoplane to me."

"Oh, I guess he can fly anything. He was picked to make some flight to Brazil that they called off. It was in the papers before you came..."

She broke off because of a sudden change of situation in the sky. After passing over them the plane had begun to circle back, and in a moment its flight resolved itself into a slowly graduated spiral which was undoubtedly intended to centre over the road a quarter of a mile ahead of them.

"What's he trying to do?" exclaimed Tom. "Drop flowers on us?"

She didn't answer. During what must have been less than a minute of time, the car and plane approached the same spot. Tom stopped the car.

"If this is one of his tricks, let's get out."

"Oh, he wouldn't—"

"But *look*!"

The plane had come out of its dive, straightened out and was headed straight for them. Tom caught at Tudy's hand, trying to pull her from the car, but he had misjudged the time and the plane was already upon them, with a roaring din – then suddenly it was over them and away.

"The fool!" Tom cried.

"He's a wonderful flyer." Her face was still and calm. "He might have killed himself."

Tom got back in the car and sat looking at her for a moment. Then he turned the car around and started back the way they had come.

For a long time they drove in silence. Then she asked:

"What are you going to do – send me home to America?"

The simplicity of her question confused him; it was impossible to punish her for an episode that was no fault of her own – yet he had intended just that when he turned the car around.

"What do you want to do?" he asked, stalling.

Her face had that fatalistic helplessness that he had seen on it one day ten months before, when he broke the news to her that her husband had left nothing. And the same wave of protective love that had swept over him then swept over him again now. In the same moment he realized that the tragedy of her marriage – which had come so quickly she scarcely knew what had happened – had not really matured her. And by protecting her from its consequences he had aided the retardation.

"You're just a girl," he said aloud. "I suppose it's my fault."

In that case his responsibility was not over, and deep in his heart he knew that in spite of her inopportune coquetry so obvious under her thin denials, he did not want it to be over. On the contrary, he seized upon it as a reason for holding her to him.

"You're making a little trip," he said as they neared town. "But not to America. I want you to go up to Paris for three or four days and shop a little. Meanwhile I'll go down to Marseille and meet Mother."

Tudy cheered up at the suggestion.

"I'll get my graduation dress and my trousseau at the same time."

"All right, but I want you to leave this afternoon. So pack your bags right away."

An hour later they stood together in the station.

"I miss my exam tomorrow," she said.

"But it'll give you a chance to come down to earth."

He hated the phrase even as it left his lips: to come down to earth – was that an appealing prospect to hold out to any woman?

"Goodbye, dearest, dearest Tom."

As the train started off he ran beside it a moment, throwing into her window a packet of two bright handkerchiefs she had liked in a bazaar.

"Thanks – oh, thanks."

It was a long platform – when he came out at its end into the sunlight he stopped. There was his heart in motion with the train; he could feel the rip when the shadow of the last car broke from under the station roof.

She wrote immediately from Paris.

Oh, I miss you so, Tom. And I miss Provence too. [Then a lot of erasing.] *I miss everything that I've grown so fond of this last year. But I don't miss any person but you!*

There are no Americans in the streets – maybe we belong at home now and always did. They have a life they never take us into. They plan their lives so differently. But our American lives are so strange that we can never figure things out ahead. Like the hurricanes in Florida and the tornadoes and floods. All of a sudden things happen to us and we hardly know what hit us.

But I guess we must like that sort of thing or our ancestors wouldn't have come to America. Does this make sense? There is a man knocking on the door with a package. More later.

Later:
Darling, it is my wedding dress and I cried on it just a little in the corner where I can wash it out. And darling, it makes me think of my other wedding dress and of how kind you have been to me and how I love you.

It is blue – oh, the frailest blue: I'm getting afraid I won't be able to get the tears out of the corner.

Later:
I did – and it is so lovely, hanging now in the closet with the door open. It's now eight o'clock – you know l'heure bleue* – *when everything is really blue – and I'm going to walk up to the Opera along the Avenue de l'Opéra and then back to the hotel.*

Before I go to sleep I'll think of you and thank you for the dress and the lovely year and the new life you're giving me.

Your devoted, your loving,

TUDY

PS: I still think I should have stayed and gone with you to meet your mother in Marseilles. She…

Tom broke off and went back to the signature: "Your devoted, your loving". Which was she? He read back over the letter, pausing at any erasure, for an erasure often means an evasion, a second thought. And a love letter should come like a fresh stream from the heart, with no leaf on its current.

Then a second the next morning:

I'm so glad for your telegram – this will reach you just before you start down to Marseille. Give your mother my dearest love and tell her how much I hate missing her and how I wish I could welcome her to Provence. [There were two lines crossed out and rewritten.] *I will be starting back day after tomorrow. How funny it is to be buying things, when I never had any money like this to spend before – \$225.00 – that's what it was, after I'd figured the hotel bill and even thought of keeping enough cash in hand so I won't arrive absolutely penniless.*

I've bought two presents, I hope you won't mind, one for your mother and one for somebody else, and that's you. And don't think I've stinted myself and that I won't be a pretty bride for you! In fact I haven't waited until my wedding day to find out. I've dressed all up half a dozen times and stood in front of the mirror.

I'll be glad when it's over. Won't you, darling? I mean, I'll be glad when it's begun – won't you, darling?

Meanwhile, on the morning after she left, Tom had run into Riccard in the street. He nodded to him coldly, still angry about the aeroplane stunt, but Riccard seemed so unconscious of any guilt, seemed to think of it merely as a trick as innocuous as the bulb under the plate, that Tom waived the matter and stood talking with him a while under the freckled poplar shadows.

"So you decided not to go," he remarked.

"Oh, I shall go, but not until tomorrow after all. And how is Madame – I mean Tudy?"

"She's gone up to Paris to do some shopping."

He felt a malicious satisfaction in seeing Riccard's face fall.

"Where does she stay there? I would like to send her a telegram of goodbye."

No, you don't, Tom thought. Aloud he lied:

"I'm not sure – the hotel where she was going to stay is full."

"When does she come back?"

"She gets here day after tomorrow morning. I'm going to meet her with the car at Avignon."

"I see." Riccard hesitated for a moment. "I hope you will be very happy," he said.

His face was sad and bright at once; he was a gallant and charming young man, and Tom was sorry for a moment that they had not met under other circumstances.

But next day, driving to Marseille, a very different idea came to him. Suppose instead of going to the airbase at Toulon today, Riccard should go to Paris. There were not an infinite number of good hotels, and in a morning's search he might find out which was Tudy's. And in the inevitable emotion of a "last meeting", who could tell what might happen.

The worry so possessed him that when he reached Marseille he put in a telephone call for the Naval Aviation Depot at Toulon.

"I'm calling Lieutenant Riccard," he said.

"I do not understand."

"Lieutenant Riccard."

"This is not Lieutenant Riccard, surely?"

"No. I want to *speak* to Lieutenant Riccard."

"Ah."

"Is he there?"

"Riccard – wait till I look in the orderly room book… Yes… he is here – or at least he *was* here."

Tom's heart turned over as he waited.

"He is here," said the voice. "He is in the mess room. One minute."

Tom put the receiver very gently on the hook. His first instinct was relief – Riccard could not make it now; then he felt ashamed of his suspicions. Strolling that morning around a seaport where so many graver things had happened, he thought again of Tudy in a key above jealousy. He knew, though, that love should be a simpler, kinder thing; but every man loves out of something in himself that cannot be changed, and if he loved possessively and jealously, he could not help it.

Before he met his mother at the steamer he wired Tudy in Paris, asking an answer with a last thought that she might not be there. Bringing his mother back to the hotel for lunch he asked the concierge:

"Have you a telegram for me?"

It was there. His hands trembled as he opened it.

WHERE ELSE SHOULD I BE STOP LEAVING AT SIX TONIGHT
AND REACHING AVIGNON TOMORROW MORNING AT FIVE
A.M.

    TUDY

Driving up through Provence with his mother in the afternoon he said:

"You're very brave to try to go around the world by yourself at seventy-eight."

"I suppose I am," she said. "But your father and I wanted to see China and Japan – and that was not to be – so I sometimes think I'm going to see them for him, as if he were alive."

"You loved each other, didn't you?"

She looked at him as if his question was a young impertinence.

"Of course." Then she said suddenly: "Tom, is something making you unhappy?"

"Certainly not. Look what we're passing, Mother – you're not looking."

"It's a river – the Rhône, isn't it?"

"It's the Rhône. And after I've settled you at the Hôtel des Thermes I'll be following this same river up to Avignon to meet my girl."

But he had a curious fear as he passed through the great gate of Avignon at four o'clock next morning that she would not be there. There had been a warning in the thin song of his motor, in the closed ominous fronts of the dark villages, in the grey break of light in the sky. He drank a glass of beer in the station buffet, where several Italian emigrant families were eating from their baskets. Then he went out on the station platform and beckoned to a porter.

"There will be a lady with some baggage to carry."

Now the train was coming out of the blue dawn. Tom stood midway on the platform trying to pick out a face at a window or vestibule as it slid to rest, but there was no face. He walked along beside the sleepers, but there was only an impatient conductor taking off small baggage. Tom went up to look at the luggage thinking maybe it was hers, that it was new and he hadn't recognized it – then suddenly the train was in motion. Once more he glanced up and down the platform.

"Tom!"

She was there.

"Tudy – it's you."

"Didn't you expect me?"

She looked wan and tired in the faint light. His instinct was to pick her up and carry her out to the car.

"I didn't know there was another *wagon-lit*,"* he said excitedly. "Thank Heaven there was."

"Darling, I'm so glad to see you. All this is my trousseau, that I told you about. Be careful of them, porter – the strings won't hold, probably."

"Put this luggage in the car," he said to the porter. "We're going to have coffee in the buffet."

"*Bien,* monsieur."

In the buffet Tudy took smaller packages from her purse.

"This is for your mother. I spent a whole morning finding this for her and I wouldn't show it to you for anything."

She found another package.

"This for you, but I won't open it now. Oh, I was going to be *so* economical, but I bought two presents for you. I haven't ten francs left. It's good you met me."

"Darling, you're talking so much you're not eating."

"I forgot."

"Well, *eat* – and drink your coffee. I don't mean hurry – it's only half-past four in the morning."

They drove back through a day that was already blooming; there were peasants in the fields who looked at them as they went by, crawling up on one knee to stare over the tips of the young vines.

"What do we do now?" she said. "Oh, yes, now we get married."

"We certainly do – tomorrow morning. And when you get married in France, you know you've been married. I spent the whole first day you were away signing papers. Once I had to forge your signature, but I gave the man ten francs—"

"Oh, Tom..." she interrupted softly. "Don't talk for a minute. It's so beautiful this morning, I want to look at it."

"Of course, darling." He looked at her. "Is something the matter?"

"Nothing. I'm just confused." She smoothed her face with her hands as if she were parting it in the middle. "I'm almost sure I left something, but I can't think what."

"Weddings are always confusing," he said consolingly. "I'm supposed to forget the ring or something by the best traditions. Now just think of that – the groom has to remember to forget the ring."

She laughed and her mood seemed to change, but when Tom saw her at intervals in the packing and preparations of the day, he noticed that the air of confusion, of vagueness, remained about her. But next morning when he called at her *pension* at nine, she seemed so beautiful to him, with her white-gold hair gleaming above her frail blue frock, that he remembered only how much he loved her.

"But don't crush my bouquet," she said. "Are you sure you want me?"

"Perfectly sure."

"Even if… even if I have been rather foolish?"

"Of course."

"Even if—"

He kissed her lips gently.

"That'll do," he said. "I know you were a little in love with Riccard, but it's all over and we won't ever mention it again – is that agreed?"

Momentarily she seemed to hesitate. "Yes, Tom."

So they were married. And it seemed very strange to be married in France. Afterwards they gave a little breakfast for a few friends at the hotel and afterwards Tudy, who had moved over from the *pension* the day before, went upstairs to change her clothes and do her last packing, while Tom went to his mother's room and sat with her for a while. She was not starting off with them, but would rest here a day or two and then motor down to Marseille to catch another boat.

"I worry about your being alone," he said.

"I know my way about, son. You just think about Tudy – remember, you've given her her head for eight months and she may need a little firmness. You're twelve years older than she is and you ought to be that much wiser…" She broke off: "But every marriage works out in its own way."

Leaving his mother's room, Tom went down to the office to pay his bill.

"Someone wishes to see Monsieur," said the clerk.

It was a French railroad conductor carrying a package.

"*Bonjour*, monsieur," he said politely. "Is it you who has just been married to the young lady who travelled on the PLM* yesterday?"

"Yes."

"I did not like to disturb Madame on such a morning, but she left this on the train. It is a cloak."

"Oh, yes," said Tom. "She just missed it this morning."

"I had a little time off duty so I thought I'd bring it myself."

"We're very much obliged. Here's a fifty – no, here's a hundred francs."

The conductor looked at the size of Tom's tip and sighed.

"I cannot keep all this. This is too generous."

"Nonsense! I've been married this morning."

He pressed the money into the man's hand.

"You are very kind, monsieur. *Au revoir*, monsieur. But wait…" He fumbled in his pocket. "I was so full of emotion at your generosity that I almost forgot. This is another article I found – it may belong to Madame or to her brother who got off at Lyon. I have not been able to figure what it is. *Au revoir* again, monsieur, and thank you. I appreciate an American gentleman…"

He waved goodbye as he went down the stairs.

Tom was holding in his hands two bulbs of an apparatus that were connected by a long tube. If you pressed one bulb the air went through the tube and inflated the other.

When he came into Tudy's room she was staring out the window in the direction of the university.

"Just taking a last look at my finishing school," she said. "Why, what's the matter?"

He was thinking faster than he ever had in his life.

"Here's your cloak," he said. "The conductor brought it."

"Oh, good! It was an old cloak but—"

"And here's this…" He showed her what he held in his hand. "It seems your brother left it on the train."

The corners of her mouth fell and her eyes pulled her young forehead into a hundred unfamiliar lines. In one moment her face took on all the anguish in the world.

"All right," she said, after a minute. "I knew I should have told you. I tried to tell you this morning. Riccard flew up to Paris in time to meet me in the station and ride south with me. I had no idea he was coming."

"But no doubt you were pleasantly surprised," he said drily.

"No, I wasn't: I was furious. I didn't see how he knew I was coming south on that train. That's all there was to it, Tom – he rode down as far as Lyon with me. I started to tell you, but you were so happy this morning and I couldn't bear to."

Their eyes met, hers wavered away from his out into the great, soft-shaking poplar trees.

"I know I can never make you believe it was all right," she said dully. "I suppose we can get an annulment."

The sunlight fell on the square corners of her bags, packed and ready to go.

"I was just getting on the train when I saw him," she said. "There was nothing I could do. Oh, it's so awful – and if he just hadn't dropped that terrible trick you'd never have known."

Tom walked up and down the room a minute.

"I know you're through with me," Tudy said. "Anyhow, you'd just reproach me all the rest of my life. So we'd better quit. We can call it off."

…We can die too, he was thinking. He had never wanted anything so much in his life as he wanted to believe her. But he had to decide now not upon what was the truth, for that he would never know for certain, but upon the question as to whether he could now and for ever put the matter out of his mind, or whether it would haunt their marriage like a ghost. Suddenly he decided:

"No, we won't quit – we'll try it. And there'll never be any word of reproach."

Her face lighted up she rose and came towards him and he held her close for a minute.

"We'll go right now," he said.

An hour later they drove away from the hotel, both of them momentarily cheered by the exhilaration of starting a journey, with the little car bulging with bags and new vistas opening up ahead. But in the afternoon as they curved down through Provence, they were silent for a while each with a separate thought. His thought was that he would never know – what her thought was must be left unfathomed – and perhaps unfathomable in that obscure pool in the bottom of every woman's heart.

Towards evening as they reached the seaboard and turned east following a Riviera that twinkled with light, they came out of their separate selves and were cheerful together. When the stars were bright on the water, he said:

"We'll build our love up and not down."

"I won't have to build my love up," she said loyally. "It's up in the skies now."

They came to the end of France at midnight and looked at each other with infinite hope as they crossed the bridge over into Italy, into the new sweet warm darkness.

Too Cute for Words

1

Bryan didn't know exactly why Mrs Hannaman was there. He thought it was something about his being a widower who should be looked after in some way. He had come home early from his office to catch up on certain aspects of his daughter.

"She has such beautiful manners," Mrs Hannaman was saying. "Old-fashioned manners."

"Thank you," he said. "We brought up Gwen in the Continental style, and when we came back here, we tried to keep up the general idea."

"You taught her languages, and all that?"

"Lord, no! I never learnt anything but waiter's French, but I'm strict with Gwen. I don't let her go to the movies, for instance…"

Had Mrs Hannaman's memory betrayed her, or had she heard her little niece Clara say that she and Gwen sat through three straight performances of *Top Hat*,* and would see it again if they could find it at one of the smaller theatres.

"We have a phonograph," Bryan Bowers continued, "so Gwen can play music of her own choice, but I won't give her a radio. Children ought to make their own music."

He heard himself saying this, only half-believing it, wishing Gwen would come home.

"She plays the piano?"

"Well, she did. She took piano lessons for years, but this year there was so much work at school that we just let it go. I mean we postponed it. She's just thirteen, and she's got plenty of time."

"Of course," agreed Mrs Hannaman drily.

66

When Mrs Hannaman left, Bryan went back to work on the apartment. They were really settled at last. At least, he was settled; it seemed rather likely that Gwen never would be settled. Glancing into his daughter's room now, he uttered a short exclamation of despair. Everything was just as it had been for the past three weeks. He had told the maid that nothing must be touched except the bed, because Gwen should do her own straightening up. She had been to camp this past summer; if this was the system she had learnt, that was time wasted. A pair of crushed jodhpur breeches lay in the corner where they had been stepped out of, a section of them rising resentfully above the rest, as if trying to straighten up of its own accord; a stack of letters from boys – a stack that had once worn a neat elastic band – was spread along the top of the bureau like a pack of cards ready for the draw; three knitted sweaters in various preliminary stages of creation and the beginnings of many tidying-ups lay like abandoned foundations about the room. The business was always to be completed on the following Sunday, but Sunday was always the day when the unforeseen came up: Gwen was invited to do something very healthy, or she had so much homework, or he had to take her out with him because he didn't want to leave her alone. For a while it had been a fine idea to let her live in this mess until she was impelled to act from within, but as October crept into November the confusion increased. She was late for everything because nothing could be found. The maid complained it had become absolutely impossible to sweep the room, save with the cautious steps of Eliza on the ice.*

He heard his daughter come in and, with the problem in his mind, went to meet her in the living room.

They faced each other in a moment of happiness. They looked alike. He had been handsome once, but middle age had added flesh in the unappealing places. When he spoke of the past, Gwen was never able to imagine him in romantic situations. She was an arresting little beauty: black-eyed, with soft bay hair and with an extraordinarily infectious laugh – a rare laugh that had a peal in it, and yet managed not to get on people's nerves.

She had thrown herself full length on a couch, scattering her books on the floor. When Bryan came in, she moved her feet so that they just projected over the side of the couch. He noted the gesture, and suggested:

"Pull down your skirt or else take it off altogether."

"Daddy! Don't be so vulgar!"

"That's the only way I can get through to you sometimes."

"Daddy, I got credit plus in geometry. Cute?

"What's credit plus?"

"Ninety-two."

"Why don't they just say ninety-two?"

"Daddy, did you get the tickets for the Harvard game?"

"I told you I'd take you."

She nodded, and remarked as if absently:

"Dizzy's father's taking her to the Harvard game and the Navy game. And her uncle's taking her to the Dartmouth game. Isn't that cute?"

"What's cute about it? Do you know what you said to Doctor Parker the other day, when he asked you if you liked Caesar? You said you thought Caesar was cute." He walked around the room in helpless laughter. "A man conquers the whole known world, and a little schoolgirl comes along a thousand years afterwards and says he's cute!"

"Two thousand years…" remarked Gwen, unruffled. "Daddy, Mr Campbell's driving them up to the Harvard game in their new car. Isn't that cu… isn't that fine?"

She was always like this in the first half-hour home from school or a party – outer worlds where she lived with such intensity that she carried it into the slower tempo of life at home like weather on her shoes. This is what made her say:

"It'd take for ever the way you drive, Daddy."

"I drive fast enough."

"Once I drove ninety miles an hour—"

Startled, he stared at her, and Gwen should have been acute enough to minimize the statement immediately. But still in her worldly daze, she continued: "—on the way to Turtle Lake this summer."

"Who with?"

"With a girl."

"A girl your age driving a car!"

"No. The girl was nineteen – she's a sister of a girl I was visiting. But I won't tell you who. Probably you'd never let me go there again, Daddy."

She was very sorry that she had ever spoken.

"You might as well tell me. I know who you've visited this summer and I can find out who's got a sister nineteen years old. I'm not going to have you mangled up against a telegraph post because some young—"

Momentarily Gwen was saved by the maid calling her father to the phone. As a sort of propitiation, she hung her overcoat in the closet, picked up her books and went on into her own room.

She examined it, as usual, with a vast surprise. She knew it was rather terrible, but she had some system of her own as to what to do about it – a system that never seemed to work out in actuality. She pounced with a cry upon the wastebasket – it was her record of 'Cheek to Cheek',* broken, but preserved to remind her to get another. She cradled it to her arms and, as if this, in turn, reminded her of something else, she decided to telephone Dizzy Campbell. This required a certain diplomacy. Bryan had become adamant on the matter of long phone conversations.

"This is about Latin," she assured him.

"All right, but make it short, daughter."

He read the paper in the living room, waiting for supper; for some time, he had been aware of a prolonged murmur which confused itself in his mind with distant guns in Ethiopia and China. Only when he turned to the financial page and read the day's quotation on American Tel. and Tel. did he spring to his feet.

"She's on the phone again!" he exclaimed to himself; but even as the paper billowed to rest in front of him, Gwen appeared, all radiant and on the run.

"Oh, Daddy, the best thing! You won't have to take me to the game, after all! I mean you *will* to the game, but not up to the game. Dizzy's aunt, Mrs Charles Wrotten Ray, or something like that – somebody that's all right, that they know about, that they can trust, and all that sort of thing..."

While she panted, he enquired politely:

"What about her? Has she made the Princeton team?"

"No. She lives up there and she has some nephews or uncles or something – it was all kind of complicated on the phone – that go to some kind of prep school that are about our age – about fifteen or sixteen—"

"I thought you were thirteen."

"The boy is always older," she assured him. 'Anyhow, she—"

"Don't ever say 'she'."

"Well, excuse me, Daddy. Well, anyhow, this sort of person – you know, not 'she', but this sort of Mrs Wrotten Ray, or whatever her name is – she wants Dizzy—"

"Now, calm yourself, calm yourself."

"I can't, Daddy: she's waiting on the phone."

"Who? Mrs Wrotten Ray?"

"Oh, that isn't her name, but it's something like that. Anyhow, Mrs Wrotten Ray wants Dizzy to bring Clara Hannaman and one other girl up to a little dance the night before the game. And Dizzy wants me to be the other girl, and can I go?"

"This is all a little sudden. I don't like such things during a school term, and you know that." He hated to refuse her, though, for, excepting an occasional indiscretion of speech, she was a trustworthy child; she made good grades in school and conscientiously wrestled with her ebullient temperament.

"Well, can I, Daddy? Dizzy's waiting; she has to know."

"I suppose you can."

"Oh, thanks. Mrs Campbell's going to call you up, but Dizzy couldn't wait to tell me. Cute?"

She vanished, and in a moment the low murmur behind the door began again.

Something told Bryan that she'd be leading a simpler life at boarding school, but didn't Helen Hannaman say something today about her old-fashioned manners? He couldn't afford it this year anyhow and, besides, she was such a bright little thing to have around the house.

But if he'd known that the movies were going to produce this *Top Hat*... She had broken the record of 'Cheek to Cheek', but there was still the one about sitting on his top hat and climbing up his shirt front...

Curiously, he opened the door to the dining room and discovered the phonograph going and his daughter in a crouching posture, arms outspread, head projecting from its proper neck, eyes half-closed. When she saw him, she straightened up.

"I thought that this 'Cheek by Jowl' was broken," he said.

"It is, but you can still play the inside a little. See, it's over already. You certainly can't object to that much of a record."

"Let's put it on again," he suggested facetiously, "and we'll dance."

She looked at him with infinite compassion.

"Who do you imagine you are, Daddy? Fred Astaire? What I want to know is if I can go to Princeton."

"I said yes, didn't I?"

"But you didn't say it like when you mean it."

"Yes, then – yes. Get enough rope and hang youself."

"Then I can go?"

"Yes, of course. Why not? Where do you think you're going? To the prom or something? Of course, you can go."

2

HAVING LUNCH ON THE TRAIN, the three girls were a little bit mad with excitement. Clara Hannaman and Dizzy Campbell were fourteen, a year older than Gwen, and Clara was already somewhat taller, but they were all dressed alike in suits that might have been worn by their mothers.

Their jewellery consisted of thin rings and chains, legacies from grandmothers, supplemented by flamboyant Koh-i-noors from the five-and-ten; and it was true that their coats might once have responded to wheedling calls of "Pussy", "Bunny", or "Nanny". But it was their attacks of hysteria that stamped them as of a certain age.

Clara had asked: "What kind of a joint is this we're going to?" She was temporarily under the spell of Una Merkel* and the hard-boiled school, and this question was enough to start a *rat-tat-tat* of laughter, to the extent that eating was suspended, napkins called into play. One word was usually enough to send them off; frequently it was a boy's name that had some private meaning to them, and for a whole afternoon or evening this single word would serve as detonator. At other times a curious soberness fell upon all of them, a sort of quietude. They faced both ways – towards a world they were fast leaving and a world they had never met – and the contradiction was externalized in the uncanny mirth.

There was a sober moment now when they all looked at the girl across the way, who was the debutante of the year and bound for the fall prom. They looked with respect, even a certain awe, impressed with her ease and tranquillity in the face of her ordeal. It made them feel very young and awkward, and they were both glad and sorry that they were too young for the prom. Last year that girl had been only the captain of the basketball team at school; now she was in the Great Game, and they had noted the men who came to see her off at the station with flowers and adjurations not to "fall for any babies up there... Be five years before they get a job."

After luncheon, the three girls planned to study – they had con-scientiously brought books along – but the excitement of the train was such that they never got any farther than the phrase "jewelled stomacher" from an English history lesson – which thereafter became their phrase for the day. They reached Princeton in an uncanny, explosive quiet, because Dizzy claimed to have forgot-ten her jewelled stomacher on the train, but their wild chuckles changed to a well-bred reserve as they were greeted on the platform by Miss Ray, young and lovely and twenty.

Where were the boys? They peered for them through the early dusk, not expecting to be greeted like prom girls, but there might have been someone of their own age, the one for whom they had dressed and dreamt and waved their locks sidewise in these last twenty-four hours. When they reached the house, Miss Ray exploded the bomb; while they took off their coats, she said:

"You're due for a disappointment. I tried to reach you by telegraphing and telephone too, but you'd already left."

Their eyes turned towards her, apprehensive, already stricken.

"Seems that Grandmother's not well, and Mother felt she had to go up to Albany. So, before I was even awake, she called off the little dance, and she'd phoned everybody. I tried to fix it up, but it was too late."

Now their faces were utterly expressionless.

"Mother was excited, that's all," continued Miss Ray. "Grandmother'll live to be a hundred. I've been on the phone all afternoon trying to find some company for you girls for this evening, but the town's a madhouse and nobody's available – the boys for the little dance were coming from New York. Lord, if I'd only waked up before eleven o'clock!"

"We don't mind," Dizzy lied gently. "Really we don't, Esther. We can amuse ourselves."

"Oh, darling, I know how you feel!"

"Yes," they said together, and Dizzy asked, "Where's Shorty? Did he have to go to Albany too?"

"No, he's here. But he's only sixteen and – I hardly know how to explain it, but he's the youngest man in his class in college, and very small, and this year he's just impossibly shy. When the party was called off, he just refused to appear as the only boy; said he'd stay in his room and study chemistry, and there he is. And he won't come out."

Gwen formed a mental picture of him. Better that he remained in his hermitage: they could have more fun without him.

"Anyhow, you'll have the game tomorrow."

"Yes," they said together.

That was that. Upstairs they took out their evening gowns, which, according to modern acceptance, were as long and as chic as any adult evening gowns, and laid them on their beds. They brought out their silk hosiery, their gold or silver sandal dancing shoes, and surveyed the glittering exhibit. At that age, their mothers would have worn ruffles, flounces and cotton stockings to brand them as adolescent. But this historical fact, dinned into them for many years, was small consolation now.

After they had dressed, things seemed better, even though they were only dressing for one another; when they went down to dinner, they gave such an impression of amiability and gaiety that they convinced even Esther Ray. It was difficult, though, when Miss Ray's escort called to take her to the Harvard-Princeton concert, and she must have seen it in their eyes.

"I've got an idea," she said. "I think we can get you into the concert, but you may have to stand up in back."

That was something indeed. They brightened. They ran for coats, and Gwen caught a sight of a very hurried young man in the upper hall with a plate in one hand and a cup in the other, but he disappeared into his room before she could see him plainly.

In any event, the concert turned out as precariously as most improvisations – it was jammed, and they were obliged to stand behind rows of taller people and to listen to tantalizing bursts of laughter and fragments of song – while from Clara's superior three inches they gathered such information as they could as to what it looked like.

When it was over, they were washed out with the happy, excited crowd, driven back to the Rays' and dumped almost brusquely on the doorstep.

"Goodnight. Thanks."

"Thanks a lot."

"It was fine!"

"Thanks. Goodnight."

Upstairs they moved around in silence, casting stray glances at themselves in the mirror and rearranging, to no purpose now, some bit of awry finery. Dizzy had even taken off her necklace of seed pearls, when Gwen said suddenly:

"I want to go to the prom."

"Who doesn't?" Clara said. Suddenly she looked at Gwen sharply and asked: 'What do you mean, Gwen?"

Gwen was drawing her lips in the mirror with Dizzy's lipstick. She would have had one along herself, save it had melted going through Alabama on the way to ranch last summer, and she had never since been able to get the top off it. Clara watched her until Gwen said:

"How would you make up if you were going to the prom?"

"Like this," Clara suggested.

In a minute they were all at it.

"Not like that; that looks very ordinary." And: "Remember, that's Esther's eye pencil. That's too much, Dizzy."

"Not with powder, it isn't."

Within half an hour they had somehow managed to age themselves by several years, and crying: "Bring on my jewelled stomacher," they minced, paraded and danced around the room.

"I'll tell you what," Gwen said. "I just sort of want to go to the outside of the prom. I mean I don't want to do anything bad, you know, but I want to see how they work it."

"Esther might see us."

"She won't," said Gwen sagely. "She's probably having herself a time, and that girl on the train too – that Marion Lamb – you know, we used to know her in school. You take a lot of these debutantes," she continued, "and when they get by themselves – pretty cute is what I would say, if you asked me."

Dizzy looked like white-pine shavings; even her eyes were so light and virginal that what she said now came as a sort of shock to the other two:

"We'll do it – we'll go to the prom. We've got more what it takes than most of those girls."

"Of course this isn't like a city," Clara suggested uncertainly. "It's perfectly all right; it's just the same as going out in your yard."

This remark was calming to their consciences, but they were really less concerned with kidnappers or molesters of womanhood than with what Gwen's plan was. Gwen had no plan. She had literally nothing on her mind except a certain disparity between the picture of herself wandering around a college campus at night with rouged lips, and a little scene that had taken place a week before, when she had argued with her father that she wanted to set up her doll's house in her room instead of having it sent to storage.

The deciding factor was that they had been cheated by their elders. Though Bryan had never met Mrs Ray, he somehow seemed to share in her disastrous excitability of the morning. This was the sort of thing that parents did as a class. The sort of thing for which they had joint responsibility. Before Gwen and Dizzy had agreed to the excursion in words, they bumped shoulders around the mirror, modifying their faces until the theatrical quality yielded to the more seemly pigmentation of an embassy ball. In the last burst of conservatism, for they might run inadvertently into Esther Ray, they cleansed the area around their eyes, leaving only the faintest patina of evening on lips and noses. The ten-cent crown jewels disappeared from ear and wrist and throat so quickly that when they went downstairs all taint of the sideshow had disappeared. Taste had triumphed.

Issuing into a clear brilliant November night, they walked along a high, exuberant street beneath the dark trees of Liberty Place – though that meant nothing to them. A dog panicked them momentarily from behind a hedge, but they met no further obstacle until it was necessary to pass beneath a bright arc on Mercer Street.

"Where are we going?" Clara asked.

"Up to where we can hear it."

She stopped. Figures had loomed up ahead, and they linked arms protectively, but it was only two coloured women carrying a basket of laundry between them.

"Come on," Gwen said.

"Come on to where?"

"To where we're going."

They reached a cathedral-like structure which Clara recognized as a corner of the campus, and by a sort of instinct they turned into an archway, threaded a deserted cloister and came out into a wider vista of terraces and Gothic buildings, and suddenly there was music in the air. After a few hundred yards, Dizzy pulled them up short.

"I see it," she whispered. "It's that big building down there with all the lights. That's the gymnasium."

"Let's go closer," said Gwen. "There isn't anybody around. Let's go till we see somebody, anyhow."

Arms linked, they marched on in the shadow of the long halls. They were getting dangerously close to the zone of activity, could distinguish figures against the blur of the gymnasium entrance, and hear the applause in the intervals. Once more they stopped, afraid either to go on or to hold their ground, for there were voices and footsteps approaching out of the darkness.

"Over at the other side," Clara suggested. "It's dark there and we can get really close."

They left the path and ran across the turf; stopped, breathless, in the haven of a group of parked cars. Here they huddled silently, feeling like spies behind the enemy lines. Within the great bulky walls, fifty feet away, a sonorous orchestra proclaimed a feeling that someone was fooling, announced that someone was its lucky star, and demanded if it wasn't a lovely day to be caught in the rain. Inside those walls existed ineffable romance – an orchid-coloured dream in which floated prototypes of their future selves, surrounded, engulfed, buoyed up by unnumbered boys. No one spoke; there was no more to say than the orchestra was saying to their young hearts, and when the music stopped, they did not speak; then suddenly they realized that they were not alone.

"We can eat later," a man's voice said.

"I don't care about it at all, when I'm with you."

The three young girls caught their breath in a gasp, clutched at one another's arms. The voices came from a car not five feet from where they stood; it was turned away from the gymnasium, so that, under cover of the music, their approach had gone unobserved.

"What's one supper," the girl continued, "when I think of all the suppers we'll have together all through life?"

"Beginning next June, darling."

"Beginning next June, darling, darling, darling."

And once again a clutching went on among the listeners. For the girl's voice was that of Marion Lamb, the debutante who had been on the train.

At this point, because it was a rather cool night and her evening cloak was thin, Dizzy sneezed – sneezed loudly – and sneezed again.

3

"BUT HOW DO WE KNOW you kids won't tell?" the man was demanding. He turned to Marion: "Can't you explain to them how important it is not to tell? Explain that it'll absolutely wreck your debut at home."

"But I don't care, Harry. I'd be proud—"

"I care. It simply can't get around now."

"We won't tell," the young girls chorused ardently. And Gwen added: "We think it's cute."

"Do you realize you're the only ones that know?" he asked sternly. "The only ones! And if it slipped out, I'd know who told, and…"

There were such sinister threats in his voice that, instinctively, the trio recoiled a step.

"That isn't the way to talk to them," said Marion. "I went to school with these girls and I know they won't tell. Anyhow, they know it's not serious – that I get engaged every few weeks or so."

"Marion," cried the young man, "I can't stand hearing you talk like that!"

"Oh, Harry, I didn't mean to hurt you!" she gasped, equally upset. "You know there's never been anyone but you."

He groaned.

"Well, how are we going to silence this gallery?" Distraught, he fumbled in his pocket for money.

"No, Harry. They'll keep quiet." But looking at those six eyes, she felt a vast misgiving. "Listen, what would you three like more than anything in the world?"

They laughed and looked at one another.

"To go to the prom, I guess," said Gwen frankly. "But of course, we wouldn't be allowed to. Our parents wouldn't let us, even if we were invited – I mean—"

"I've got the idea," said Harry. "I'll tell you what I'll do. I know a side entrance that leads up to the indoor track. How would you like to sit up there in the dark and look on awhile without anybody seeing you?"

"Whew!" said Dizzy.

"If I take you up there, will you give me your sacred words of honour that you'll never breathe a word of what you heard tonight?"

"Will we!" they exclaimed together.

4

LEAVING THEM ON THE RUNNING TRACK, the focusing eye must move down momentarily to the thick of the dance below. Or rather to its outskirts, where a person had just appeared who has hitherto played a small and sorry part in this history, and there he stood uncertainly, his view obscured by a throbbing Harvard-Princeton stag line. If, half an hour before, anyone had told Shorty Ray that eleven o'clock would find him in his present situation, he would not even have said, "Huh!" Some boys of inconsiderable height are compensated by an almost passionate temerity. Not Shorty: since adolescence, he never had been able to face girls with a minimum of dignity.

The dance at home was part of a campaign to break him of his shyness, and it had seemed a stroke of luck to him that if his grandmother's health were going to fail anyhow, it should have chosen this particular day.

As if in retribution for this irreverence, a telegram from Albany addressed to his sister had come to the house at the very moment when he had started to turn out his lights.

An older man would have torn open the telegram and read it, but anything sealed was sacred to him, and such telegrams spelled emergencies. There was nothing for it save to get it to Esther in the gymnasium as quickly as possible.

One thing he knew – he would not go upon the dance floor in search of her. After he had argued his way past the doorkeeper, he was simply standing there feeling helpless, when Dizzy spied him from above.

"There's Tommy!" she exclaimed.

"Where?"

"The short boy by the door. Well, that's pathetic, if you ask me! He wouldn't even come out and look at us, and then he goes to the prom."

"He doesn't seem to be having much of a time," said Clara.

"Let's go down and cheer him up," Gwen suggested.

"Not me," said Dizzy. "For one thing, I wouldn't want the Rays to know we were here."

"I forgot about that."

"Anyhow, he's gone now."

He was gone, but not, as they supposed, into the delirious carnival. Irresolute, he had finally conceived the idea of mounting to the running track and trying to locate Esther among the dancers. Even as Dizzy spoke, he was there at her elbow, to their mutual surprise.

"I thought you were in bed!" he exclaimed, as he recognized his cousin.

"I thought you were studying."

"*I was* studying when a telegram came, and now I've got to find Esther."

He was introduced with great formality; Gwen and Clara immediately adopting the convention that they had not known of his existence in the same town.

"Esther was in one of the boxes a while ago," said Gwen. "Number Eighteen."

Grasping at this, Tommy turned to Dizzy.

"Then I wonder if you'd mind going over and giving her this telegram?"

"I would so mind," said Dizzy. "Why don't you give it to her yourself? We're not supposed to be here."

"Neither am I; they let me in. But I can't just walk across there all by myself, and you can," he said earnestly.

Gwen had been looking at him in a curiously intent way for some moments. He was not at all the person she had pictured – in fact, she decided that he was one of the handsomest boys she had ever seen in her life.

"I'll take it to her," she said suddenly.

"Will you?" For the first time he seemed to see Gwen – a girl who looked like the pictures in the magazines, and yet was smaller than himself. He thrust the telegram at her. "Thanks! Gosh, I certainly am—"

"I'm not going downstairs alone," she interrupted. "You've got to take me part way."

As they descended, he looked at her again out of the corner of his eye; at the big arch he paused.

"Now you take it the rest of the way," he said.

"The best way would be to do it together."

"Oh, no!" he exclaimed. "You didn't say that. I'm not going to walk across the floor."

"I didn't mean walk. If we walked, everybody'd kind of look at us, but if we danced across to the box, nobody would notice it."

"You said you'd take it!" he said indignantly.

"I will, but you've got to take me." And she added innocently, "That makes it easy for us both."

"I won't do it," he declared.

"Then you can take it yourself."

"I never—"

Suddenly, before he realized it, she was in the circle of his arm, his hand was on what was apparently a forgotten seam in her dress just between shoulder blades, and they were moving across the floor.

Through the line of stags and out into the kaleidoscope. Gwen was at home; all hesitancy at the daring of her idea vanishing like the tension of a football player after the kick-off. By some inexorable right, this was her world. This was, perhaps, not the time set for entering it but, maybe because her generation had ceased to move in the old Euclidean world, her age ceased to matter after a moment. She felt as old as any girl on the floor.

And now, miracle of miracles, the lights dimmed, and at the signal the divine spark passed from one orchestra to another, and Gwen was dancing onward in a breathless trance to the melody of 'Cheek to Cheek'.

In the Laurel Club box, the ladies were growing weary. Chaperonage, they decided, was too lightly undertaken, too poorly compensated for. They were tired of the parade of animation, of lovely, confident faces, and one of them said as much to the middle-aged man who sat at her side. He too wore the look of speculating upon the texture of cool pillowcases and the beatitude of absolute quiet.

"I had to come," she said, "but I still don't understand why you came."

"Perhaps because I saw in the morning paper that you'd be here, after all these years."

"This is no place to say that to a woman of my age; the competition makes me feel very old. Look at that odd-looking couple – like a pair of midgets. I haven't seen them before."

He looked, but they seemed like just the sort of eccentrics to wander into any doze, so, after vaguely replying, "Aren't they cute?" he glazed his eyes for a while, until she commented: "There they are again. Such little people. That girl – why, she can't be more than fourteen, and she's like a blasé, world-weary woman of twenty. Can you imagine what her parents could have been thinking of, to let her come here tonight?"

He looked again; then, after a long pause, he said, rather wearily: "Yes, I can imagine."

"You think it's all right then?" she demanded. "Why, it seems to me—"

"No, Helen, I just meant I can imagine what they would be thinking if they knew about it. Because the girl seems to be my daughter."

5

IT WAS NOT IN BRYAN'S NATURE to rush out and snatch Gwen from the floor. Should she pass near him again, he intended to bow to her very formally indeed and let the next step be hers. He was not angry with her – he supposed her hostess was behind the matter – but he was angry at a system which permitted a baby disguised as a young woman, a marriageable young woman, to dance at a semi-public ball.

At his undergraduate club the next day, he wended his way from group to group, stopping to chat momentarily here and there, but with his eye always out for Gwen, who was to meet him there. When the crowd was drifting out and down to the stadium, he called the Rays' house, and found her still there.

"You better meet me at the game," he said, glad he had given her the ticket. "I want to go down now and see the teams practise."

"Daddy, I hate to say it but I've lost it." Her voice was hushed and solemn. "I searched and searched, and then I remembered I stuck it in the mirror at home with some invitations, to see how it would look, and forgot to—"

The connection was broken, and a male voice demanded if there were rooms at the club tonight and if the steward had delivered a brown lunch basket to Thomas Pickering, ninety-six. For ten minutes more he jangled the receiver; he wanted to tell her to buy a bad seat in the end stand and work her way around to him, but the phone service in Princeton shared the hysteria of the crowd.

People began going by the booth, looking at their watches and hurrying to get to the kick-off; in another five minutes there was no one going by the booth, and there was sweat upon Bryan's brow. He had played freshman football in college; it meant to him what war or chess might have meant to his grandfather. Resentment possessed him suddenly.

"After all, she had her fun last night, and now I have a right to mine. Let her miss it. She doesn't care, really."

But on the way to the stadium he was torn between the human roar that went up at momentary intervals behind that massive wall and the picture of Gwen making a last desperate search for that precious counter that gleamed uselessly in a mirror at home.

He hardened himself.

"It's that disorderliness. This will be a better lesson than any lecture."

Nevertheless, at the very gate Bryan paused once more; he and Gwen were very close, and he could still go after her, but a huge swelling cry from the arena decided him: he went in with the last dribble of the crowd.

It was as he reached his seat that he saw that there was a hand signalling him, heard a voice hailing him.

"Oh, Daddy, here we are! We thought maybe you'd—"

"Sit down," he whispered, breathlessly slipping into his place. "People want to see. Did you find your ticket?

"No, Daddy. I had a terrible time – but this is Tommy Ray, Daddy. He hasn't got a seat here: he was just keeping your seat till you came. He can sit anywhere because he—"

"Be quiet, baby! You can tell me later. What's happened on the field? What's on that scoreboard?"

"What scoreboard?"

From the aisle steps whither he had moved, Tommy supplied the information that it was nothing to nothing; Bryan bent his whole attention upon the game.

At the quarter, he relaxed and demanded:

"How did you manage to get in?"

"Well, you see, Tommy Ray" – she lowered her voice – "this boy beside me – he's one of the ticket-takers. And I knew he'd be somewhere, because he told me last night that was why he had to go home—"

She stopped herself.

"I understand," Bryan said drily. "I wondered what you found to talk about in that remarkable dancing position."

"You were there?" she cried in dismay. "You—"

"Listen to that Harvard band," he interrupted, "jazzing old marching songs – seems sort of irreverent. Of course, you'd probably like them to play 'Cheek by Jowl'."

"Daddy!"

But for a moment her eyes were far off on the grey horizon, listening, not to the band, to that sweeter and somehow older tune.

"What did you think?" she asked, after a moment. "I mean when you saw me there?"

"What did I think? I thought you were just too cute for words."

"You didn't! I don't care how you punish me, but please don't ever say that horrible word again!"

Inside the House

1

WHEN BRYAN BOWERS CAME HOME in the late afternoon, three boys were helping Gwen to decorate the tree. He was glad, for she had bought too big a tree to climb around herself, and he had not relished the prospect of crawling over the ceiling.

The boys stood up as he came in, and Gwen introduced them:

"Jim Bennett, Daddy, and Satterly Brown you know, and Jason Crawford you know."

He was glad she had said the names. So many boys had been there throughout the holidays that it had become somewhat confusing.

He sat down for a moment.

"Don't let me interrupt. I'll be leaving you shortly."

It struck him that the three boys looked old, or certainly large, beside Gwen, though none was over sixteen. She was fourteen, almost beautiful, he thought – would be beautiful, if she had looked a little more like her mother. But she had such a pleasant profile and so much animation that she had become rather too popular at too early an age.

"Are you at school here in the city?" he asked the new young man.

"No, sir. I'm at St Regis; just home for the holidays."

Jason Crawford, the boy with the wavy yellow pompadour and horn-rimmed glasses, said with an easy laugh:

"He couldn't take it here, Mr Bowers."

Bryan continued to address the new boy:

"Those little lights you're working at are the biggest nuisance about a Christmas tree. One bulb always misses and then it takes for ever to find which one it is."

"That's just what happened now."

"You said it, Mr Bowers," said Jason.

Bryan looked up at his daughter, balanced on a stepladder.

"Aren't you glad I told you to put these men to work?" he asked. "Think of old Daddy having to do this."

Gwen agreed from her precarious perch: "It would have been hard on you, Daddy. But wait till I get this tinsel thing on."

"You aren't old, Mr Bowers," Jason offered.

"I feel old."

Jason laughed, as if Bryan had said something witty.

Bryan addressed Satterly:

"How do things go with you, Satterly? Make the first hockey team?"

"No, sir. Never really expected to."

"He gets in all the games," Jason supplied.

Bryan got up.

"Gwen, why don't you hang these boys on the tree?" he suggested. "Don't you think a Christmas tree covered with boys would be original?"

"I think—' began Jason, but Bryan continued:

"I'm sure none of them would be missed at home. You could call up their families and explain that they were only being used as ornaments till after the holidays."

He was tired, and that was his best effort. With a general wave, he went towards his study.

Jason's voice followed him:

"You'd get tired seeing us hanging around, Mr Bowers. Better change your mind about letting Gwen have dates."

Bryan turned around sharply. "What do you mean about 'dates'?"

Gwen peeked over the top of the Christmas tree. "He just means about dates, Daddy. Don't you know what a date is?"

"Well now, will one of you tell me just exactly what a date is?"

All the boys seemed to begin to talk at once.

"Why, a date is—"

"Why, Mr Bowers—"

"A *date*—"

He cut through their remarks:

"Is a 'date' anything like what we used to call an engagement?"

Again the cacophony commenced.

"…No, a date is…"

"…An engagement is…"

"…It's sort of more…"

Bryan looked up at the Christmas tree from which Gwen's face stared out from the tinsel somewhat like the Cheshire cat in *Alice in Wonderland*.

"Heaven's sakes, don't fall out of the tree about it," he said.

"Daddy, you don't mean to say that you don't know what a date is?"

"A date is something you can have at home," said Bryan. He started to go to his study but Jason supplied: "Mr Bowers, I can explain to you why Gwen won't fall out of the tree—"

Bryan closed his door on the remark and stood near it.

"That young man is extremely fresh," he thought.

Stretched out on his divan for half an hour, he let the worries of the day slip from his shoulders. At the end of that time there was a knock, and he sat up, saying:

"Come in… Oh, hello, Gwen." He stretched and yawned.

"How's your metabolism?"

"What's metabolism? You asked me that one the other afternoon."

"I think it's something everybody has. Like a liver."

She had a question to ask him and did not pursue the subject further: "Daddy, did you like them? Those boys?"

"Sure."

"How do you like Jason?"

He pretended to be obtuse.

"Which one was he?"

"You know very well. Once you said he was fresh. But he wasn't this afternoon, did you think?"

"The boy with all the yellow fuzz?"

"Daddy, you know very well which one he was."

"I wasn't sure. Because you told me if I didn't let you go out alone at night, Jason wouldn't come to see you again. So I thought this must be some boy who looked like him."

She shook off his teasing.

"I do know this, Daddy: that if I'm not allowed to have dates, nobody's going to invite me to the dance."

"What do you call this but a date? Three boys. If you think I'm going to let you race around town at night with some kid, you're fooling yourself. He can come here any night except a school night."

"It isn't the same," she said mournfully.

"Let's not go over that. You told me that all the girls you knew had these dates, but when I asked you to name even one—"

"All right, Daddy. The way you talk you'd think it was something awful we were going to do. We just want to go to the movies."

"To see Peppy Velance again."

She admitted that was their destination.

"I've heard nothing but Peppy Velance for two months. Dinner's one long movie magazine. If that girl is your ideal, why don't you be practical about it and learn to tap like her? If you just want to be a belle—"

"What's a belle?"

"A belle?" Bryan was momentarily unable to understand that the term needed definition. "A belle? Why, it's what your mother was. Very popular – that sort of thing."

"Oh. You mean the nerts."

"What?"

"Being the nerts – having everybody nerts about you."

"What?" he repeated incredulously.

"Oh, now, don't get angry, Daddy. Call it a belle then."

He laughed, but as she stood beside his couch, silent and a little resentful, a wave of contrition went over him as he remembered that she was motherless. Before he could speak, Gwen said in a tight little voice:

"I don't think your friends are so interesting! What am I supposed to do – get excited about some lawyers and doctors?"

"We won't discuss that. You have the day with your friends. When you're home in the evening, you've got to be a little grown-up. There's a lawyer coming here tonight to dinner, and I'd like you to make a good impression on him."

"Then I can't go to the movies?"

"No."

Silent and expressionless, save for the faint lift of her chin, Gwen stood a moment. Then she turned abruptly and left the room.

2

M R EDWARD HARRISON was pleased to find his friend's little girl so polite and so pleasant to look at. Bryan, wanting to atone for his harshness of the afternoon, introduced him as the author of 'The Music Goes Round and Round'.

For a moment, Gwen looked at Mr Harrison, startled. Then they laughed together.

During dinner, the lawyer tried to draw her out:

"Do you plan to marry? Or to take up a career?"

"I think that I'd like to be a debutante.' She looked at her father reproachfully. "And maybe have dates on the side. I haven't got any talents for a career that I know about."

Her father interrupted her:

"She has though. She ought to make a good biologist – or else she could be a chemist making funny artificial fingernails." He changed his tone: "Gwen and I had a little run-in on the subject of careers this afternoon. She's stage-struck, and I'd rather have her do something about it than just talk."

Mr Harrison turned to Gwen. "Why don't you?" he asked. "I can give you some tips. I do a lot of theatrical business. Probably know some of your favourites."

"Do you know Peppy Velance?"

"She's a client of mine."

Gwen was thrilled.

"Is she nice?"

"Yes. But I'm more interested in you. Why not go in for a career if your father thinks you have the necessary stuff?"

How could Gwen tell him it was because she was happy the way things were? How could she explain to him what she hardly knew herself – that her feeling for Peppy Velance only stood for loveliness – enchanted gardens, ballrooms through which to walk with enchanted lovers? Starlight and tunes.

The stage! The very word frightened her. That was work, like school. But somewhere there must exist a world of which Peppy Velance's pictures were only an echo, and this world seemed to lie just ahead – proms and parties of people at gay resorts. She could not cry out to Mr Harrison, "I don't want a career, because I'm a romantic little snob. Because I want to be a belle, a belle, a belle" – the word ringing like a carillon inside her.

So she only said:

"Please tell me about Peppy Velance."

"Peppy Velance? Let's see."

He thought for a moment. "She's a kid from New Mexico. Her name's really Schwartze. Sweet. About as much brains as the silver peacock on your buffet. Has to be coached before every scene, so she can talk English. And she's having a wonderful time with her success. Is that satisfactory?"

It was far from being satisfactory to Gwen. But she didn't believe him.

He was an old man, about forty, like her father, and Peppy Velance had probably never looked at him romantically.

The important thing was that Jason would arrive presently, and maybe two other boys and a girl. They would have some sort of time – in spite of the fact that a sortie into the world of night was forbidden.

"One girl at school knows Clark Gable," she said, switching the subject. "Do you know him, Mr Harrison?"

"No," Mr Harrison said in such a funny way that both father and daughter looked at him. His face had turned grey.

"I wonder if I could ask for a cup of coffee?"

The host stepped on the bell.

"Do you want to lie down, Ed?"

"No, thanks. I brought a briefcase of work to do on the train and the strain on the eyes always seems to affect the old pump."

Being one of those who had made an unwelcome breakfast of chlorine gas eighteen years before, Bryan understood that Mr Harrison could never be quite sure. As the other man drank his coffee, the world was still swimming and he felt the need of telling this pretty little girl something – before the tablecloth got darker.

"Were you offended at what I said about Peppy Velance? You were. I saw you wondering how an old man like me would dare even talk about her."

"Honestly—"

He waved her silent with a feeling that his own time was short.

"I didn't want to give you the idea that all actresses are as superficial as Peppy. It's a fine career. Lots of intelligent women go into it now."

What was it that he wanted to tell her? There was something in that eager little face that he longed to help.

He shook his head from side to side when Bryan asked him once more if he would like to lie down.

"Of course, it's better to do things than to talk about them," he said, catching his breath with an effort.

He choked on the coffee. "Nobody wants a lot of bad actresses. But it would be nice if all girls were to do something."

As his weakness increased he felt that, perhaps, it was this pretty little girl's face he was fighting. Then he fainted.

Afterwards he was on his feet with Bryan's arm supporting him.

"No… Here on Gwen's sofa… till I can get the doctor… Gently… There you are… Gwen, I want you to stay in the room a minute."

She was thinking:

"Jason will be here any time now." She wished her father would hurry at the phone. Growing up during her mother's illness had inevitably made her callous about such things.

Their doctor lived almost across the street. When he arrived, she and her father retired to his study.

"What do you think, Daddy? Will Mr Harrison have to go to a hospital?"

"I don't know whether they'll want to move him."

"What about Jason then?"

Abstracted, he only half-heard her. "I hope it's nothing serious about Mr Harrison, but did you notice the colour of his face?"

The doctor came into the study and held a quiet conversation with him, from which Gwen caught the words "trained nurse" and "I'll call the drugstore".

As Bryan started into the other room, she said:

"Daddy, if Jason and I went out—"

She broke off as he turned.

"You and Jason aren't going out. I told you that."

"But if Mr Harrison's got to stay in the guest room right next door, where you can hear every word…"

She stopped again at the expression in her father's face when what she was saying dawned on him.

"Call Jason right away and tell him not to come," he said. He shook his head from side to side: "Good Lord! Whose little girl are you?"

3

SIX DAYS LATER GWEN CAME HOME, propelling herself as if she were about to dive into a ditch just ahead. She wore a sort of hat that evidently Heaven had sent down upon her. It had lit as an ornament on her left temple, and when she raised her hand to her head, it slid – the impression being that it was held by an invisible elastic, which might snap at any moment and send it, with a zip, back into space.

"Where did you get it?" the cook asked enviously as she came in through the pantry entrance.

"Get what?"

"Where did you get it?" her father asked as she came into his study.

"This?" Gwen asked incredulously.

"It's all right with me."

The maid had followed her in, and he said, in answer to her question:

"We'll have the same diet ordered for Mr Harrison. Wait a minute – if Gwen's hat floats out the window, take a shotgun out of the closet – and see if you can bring it down, like a duck."

In her room, Gwen removed the article of discussion, putting it delicately on her dresser for present admiration. Then she went to pay her daily visit to Mr Harrison.

He was so much better that he was on the point of getting up. When Gwen came in, he sent the nurse for some water and lay back momentarily. To Gwen he looked more formidable as he got better. His hair, from lack of cutting, wasn't like the smooth coiffures of her friends. She wished her father knew handsomer people.

"I'm about to get up and make my arrangements to go back to New York to work. Before I go, though, I want to tell you something."

"All right, Mr Harrison. I'm listening."

"It's seldom you find beauty and intelligence in the same person. When you do, they have to spend the first part of their life terribly afraid of a flame that they will have to put out some day—"

"Yes, Mr Harrison—"

"—and sometimes they spend the rest of their life trying to wake up that same flame. Then it's like a kid trying to make a bonfire out of two sticks – only this time one of the sticks is the beauty they have lost and the other stick is the intelligence they haven't cultivated – and the two sticks won't make a bonfire – and they just think that life has done them a dirty trick, when the truth is these two sticks would *never* set fire to each other. And now go call the nurse for me, Gwen." As she left the room he called after her, "Don't be too hard on your father."

She turned around from the door – "What do you mean, don't be hard on Father?"

"He loved somebody who was beautiful, like you."

"You mean Mummy?"

"You do look like her. Nobody could ever actually be like her." He broke off to write a cheque for the nurse, and as if he was impelled by something outside himself he added, "So did many other men." He brought himself up sharply and asked the nurse, "Do I owe anything more to the night nurse?" Then once again to Gwen:

"I want to tell you about your father," he said. "He never got over your mother's death, never will. If he is hard on you, it is because he loves you."

"He's never hard on me," she lied.

"Yes, he is. He is unjust sometimes, but your mother…" He broke off and said to the nurse, "Where's my tie?"

"Here it is, Mr Harrison."

After he had left the house in a flurry of telephoning, Gwen took her bath, weighted her fresh, damp hair with curlers and drew herself a mouth with the last remnant from a set of vari-coloured lipsticks that had belonged to her mother. Encountering her father in the hall, she looked at him closely in the light of what Mr Harrison had said, but she only saw the father she had always known.

"Daddy, I want to ask you once more. Jason has invited me to go to the movies with him tonight. I thought you wouldn't mind – if there were four of us. I'm not absolutely sure Dizzy can come, but I think so. Since Mr Harrison's been here I haven't been able to have any company."

"Don't do anything about it until you've had your dinner," Bryan said. 'What's the use of having an admirer if you can't dangle him a little?"

"Dangle how, what do you mean?"

"Well, I just meant make him wait."

"But, Daddy, how could I make him wait when he's the most important boy in town?"

"What is this all about?" he demanded. "Seems to be a question of whether this prep-school hero has his wicked way with you or whether I have mine. And anyhow, it's just possible that something more amusing will turn up."

Gwen seemed to have no luck that night – on the phone Dizzy said:

"I'm almost sure I can go, but I don't know absolutely."

"You call me back whatever happens."

"You call me. Mother thinks I can go, but she doesn't think she can do anything now, 'cause there's something under the sink and Father hasn't come home."

"The sink!"

"We don't know exactly what it is; it may be a water main or something. That's why everybody's afraid to go downstairs. I can't tell you anything definite until Father comes home."

"Dizzy! I don't know what you're talking about."

"We're so upset out here too. I'll explain when I see you. Anyhow, Mother's telling me to put the phone down" – there was a momentary interruption – "so they can get to the plumber."

Then the phone hung up with an impact that suggested that all the plumbers in the world were arriving in gross.

Immediately the phone rang again. It was Jason.

"Well, how about it, can we go to the movies?"

"I don't know. I just finished talking to Dizzy. The water main's busted and she has to have a plumber."

"Can't you go to the picture whether she can or not? I've got the car and our chauffeur."

"No, I can't go alone and Dizzy's got this thing."

The impression in Gwen's voice was that plague was raging in the suburbs.

"What?"

"Never mind, never mind. I don't understand it myself. If you want to know more about it, call up Dizzy."

"But Peppy Velance is in *Night Train* at the Eleanora Duse Theatre – you know, the little place just about two blocks from where you live."

There was a long pause. Then Gwen's voice said:

"A-l-l right. I'll go whether Dizzy can go or not."

She met her father presently with a guilty feeling, but before she could speak he said:

"Put on your hat – *and* your rubbers; feels stormy outside; plans are changed and we're dining out."

"Daddy, I don't want to go out. I've got homework to do."

He was disappointed.

"I'd rather stay here," Gwen continued. "I'm expecting company."

At the false impression she was giving she felt something go out of her. With an attempt at self-justification she added, "Daddy, I get good marks at school, and just because I happen to like some boys..."

Bryan tied his muffler again and bent over to pull on his over-shoes. "Goodbye," he said.

"What do you mean?" enquired Gwen uncertainly.

"I merely said goodbye, darling."

"But you kind of scared me, Daddy – you talk as if you were going away for ever."

"I won't be late. I just thought you might come along, because someone amusing might be there."

"I don't want to go, Daddy."

4

BUT AFTER HER FATHER HAD GONE, it was no fun sitting beside the phone waiting for Jason to call. When he did phone, she started downstairs to meet him – she was still in a bad humour – a fact that she displayed to one of the series of trained nurses that had been taking care of Mr Harrison. This one had just come in and she wore blue glasses, and Gwen said with unfamiliar briskness:

"I don't know where Mr Harrison is; I think he was going to meet Daddy at some party and I guess they will be back some time."

On her way down in the elevator she thought: "But I do know where Daddy is."

"Stop!" she said to the elevator man. "Take me upstairs again."

He brought the car to rest.

But a great stubbornness seemed to have come over Gwen with her decision to be disobedient.

"No, go on down," she said.

It haunted her, though, when she met Jason and they trudged their way through the gathering snowstorm to the car.

They had scarcely started off before there was a short struggle.

"No, I won't kiss you," Gwen said. "I did that once and the boy that kissed me told about it. Why should I? Nobody does that any more – at my age anyhow."

"You're fourteen."

"Well, wait till I'm fifteen then. Maybe it'll be the thing to do by that time."

They sank back in opposite corners of the car. "Then I guess you won't like this picture," said Jason, "because I understand it's pretty hot stuff. When Peppy Velance gets together with this man in the dive in Shanghai, I understand—"

"Oh, skip it," Gwen exploded.

She scarcely knew why she had liked him so much an hour before.

The snow had gathered heavily on the portico of the theatre with the swirl of a Chesapeake Bay blizzard, and she was glad of the warmth within. Momentarily, as the newsreel unwound, she forgot her ill humour, forgot her unblessed excursion into the night – forgot everything except that she had not told the nurse where her father could be found.

At the end of the newsreel she said to Jason:

"Isn't there a drugstore where I could phone home, where we could go out to for just a minute?"

"But the feature's going on in just a minute," he objected, "and it's snowing so hard."

All through the shorts, though, it worried her – so much that in a scene where Mickey Mouse skated valiantly over the ice she seemed to see snow falling into the theatre too. Suddenly she grabbed Jason's arm and shook him as if to shake herself awake – though she didn't feel asleep – because the snow was falling. It was falling in front of the screen in drips and then in large pebble-like pieces and then in a scatter of what looked like snowballs. Other people must have noticed the same phenomenon at the same time, for the projecting machine went off with a click and left the house dark; the dim house lights went on and the four ushers on duty in the little picture house ran down the aisles with confused expressions to see what the trouble was.

Gwen heard a quick twitter of alarm behind her; a stout man who had stumbled over them coming in said in an authoritative voice, "Say, I think the ceiling is caving in." And immediately several people rose around them.

"Hold on," the man cried. "Don't anybody lose their heads."

It was one of those uncertain moments in a panic where tragedy might intervene by an accidental word and, as if realizing this, a temporary hush came over the crowd. The ushers stopped in their tracks. The first man to see and direct the situation was the projector operator, who came out from his booth and leant over the balcony, crying down:

"The snow has broken through the roof. Everybody go out the side exits marked with the little red lights. No, I said the side exits – the little red lights." Trouble was developing at the main entrance too, but he didn't want them to know about it. "Don't rush – you're just risking your own lives. You men down there crack anybody that even looks as if they were going to run."

After an uncertain desperate moment, the crowd decided to act together.

They filed slowly out through the emergency exits, some of them half afraid even to look towards the screen, now only a white blank almost imperceptible through the interior snowstorm that screened it in turn. They all behaved well, as American crowds do, and they were out in the adjoining street and alley before the roof gave way altogether.

Gwen went out calmly.

What she felt most strongly in the street with the others was that the durn snow might have waited a little longer, because Peppy Velance's picture was about to start.

5

THE MANAGER HAD BEEN THE LAST TO LEAVE, and he was now telling the anxious crowd that everyone had left the theatre before the roof fell in. It was only then that Gwen thought of Jason and realized that he was no longer with her...

That, in fact, from the moment of the near calamity he had not been beside her at all – but just might have been snowed under by the general collapse. Then – as she joined the throng of those who had lost each other and were finding each other again in the confusion – her eye fell upon him on the outskirts of the crowd and she started towards him.

She ran against policemen coming up, and small boys rushing towards the accident, and she was held up by the huge drift of snow that still gathered about the fallen portico.

When she was clear of the crowd, Jason was somehow out of sight. But she had a dollar in her pocket, and she hesitated between trying to get a taxi or walking the few blocks home. She decided on the latter.

The snow that had brought down the movie house continued. She had meant to be home surely before her father, and had calculated on only one hour of time that she would never be able to account for to herself – but time she knew that sooner or later she would account for to her father.

As she walked along she thought that she had made the nurse wait too, but now she was almost home and she could straighten that out. As she passed the second block she thought of Jason with contempt, and thought:

"If *he* couldn't wait for me, why should I wait for *him*?"

She reached the apartment, prepared to face her father with the truth and what necessary result would evolve.

6

THERE WAS A COAT OF SNOW on her shoulders as she came into the apartment.

Her father in the sitting room heard her key in the lock and came to the door before she opened it. "I have been worried," he said. "You've never gone out before against my orders. What happened?"

"We went to see Peppy Velance at the small theatre just over a couple of blocks from here and, Daddy, the roof fell in."

"What roof?"

"The roof of the theatre."

"What!"

"Yes, Daddy, the roof fell in."

"Was anybody killed?"

"No, they got us all out first; Jason didn't bring me home, but I saw him afterwards and I know that he's all right, and the man said nobody was hurt."

"I'm glad I didn't think of all that."

"It was the snow," said Gwen. "I know you're pretty sore, but it's been so dull this whole week, with Mr Harrison sick and this is the last time Peppy Velance was going to be at the Eleanora Duse—"

"Peppy Velance was here. She left ten minutes ago. She was waiting to see you."

"What?"

"You saw her tonight, even if you didn't know it. She flew down from New York to see Mr Harrison about some business, but you seemed to be in an awful hurry. Mr Harrison didn't expect her so soon. We brought her back here because I knew that you might like to meet her properly."

"*Daddy!*"

"I suppose you didn't recognize her because she had on blue glasses, but she took them off, and when she's got them off she looks just as human as anyone else."

Stricken, Gwen sat down and repeated. "Was she here, Daddy?"

"Well, Mr Harrison seems to think so, and he ought to know."

"Where is Peppy Velance now?"

"She and Mr Harrison had plans to catch the midnight train to New York. He left you his regards. Say, you haven't caught cold, have you?"

Gwen brushed at her eyes. "No, these are only snowflakes. Daddy, do you mean that she was honestly here all that time while I was out?"

"Yes, daughter, but don't cry about it. She left you a little box of lipstick with her name on it and it's on the table."

"I never thought of her like that," Gwen said slowly. "I thought there were always a lot of – you know – a lot of attractive men hanging around her. I guess why I didn't recognize her was because there weren't any men hanging around her. Go on, Daddy: tell me – at least, was she attractive – like Mummy was?"

"She wasn't like Mummy, but she was very nice – I hope you didn't catch cold."

"I don't think so." She sniffed experimentally. "No, I'm sure I didn't. Isn't it funny I went out and the blizzard came? I wish I'd stayed here where it was safe and warm..." On her way to her room she ruminated aloud:

"I guess most important things happen inside the house, don't they, Daddy?"

"You go to bed."

"All right, Daddy."

Her door closed gently. What went on behind it he would never know. He wrote her a short note saying:

Peppy Velance and Mr Harrison are coming to dinner tomorrow night.

He stood it up against the English history book on the table. Then he moved it to rest against the little tin satchel that the maid would fill with sandwiches for school in the morning.

Three Acts of Music

1

THEY COULD HARDLY HEAR IT for a while. It was a slow gleam of pale blue and creamy pink. Then there was a tall room where there were many young people, and finally they began to feel it and hear it.

What were they – no. This is about music.

He went to the bandstand; the piano player let him lean over his shoulder to read:

"From *No, No, Nanette* by Vincent Youmans."*

"Thank you," he said. "I'd like to drop something in the horn, but when an intern has a dollar bill and two coins in the world he might get married instead."

"Never mind, doctor. That's about what I had when I got married last winter."

When he came back to the table she said:

"Did you find out who wrote that thing?"

"*No!* When do we go from here?"

"When they stop playing 'Tea for Two'."

Later, as she came out of the women's dressing room, she asked the man: "Who played it?"

"My God, how do I know? The band played it."

It dripped out the door now:

> *Tea...*
>   *...two*
> *Two...*
>   *...tea*

"We can never get married. I'm not even a nurse yet."

"Well, let's kill the idea – let's spend the rest of our lives going around and listening to tunes. What did you say that writer's name was?"

"What did *you* say? You went over and looked, dint you?"

"*Didn't* you," he corrected her.

"You're so swell all the time."

"Well, at least I found out who wrote it."

"Who?"

"Somebody named Vincent Youmans."

She hummed it over:

> *And you...*
>   ...for me
> *And me...*
>   ...for you
>   *Al—o-*
>   *o-*
>   *n-n...*

Their arms went about each other for a moment in the corridor outside the red room.

"If you lost the dollar bill and the other nickel, I'd still marry you," she said.

2

THIS IS NOW YEARS LATER, but there was still music. There was 'All Alone' and 'Remember' and 'Always' and 'Blue Skies' and 'How about Me'.* He was back from Vienna, but it didn't seem to matter so much as it had before.

"Wait in here a moment," she said outside the operating room. "Turn on the radio if you want to."

"You've got mighty important, haven't you?"

He turned on:

Re-mem-ber
> *the night*
> *the night*
> *you said…*

"Are you high-hatting me?" she enquired. "Or did medicine begin and end in Vienna?"

"No it didn't," he said humbly. "I'm impressed – evidently you can supervise the resident or the surgeons—"

"I've got an operation of Doctor Menafee's coming in and there's a tonsillectomy that's got to be postponed. I'm a working girl. I'm supervising the operating room."

"But you'll go out with me tonight – won't you? We'll get them to play 'All Alone'."

She paused, regarding him.

"Yes, I've been all alone for a lot of time now. I'm somebody – you don't seem to realize it. Say, who is this Berlin* anyhow? He was a singer in a dive, wasn't he? My brother ran a roadhouse and he gave me money to get started with. But I thought I was away from all that. Who is this Irving Berlin? I hear he's just married a society girl—"

"He's just married—"

She had to go: "Excuse me. I've got to fire an intern before this gets going."

"I was an intern once. I understand."

They were out at last. She was making three thousand a year now and he was still being of a conservative old Vermont family.

"This Irving Berlin now. Is he happy with this Mackay girl?* Those songs don't sound—"

"I guess he is. The point is, how happy are you?"

"Oh, we discussed that so long ago. What do I matter? I matter in a big way – but when I was a little country girl your fambly decided… Not *you*," she said at the alarm in his eyes. "I know you never did."

"I knew something else about you. I knew three things – that you were a Yonkers girl – and didn't pronounce the language like I did—"

"And that I wanted to marry you. Let's forget it. Your friend Mr Berlin can talk better than we can. Listen to him."

"I'm listening."

"No. But *lis*den, I mean."

Not for just a year but…

"Why do you say my friend Mr Berlin? I never saw the guy."

"I thought maybe you'd met him in Vienna in all these years."

"I never saw him."

"He married the girl – didn't he?"

"What are you crying about?"

"I'm not crying. I just said he married the girl – didn't he? Isn't that all right to say? When you've come so far – when—"

"You are crying," he said.

"No, I'm not. Honest. It's this work. It wears down your eyes. Let's dance."

…o
  …ver
    …head

They were playing.

Blue
  skies
    o
      ver
        head

She looked up out of his arms suddenly.

"Do you suppose they're happy?"

"Who?"

"Irving Berlin and the Mackay girl?"

"How should I know whether they're happy? I tell you I never knew them – never saw them."

A moment later she whispered:

"We all knew them."

3

THIS STORY IS ABOUT TUNES. Perhaps the tunes swing the people or the people the tunes. Anyhow:

"We'll never do it," he remarked with some finality.

"Smoke gets in your eyes," said the music.

"Why?"

"Because we're too old. You wouldn't want to anyhow – you've got that job at Duke's hospital."

"I just got it."

"Well, you've just got it. And it's going to pay you four thousand."

"That's probably half what you make."

"You mean you want to try it anyhow?"

When your heart's on fire

"No. I guess you're right. It's too late."

"…Too late for what?"

"Just too late – like you told me."

"But I didn't mean it."

"You were right though… Be quiet:"

> *Lovely*
>   *to look at,*
>   *Romantic*
>   *to know**

"You're all those things in the song," he said passionately.

"What? Lovely to look at and all that? You should have told me that fifteen years ago. Now I'm superintendent of a woman's hospital." She added: "And I'm still a woman." Then she added: "But I'm not the woman you knew any more. I'm another woman."

...lovely to look at

the orchestra repeated.

"Yes, I was lovely to look at when I was nothing – when I couldn't even talk plain—"

"I never knew—"

"Oh let's not go over it. Listen to what they're playing."

"It's called 'Lovely to Look At'."

"Who's it by?"

"A man named Jerome Kern."*

"Did you meet *him* when you went back to Europe the second time? Is he a friend of yours?"

"I never saw him. What gives you the impression I met all these big shots? I'm a doctor. Not a musician."

She wondered about her own bitterness.

"I suppose because all those years I met nobody," she said finally. "Sure, I once saw Doctor Kelly at a distance. But here I am – because I got good at my job."

"And here I am, because—"

"You'll always be wonderful to me. What did you say this man's name was?"

"Kern. And I didn't say it *was*. I said it *is*."

"That's the way you used to talk to me. And now both of us are fat and – sort of middle-aged. We never had much. Did we?"

"It wasn't my fault."

"It wasn't anybody's fault. It was just meant to be like that. Let's dance. That's a good tune. What did you say was this man's name?"

"Kern."

They
    asked me how I
        knew-ew-ew—

"We've had all that anyhow, haven't we?" she asked him. "All those people – that Youmans, that Berlin, that Kern. They must have been through hell to be able to write like that. And we sort of listened to them, didn't we?"

"But my God, that's so little—" he began, but her mood changed and she said:

"Let's not say anything about it. It was all we had – everything we'll ever know about life. What were their names – you knew their names."

"Their names were—"

"Didn't you ever know *any* of them in that fifteen years around Europe?"

"I never saw one of them."

"Well, I never will." She hesitated before the wide horizon of how she might have lived. How she might have married this man, borne him children, died for him – of how she had lived out of sordid poverty and education – into power – and spinsterhood. And she cared not a damn for her man any more, because he had never gone off with her. But she wondered how these composers had lived – Youmans and Irving Berlin and Jerome Kern – and she thought that if any of their wives turned up in this hospital she would try to make them happy.

An Author's Mother

S HE WAS A HALTING OLD LADY in a black silk dress and a
rather preposterously high-crowned hat that some milliner
had foisted upon her declining sight. She was downtown with a
purpose; she only shopped once a week now, and always tried to
do a lot in one morning. The doctor had told her she could have
the cataracts removed from her eyes, but she was over eighty and
the thought of the operation frightened her.

Her chief purpose this morning was to buy one of her sons a
birthday present. She had intended to get him a bathrobe, but
passing through the book department of the store and stopping
"to see if there was anything new", she saw a big volume on
Niaco, where she knew he intended to spend the winter – and
she turned its pages, wondering if he wouldn't like that instead,
or if perhaps he already had it.

Her son was a successful author. She had by no means abetted
him in the choice of that profession, but had wanted him to be an
army officer, or else go into business like his brother. An author
was something distinctly peculiar – there had been only one in the
Midwestern city where she was born, and he had been regarded
as a freak. Of course, if her son could have been an author like
Longfellow, or Alice and Phoebe Cary,* that would have been different, but she did not even remember the names of who wrote
the three hundred novels and memoirs that she skimmed through
every year. Of course she remembered Mrs Humphry Ward and
now she liked Edna Ferber,* but as she lingered in the bookstore
this morning her mind kept reverting persistently to the poems of
Alice and Phoebe Cary. How lovely the poems had been! Especially
the one about the girl instructing the artist how to paint a picture
of her mother. Her own mother used to read her that poem.

But the books by her son were not vivid to her, and while she was proud of him in a way, and was always glad when a librarian mentioned him or when someone asked her if she was his mother, her secret opinion was that such a profession was risky and eccentric.

It was a hot morning and, feeling suddenly a little faint after her shopping, she told the clerk she would like to sit down for a moment.

He got her a chair politely and, as if to reward him by giving him business, she heard herself asking: "Have you got the poems of Alice and Phoebe Cary?"

He repeated the names.

"Let me see. No – I don't believe we have. I was just looking over the poetry shelves yesterday. We try to keep a few volumes of all the modern poets in stock."

She smiled to herself at his ignorance.

"These poets have been dead many years," she said.

"I don't believe I know of them – but I might be able to order them for you."

"No – never mind."

He seemed an obliging young man, and she tried to focus her eyes upon him, for she liked polite young men, but the stacks of books were blurring up a little and she thought she had better go back to her apartment and perhaps order a bathrobe for her son over the telephone.

It was just at the entrance of the store that she fell. There were a few minutes when she was just barely conscious of an annoying confusion centring on her, and then she became gradually aware that she was lying on a sort of bed in what seemed to be an automobile.

The man in white who rode with her spoke to her gently:

"How do you feel now?"

"Oh, I'm all right. Are you taking me home?"

"No, we're taking you to the hospital, Mrs Johnston – we want to put a little dressing on your forehead. I took the liberty of looking in your shopping bag and finding out your name. Will you tell me the name and address of your nearest relatives?"

Once again consciousness began to slip away and she spoke vaguely of her son who was a businessman in the West, and of a granddaughter who had just opened a millinery shop in Chicago. But before he could get anything definite, she dismissed the subject as if it were irrelevant, and made an effort to rise from the stretcher.

"I want to go home. I don't know why you're taking me to a hospital – I've never been in a hospital."

"You see, Mrs Johnston, you came out of the store and tripped and fell down some stairs, and unfortunately you have a cut."

"My son will write about it."

"What!" asked the intern, rather surprised.

The old woman repeated vaguely: "My son will write about it."

"Is your son in the journalistic business?"

"Yes – but you mustn't let him know. You mustn't disturb—"

"Don't talk for just a moment, Mrs Johnston – I want to keep this little cut together till we can make a suture."

Nonetheless, she moved her head and said in a determined voice:

"I didn't say my son was a suture – I said he was an author."

"You misunderstood me, Mrs Johnston. I meant about your forehead. A 'suture' is where someone cuts themselves a little…"

Her pulse fluttered and he gave her spirits of ammonia to hold her till she got to the hospital door.

"No, my son is not a suture," she said. "Why did you say that? He's an *au*thor." She spoke very slowly as if she was unfamiliar with the words coming from her tired mouth. "An author is someone who writes books."

They had readied the hospital and the intern was busy trying to disembark her from the ambulance. "…Yes, I understand, Mrs Johnston. Now try and keep your head quite still."

"My apartment is three-o-five," she said.

"We just want you to come into the hospital a few hours. What sort of books does your son write, Mrs Johnston?"

"Oh, he writes all sorts of books."

"Just try to hold your head still, Mrs Johnston. What name does your son write under?"

"Hamilton T. Johnston. But he's an author, not a suture. Are you a suture?"

"No, Mrs Johnston, I'm a doctor."

"Well, this doesn't look like my apartment." In one gesture she pulled what was left of her together and said: "Well, don't disturb my son John or my son-in-law or my daughter that died or my son Hamilton who…" She raised herself to a supreme effort and, remembering the only book she knew really in her heart, announced astonishingly, "…my son, Hamilton, who wrote *The Poems of Alice and Phoebe Cary*…" Her voice was getting weaker, and as they carried the stretcher into the elevator her pulse grew feebler and feebler and the intern knew there would not be any suture, that nature had put its last stitch in that old forehead. But he could not know what she was thinking at the last, and would never have guessed it was that Alice and Phoebe Cary had come to call upon her, and taken her hands, and led her back gently into the country she understood.

"Trouble"

1

T HE ANNUAL TURTLE RACE at Luke Harkless Hospital once attained considerable celebrity because it was newsreeled and broadcast on an Eastern hook-up, but this year the hospital's governing board put its collective foot down. The race gave an undesirable brand of publicity to a great, serious institution, looked like advertising and so on, and had better remain what it was in the beginning – a June-day diversion organized by some ingenious interns a dozen years ago.

As a result of this decision, Trouble's tumble off the sun deck into the arms of Dr Dick Wheelock, Resident in Orthopaedics, is officially unrecorded. And that is a pity, for it would be nice to have preserved the expression on her lovely face.

It happened like this:

Doctor Wheelock was one of four judges, attired in tail coats and top hats, who were stationed at the four corners of the tennis court where the race takes place. Their business was to see which one among the dozen turtles released simultaneously from a cage in the centre first finds its way to the rim of a surrounding chalk circle – a voyage, if navigated in a straight line, of about fifteen feet.

There were other officials: an announcer with a mike, a bookie – for each turtle represents one section of the hospital – and a remarkable jazz band made up of members of the staff and composed that year of the Spirit of Seventy-Six, Haile Selassie* under an umbrella, a guitar and bass drum and two coloured urchins, who furnished the only real music with lively harmonicas.

But the judges, wilting damply in their finery, were by far the most conspicuous. It was thus that Trouble had been impelled to fix her eyes upon Doctor Wheelock's profile during the intervals between heats; so that by the time she fell into his arms she was well acquainted with the handsome and rather haughty profile, with the back of his head and the top of his hat, that glistened in the June sun.

Trouble was a trained nurse, at present on general night duty in the private wards. Her real name was Glenola McClurg, but though she was considered an excellent young nurse, she had somehow acquired the nickname "Trouble" and was never known by any other name. Men encountering her in a corridor often thought they knew why. She was Trouble all right, all right. Starting to smile a hundred feet away, she would breeze along, stop and wheel, smart as the military, and come up to the interns, or whoever it was, and figuratively press against them. All she had to say was: "Good morning, Doctor This; good morning, Doctor That" – and then, knowing she'd registered, lean back for a moment against the wall, conscious – oh, completely conscious – of what she had done to their next hours.

Her face was rather like the autumn page from the kitchen calendars of thirty years ago – vivid October eyes, a hazel canopy full of grief that looked down over a tiny childhood scar to her mouth, as if to shadow its smallest sadness and light up its faintest joy.

But this depth of feeling in her face rather belied her, for she was a light-hearted, sensuous, hard-working girl with iron nerves and a passionate love of life – one who had grown up in sordid poverty, to whom the hospital was the opening-up of a wide, radiant world. This was before she fell into Doctor Wheelock's arms.

It was not deliberate, though certain malicious spirits intimated later that it was. The central campus of the hospital was jammed. Two thousand doctors and patients and visitors and nurses and probationers swarmed over the sun deck, packed like cigarettes around the tennis court, or leant from a hundred windows, while on the old bell tower above, a solitary steeplejack quit his work and looked down precariously, overcome with wonder. Trouble and some other nurses had crawled between two wheelchairs on the sun deck and sat with their feet dangling over the edge, while the voices of the crowd rang around them, cheering on their favourite entry:

"Come on, Pathology!"

"Shake it up, Surgery!"

"Come on, Hick's Memorial!"

"Hey, Eye-and-Ear! Don't turn around! You're at the line! You're at the *line*!"

...as the turtles rushed, wavered, spun, reversed or sometimes settled unconcernedly to sleep.

It was a huge hospital, and there were thirty entries, from the offices to the nurses' training school, so that there were numerous heats, and many people had waited for the final before appearing. Now, as the afternoon waned, they hurried forth from duties in the building and pressed forward upon those in front. Trouble, concealed by the back of the wheelchair, felt it slide suddenly from her grasp, felt what seemed a mighty knee in her back, and then, with a sort of yelp, flung off into space, clawing desperately at unsubstantial air.

Dr Dick Wheelock was not a stiff man, but he was formidable in rather an old-fashioned way. You might say that at twenty-eight he was already the sort of man to whom no stranger would have shown any familiarity, even if he had entered an Oregon logging camp in a morning coat and spats. This was because he had a certain dignity of heart that went deeper than his proud carriage, and his first concern was to find out if Trouble were hurt. She had, in fact, twisted her ankle, but she scarcely knew it at the time.

"I'm all right!" she said breathlessly. "Oh, for Heaven's sakes, how shall I get out of here? Everybody's looking and laughing at me!"

Dick Wheelock laughed himself.

"I guess they're laughing at both of us." He escorted her towards the sideline. "I think we've made quite a contribution to the afternoon, don't you?"

She looked at him, and her heart went out of her and she adored him.

"Are you sure you're not hurt?" he asked again.

"Oh, no, I'm all right."

And suddenly, for a minute, just before he left her, she looked him in the eye and became Trouble for him – Trouble so white, so lovely that it didn't immediately identify itself as such. It was sheer Trouble. It was the essence of Trouble – Trouble personified, challenging!

Trouble.

"Oh, I'm so much obliged," she said.

He tipped his silk hat.

"I've got to get back to my duties. This is the final heat." He threw back his head with a faint chortle. "Excuse me, but it was funny! An angel dropping out of heaven into my arms!"

All that afternoon she remembered just those words. Somehow they took all the humiliation out of the experience. Trouble was not one to brood, but the absurdity of the situation was extreme, and in half a dozen words he had made it all right. Long before supper, in spite of the kidding to which she was inevitably subjected, she was glad it happened.

She did not get far with supper that night, however. Halfway through the main course, a waitress brought word that a lady wanted to see her in the sitting room.

"A lady? What lady?"

After some concentration, the waitress repeated a name, and a curious expression came over Trouble's face. She threw down her napkin and got up. Going through the corridor, she took a quick look at her hair in a glass door, and she was glad she had replaced her mussed uniform after the catastrophe of the afternoon.

Her visitor arose to greet her, and the two women exchanged instantaneous appraising glances, but while Trouble's expression continued to hold a touch of suspicion, the older woman's melted into a soft charm, and she spoke in a quiet, cultivated voice:

"I've wanted to meet you, Miss McClurg. My son, Frederic Winslow, has talked so much of you."

"Oh, yes, we've got to be quite good friends."

"Can we sit down for a minute? I hope I'm not too close to your dinner hour."

"Oh, no," lied Trouble.

"I tried to find you earlier, but the field there was so full of people for that potato race."

"It was a turtle race."

"Oh, a turtle race? I didn't know that turtles raced."

"Yes," said Trouble uncomfortably, "they do. Very slowly though."

"It must be interesting. My son told me he considered coming, but I thought he said it was potatoes."

Recovering her poise somewhat, Trouble couldn't help saying: "They'd go even slower than turtles."

"What? Oh, yes." Mrs Winslow's expression became graver. "Miss McClurg, I've always been in my son's confidence, and many times in the year that Fred's known you he's talked about you and told me how desperately in love with you he is."

"He just thinks he is," said Trouble.

"Oh, no. He loves you. And you're the only person that can do anything with him – I know that too. The six months he didn't drink were entirely due to you. At first I thought it was just an infatuation – and then, even without seeing you, I began to realize it wasn't. Miss McClurg, why did you throw him over?"

"Why, I didn't!" exclaimed Trouble. "We just had a little quarrel because he didn't want me to see any man but him. Or, he said, he'd start drinking again."

"And you said, 'Go ahead.'"

"Of course I did!" exclaimed Trouble. "Did he expect me to go down on my knees and beg him? Mrs Winslow, I'm not in love with your son; I like him tremendously when he… behaves himself, but I'm not in love with him, and I never pretended I was."

"He told me that too."

Liking the woman, Trouble spoke frankly:

"I think Fred thought I'd jump at the chance when he first asked me to marry him, because you're sort of" – a faintly defiant look came into her eyes – "because you're sort of rich, and society people, and all that, but I couldn't marry a man I didn't love."

"I see." Mrs Winslow hesitated. "I thought maybe it was because you were afraid of us – because you thought we were snobbish and – what is it they say now? – high-hat and all that. I asked him to bring you to see us half a dozen times, but he said you wouldn't come."

"No, it wasn't that," denied Trouble. She, in turn, hesitated. "It's partly because he goes on these bats, and I wouldn't want to be nurse to my husband, and it's partly what I said."

Mrs Winslow nodded.

"I understand. And I see you've made up your mind – and I see you're a girl after my own heart. But I hope you'll find time to see Fred sometimes, and if things do happen to clear up, I hope some day, perhaps..."

She left the sentence in mid-air.

"Oh, I don't mind seeing him, Mrs Winslow. I'd love to – any time I'm free."

"Thank you." The older woman rose. "I won't keep you any longer; it must be near your dinner hour. And please don't mention to him that I called. He wouldn't like it."

"No, I won't, Mrs Winslow."

They shook hands, and Mrs Winslow went down the corridor thinking that this oddly attractive little country girl with the gorgeous eyes and the square little chin might be just the person for her son, and hoping she would think of him differently later.

But all Trouble was thinking on her way back to her supper was:

"An angel dropping out of heaven into my arms – an angel dropping..."

2

D R DICK WHEELOCK had an odd scepticism about trained
nurses – a scepticism shared by many men in his profession. He thought that a true scientific vocation would have made
them take the extra year to obtain an MD – forgetting that few of
them had the necessary preliminary education and still fewer the
necessary money. His feeling was less than logical and can best be
illumined as a facet of the struggle between the sexes – the man
insisting upon mastery and then being faintly contemptuous of
the slave he has made.

So he had tried conquests in that direction, and even those were
several years in the past. The peculiar force of Trouble's personality had come as a shock on the day of the turtle race, and he had
asked her name, but after that, a press of work drove her from his
mind. A few days later, having occasion to pass through the private
wards, he nearly went by her in the corridor without speaking.

Then he remembered and turned back.

"Hello."

"Hello, Doctor Wheelock. I thought you'd forgotten me."

"Certainly not. I meant to find out if you'd broken anything
when you made that spectacular dive."

"And you were the victim."

"I thought maybe it was the turtles made you do it. You began
to think there was a lake down there."

She laughed.

"Maybe. Or maybe it was just an original way of attracting
your attention."

She looked him straight in the eye, and he smiled, rather
attracted by the boldness of the invitation.

"I did sprain my ankle," she said, "but I didn't realize it till I
got out of bed next morning."

He hesitated, uncertain whether to pursue the acquaintance
further, yet unable to move on down the corridor.

"Have you done anything about it?"

"No, but I ought to."

"Come over to the orthopaedic clinic when you're off duty and I'll strap it up for you."

"Now?"

"No. I can't now. Some time this afternoon or tomorrow morning."

"That's very nice of you, doctor. I've developed a nice little limp – and it's a nuisance because I'm the number they always call in a hurry. There's one on every ward."

She was not boasting. It was always: "Miss McClurg can find it" or "Trouble knows where the key is" or "Trouble, for Heaven's sake, go and see what's the matter in B16 and take care of it yourself". She really was a crack nurse – tireless, quick and resourceful – and they were thinking of shifting her to the accident room, where those qualities were much in demand. But the new superintendent of nurses was a somewhat austere lady who had taken one look at Trouble and decided that no girl that pretty could be very serious.

On warm evenings Doctor Wheelock frequently went out into the campus and stood by the grille gate, smoking a few minutes and listening to the click and scrape of roller skates on the pavement outside and to the Negro patients singing in their building across the way. Tonight, their spirituals, lying suspended on the sweet June air, seemed to have a peculiar melancholy, and he wondered if they were mourning for someone who had departed that day. He recognized the deep bass of Doofus, who had been there two years, and who, Doctor Wheelock had been told, was about to die; his place in the dark choir would be hard to fill.

He threw away his cigarette and started back towards the Orthopaedic Clinic. A nurse was going up the steps as he came near, and he saw, first, that she was limping and, second, that it was Trouble.

"Hello!" he called out of the darkness. At the sound of his voice, she wheeled on the steps and almost fell.

"Take it easy," he said. "You've got a real limp there."

"I guess I have, doctor. I tried to come over this afternoon, but everything seemed to happen at once. If it gets worse, I won't be fit for duty."

"Well, come on up to an operating room and we'll take a look at it."

The elevator hummed upward. He switched on a light and the room sprang into sparse, sterile whiteness.

"Now, if you'll just hop up on this table and get off your stocking, I'll wash my hands and look it over."

He pulled off the adhesive tape and went over the injured member.

"Does that hurt?"

"No... Ouch! That does!"

"You've got a sprain there, all right. A little one, but a sprain. Why don't you lay off for a day?"

"I can't. Everybody's on vacation."

"Well, make the probationers run around for you and save yourself some steps."

He began tearing large strips from a roll of adhesive and sticking them to the side of the table.

"I'm going to make you a regular plaster cast, anyhow, that'll keep you from running away from us."

"Ouch!"

"That's all right. It'll ease up. I wanted to bind it tight. Haven't you got a friend that wears a big shoe you could borrow?"

Suddenly they were not alone. The door swung open and a figure stood there, white against the darkness of the hall.

"Come in, Mrs Johnston," he said. "I was just strapping an ankle."

"So I see, Doctor Wheelock," said the new superintendent of nurses in a dry, hard voice... "And since when have you been stationed on the orthopaedic ward, Miss McClurg?"

"Why, I didn't—"

"I have stood three or four serious breaches of discipline lately, but I simply am not going to permit my nurses to go up into operating rooms with doctors at night."

"Come now, Mrs Johnston—" began Dick Wheelock, but her voice cut through his:

"Miss McClurg, you might do me the courtesy to stand up when I come in."

Trouble began to roll from the table, but her ankle, half-bandaged, caught in the waiting strips of adhesive tape, tangled for a minute, tripped her, and something snapped as she pitched sideways on the floor with her foot still caught above. In a moment Dick had disentangled her and helped her to feet, but the leg gave way beneath her and she exclaimed aloud as a burst of pain shot through the ankle joint.

"Now I have got something!" she exclaimed. "I could feel it snap."

"Get back here." Doctor Wheelock boosted her onto the table and his deft fingers went over the ankle bone.

"You certainly have." He turned swiftly on Mrs Johnston. "Will you kindly get out of here? You've managed to make the girl hurt herself seriously. It's not your province to interfere with a doctor on duty."

"Oh, she's an old busybody!" exploded Trouble, her eyes filling with tears of pain. "Everybody thinks so."

"Oh, they do, do they?" said Mrs Johnston.

Without another word, she turned swiftly and left the room.

3

"SO THEN," MRS JOHNSTON CONCLUDED, "I turned and walked out. With Doctor Wheelock looking after me as if he wanted to shoot me."

"What time last night was it?" the superintendent asked.

"About nine o'clock. But there are definite orders about nurses' whereabouts, and Miss McClurg knew perfectly well she should have applied for permission and had another nurse go along with her. At the Medical Centre that never would have been tolerated, Doctor Compson."

"Yes, I understand. I understand," said Doctor Compson meditatively. "And I know we can't have nurses saying things like that, or we wouldn't have any discipline at all. She's got to go, all right." He sighed and drummed his fingers on the table. "It's too bad. I've heard she was a good nurse. Someone was suggesting her for the accident room."

"I think that's more her face than her competence," said Mrs Johnston. "She has the sort of way about her that might be particularly attractive – to young doctors. Perhaps you know that her nickname is 'Trouble'."

"All right – all right. I understand. Bring her in to me and let her speak a word for herself."

"One more thing, Doctor Compson: it's hard for me to keep my nurses in line unless the doctors cooperate by behaving with propriety. At the Medical Centre—"

"That's rather in my sphere of judgement, Mrs Johnston," he interrupted drily.

Trouble was half-expecting the call, but with no particular apprehension. She knew she had lost her temper, but she had seen nurses do that before; and as for being in the operating room, she had no sense of guilt at all, and she knew that Doctor Wheelock would stand behind her.

But when she entered the office and saw the very serious look on Doctor Compson's face and saw Mrs Johnston standing beside the desk with the face of a gargoyle, she began to feel a faint uneasiness.

"Sit down, Miss McClurg. You seem a little lame."

Discreetly, Trouble answered, "I turned my ankle at the turtle race, doctor. I fell off the sun deck."

"Oh, yes, I heard something about that, but I didn't know it was you." Again he hesitated. "Miss McClurg. I have a difficult duty to perform. Last night you used some insulting words to your superior when she was engaged in the performance of her duty."

They were going to ask for an apology, Trouble guessed. She hated the idea, but she had undoubtedly spoken out of turn. She was utterly unprepared for what followed.

"I'm afraid we have no place for you here, Miss McClurg. The tradition of this institution is one of the most rigid discipline. An incident of this sort, if it took place under other circumstances, might result in serious harm to patients. You were clearly in the wrong. Even that might be forgiven, but your defiance, in the face of a just rebuke, leaves us no alternative."

She stared at him aghast.

"Oh, my!" she exclaimed.

"We're very sorry."

Then she blundered again:

"Didn't Doctor Wheelock—"

"We won't discuss Doctor Wheelock. He has nothing whatever to do with the supervision of nurses."

"Then you mean I have to leave?"

"I'm afraid I do, Miss McClurg."

"Even if… even if I apologize?"

Mrs Johnston addressed herself to the doctor: "After this affair, I don't think I could continue to keep discipline with Miss McClurg on my staff."

And now Trouble's eyes did not look like October on a calendar. There was December in them – desolation and bleak hail. She was shaking so that she could scarcely trust herself to speak.

"Is that all?" she asked in a dulled voice.

"Unless you have something you want to say."

She shook her head; then, throwing up her chin so that she could avoid looking at Mrs Johnston, she walked from the room. She walked very slowly, gritting her teeth so as not to limp.

Whatever her faults, Trouble had never lacked character.

Back on the ward there was a note waiting for her at the desk, and with a quick breath of relief, she guessed from whom it came. It read:

Dear Miss McClurg: I'm going away for a few days on a semi-vacation. If it were a real vacation, I'd have stayed over to look after your ankle. But this is a friend and patient that I long ago arranged to see. However, I've spoken to Doctor Donowska and he will look at the ankle every day, and if you decide to lie up, he will come to you.

Yours,

R.H. WHEELOCK

A wave of panic swept over her. She realized that she had counted on his doing something, though what he could do she did not know. Holding tight to the note, she hurried as fast as she could down the corridor, down an inclined walk onto the campus and across a short cut to the orthopaedic clinic.

The girl at the desk yielded her attention with maddening leisure.

"Doctor Wheelock? He left not two minutes ago. He was going away for..."

But Trouble was out the door and hastening to the gate where the doctors parked their cars.

Then, twenty feet from the gate, she stopped suddenly. Doctor Wheelock was there indeed, but not alone. He was far from being alone. A lovely shining girl, all shining with blond hair under the sort of hat that wouldn't be in the department stores for another month, the very girl for whom such things were made, sat at the wheel of a long, glittering open car and a purely ornamental chauffeur was stowing Doctor Wheelock's bag in the back seat. As Doctor Wheelock got in beside the girl, Trouble saw them look at each other, and saw that the girl's eyes were starry and expectant; Doctor Wheelock's eyes she could not see.

The car moved off in powerful silence, and Trouble stood for a moment struck motionless by the first doubt she had ever had that life was good. Then she hobbled on across the street towards her room in Nurses' Row. She felt as if she were trailing behind her the ruin of her little career, like a tattered train in the street.

4

I T WAS NOT SO BAD AS ALL THAT, she thought next morning. The Luke Harkless no longer stood alone as the one inspired hospital of America. In placing herself elsewhere, she had only to say truthfully that she had quarrelled with the superintendent of nurses on a personal matter. The former superintendent – oh, many others would speak for her, she felt sure, even Doctor Wheelock; but when the name came into her mind, the world turned dark and incomprehensible. It was as if in the space of a week he had become a symbol of all she loved here; he was the fresh strength of coming on duty in the morning; he was the busy silence of the corridor at night; he was the summer sunlight on the red buildings across from her window, and the thrill of hurrying through the winter night just pleasantly a little cold in her thin nurse's cape. He was the majesty of duty she had seen through her young probationer's eyes; the skill of hands, the strength of nerve; he was all that it meant to be ever fearless and never tired. Even, she thought – with horror at the blasphemy – he was the great stone Christ in the entrance hall...

But he had turned from her. She had aspired too high.

All afternoon her foot throbbed, but she could not bring herself to go and see Doctor Donowska over the way. When the phone rang at eight o'clock, and it was Fred Winslow, sounding entirely sober and asking her to go riding, she answered: "Yes, I will," and then, because her voice sounded listless, she raised herself to an effort: "Yes, I would love to, Fred, I certainly will."

5

W HEN SHE WENT TO DINNER at the Winslows' country place two nights later, she did not feel it necessary to explain what had happened: her injured ankle accounted well enough for the few days she was taking off.

"Yes, I heard about it," said Fred, on their way out in the car. "Some doctor caught you when you fell. They mentioned it in the newspaper account of the race."

"Oh, did they? I didn't see it."

"It didn't have your name. It just said it was a very pretty nurse and that the doctor didn't seem to mind it a bit."

"I'd like to have read it."

"Did you ever see the doctor again? Who was he?"

"Oh, he was... he was" – she struggled with the name – "a doctor named Wheelock."

Fred Winslow's eyes narrowed a little as he detected the heightened inflections of her voice.

"I bet he's been rushing you ever since."

Trouble groaned.

"Fred, are you going to start that again?"

"I'm sorry." After a minute he added, "But when you're so crazy about a girl that nothing else in the world matters one bit..."

She was silent. It was pleasant to be out in the rushing night in the long open car, not unlike the car in which Doctor Wheelock had embarked on his semi-vacation two days before. It occurred to her that it might be pleasant to drive up to the hospital some time as a patient, not a very sick patient, in just such a car, and a hat from Paris, and say, rather aloofly, but without any reproach in her voice:

"I think I should prefer to occupy the room we endowed – the Frederic Winslow room. My own doctor is flying down from New York because I'd heard that methods in other cities have become... well, a little antique. Of course, I wanted to come to this funny old dump for old times' sake."

This didn't sound quite right, and she knew there was no hospital like this in the world, from the moment it was built solidly on men instead of bricks – and another image began creeping into her chain of imaginings, so she broke it off. She was a very practical person, Trouble. She would always rather do a thing than think or talk about it.

That was why she was glad that everything was so matter-of-fact at the Winslows' that night. Mrs Winslow didn't press her hand, as if Trouble had somehow come around to reason; on the contrary, she was accepted as casually as a guest who had often visited there before.

Trouble had done little private nursing, and on only one other occasion had she ever entered such a house – to be treated as a goddess when the patient was very sick and as an upper servant when the patient began to grow well. That was all in the game, she knew, but anyhow this was quite different. Mr Winslow teased her about the incident at the turtle race.

"What I want to know is whether you picked your doctor or whether you just jumped at a whole crowd of them."

He seemed to know one or two of the big doctors quite well, appreciating them – and, looking from father to son, Trouble could not help wishing that Fred was like his father, but as the evening waned that seemed to matter less and less.

The great rooms blurred into a symphony of a thousand notes that she had never heard and did not understand – notes that no radio ever carried into small Virginia villages – from the flashing moment of a single Florentine to the lifelong labour over warp and woof of a whole Circassian family on a carpet, from the porcelains of Jingdezhen, which left their factory fifteen hundred years ago, to the latest magnetic rod which Mr Winslow played like a violin by merely moving a wand near it.

It was all equally incomprehensible to Trouble in detail, but she was quick, and as a whole she understood. Later in the evening, as if at Mrs Winslow's command, a wild summer storm broke out and ranged in white light and thunder up and down the valley, and they insisted she spend the night; the bedroom and the borrowed clothes and the bathroom all went into the gorgeous blur, like the gardens and pools and stables and trout streams next morning.

It was rather terrible to her: it was not austere, it was not a ship cleared for action, but she wanted to forget something and she let the mist settle, growing thicker and thicker.

Forty-eight hours later, on Trouble's insistence that there should be no big wedding, it was agreed that she and Fred would be married next week.

6

IN GENERAL, TROUBLE HAD FOUND all attractive men equally attractive – the point of view of a man fancy-free. Here was Fred, for instance, the very magazine cover of an athlete – he had, in fact, played baseball in college – with a fresh, boyish and rather wistfully appealing face. Sitting opposite him at breakfast at his parents' house a few days after she had reached her decision, he seemed to her as desirable as the others, even a little more so as she began to identify her destiny with his.

Mr Winslow had been talking with the butler about terrapin, and the subject raised once more a discussion of the turtle race – a matter that apparently refused to die of itself.

It seemed to haunt Fred especially, and when they were alone together, he said:

"I certainly wish I'd been there to catch you. Maybe I'll be able to save your life some time and then you'll really fall in love with me."

"You don't fall in love with people that save you."

"Are you sure you don't?" He turned to the butler. "Bring me a bottle of beer, Phillips."

"What?" exclaimed Trouble, rather shocked. "Beer at breakfast?"

"Why not? My grandfather always used to start the day with a snifter, but never anything after that."

"You're not your grandfather," said Trouble. "You wouldn't do that way."

"I won't take it if you don't like."

But she shook her head, declining the suggestion.

"Oh, no. I'm not going to be your schoolteacher. Let's get that straight. It's absolutely up to you."

"Trouble, you'll see I'll never abuse liquor again."

She tried to think so, but when they started to town later in the day, she could not help suspecting that he had had a few more. When he opened the car door for her, he forgot the bad ankle until Trouble exclaimed: "Ouch! Wait a minute!"

And then he was too profusely apologetic.

"Why don't you do something about your ankle?" he demanded.

"I'm going to, if it doesn't get better." She had told him a diluted story of her quarrel with the superintendent of nurses and of quitting the hospital, and now she said, "It's not going to be treated at Harkless, though."

Nevertheless, she was going there today for a few minutes to get her back salary and collect a few articles out of her locker.

"Don't be long," Fred said impatiently, when she left the car. "We've got to meet Mother for tea."

"We've got hours."

"You want me to come in with you?"

"Oh, no."

"Well, you stay away from that doctor."

She saw that he was not quite joking, and it annoyed her.

"You'll end by putting ideas in my head," she answered.

Though it had been less than a week, she felt as though she had been away from the hospital for years; crossing the campus, she was rather surprised at seeing the same activities continuing. On the court, two interns played tennis under the supervision of convalescents on the sun deck; the male patients of the psychiatric clinic were doing something with a basketball in their yard, and outside the paediatric clinic a mother was playing with her child. The grass on the campus already looked a little baked with the summer; the first fresh green was gone.

Only a single nurse was at the desk.

"Trouble! You're not leaving us?"

"I'm afraid I am."

"But why? Where are you going?"

"I'm not sure yet."

"I thought you were just laid up with your ankle."

She collected her things and stopped at the office for the money due her. Then out past the statue that stretched out its arms for the last time; only when she reached the gate did she realize that there were tears on her cheeks. Trouble had been very happy here, put in so much effort and spent so much youth.

Save for the manner of her leaving, she had no regret for anything that had ever happened to her in that square block of hardship and surcease. The endless hum of it would continue when her faint footsteps had long died away – nurses, interns, doctors would change; only the frailty of human flesh would continue, and the communal intelligence of many generations of men to fight against it.

When she reached the car, Fred was not there. Supposing he had gone down to the drugstore on the corner, she waited a moment; then she went after him. He was not there either, nor was he in the little grill bar next door – but, on an impulse, she described him and was told that he had just left. Trouble knew the waitress by sight, and she asked frankly:

"Did he have anything to drink?"

"Yes, he had three drinks very quick."

Trouble returned to the car. After five more minutes of waiting, it was borne in on her with increasing apprehension that he had gone into the hospital seeking her. His morbid jealousy had come to the fore, and it was more than probable that his destination was Doctor Wheelock's office. Relegating the ache of her ankle to the world of unimportant things, she set off once more towards the gates she had thought to leave behind.

At the office in the orthopaedic clinic she found that a man answering Fred's description had asked for Doctor Wheelock and, on being told he was busy, announced himself as a physician and said that he would wait outside the operating room. In a panic, Trouble hurried to the elevator; she arrived upstairs just a minute too late.

As she paused for breath at the door of the ante-room, she saw Fred arguing violently with an orderly who held him by an arm, while a nurse looked on in shocked surprise. Even as Trouble watched, heart in her mouth, the door of the operating room flung open and a doctor came out, tearing the mask from his face and walking directly up to Fred.

"All right, I'm Doctor Wheelock. I don't know what you want of me, but if you try to force your way into an operating room you're likely to get in difficulties. Now what is it?"

At the moment when she started towards them, she saw a reflex in Fred's shoulder, saw the orderly try to pinion him; then she was between the two men at the instant that Fred broke away, and the force of his rush sent her back against Doctor Wheelock, who caught her – for the second time in their lives. Seeing her, Fred stood dead still, breathing hard, and for just a moment it seemed that anything could happen – when there was a sudden interruption.

The door of the operating room opened again, and a nurse came out, preceding a rolling table pushed by another nurse, which bore a recumbent form swathed in white. For two minutes there was not a sound in the room except the faint noise of the rubber wheels; even the gasp of Fred's breathing stopped, and with a slow, soundless movement Trouble leant out and away from Doctor Wheelock and regained her balance.

The rolling table disappeared out the farther door and, as if it were a signal, they all relaxed at once and the silence was broken.

"I'm very sorry," said Fred in a dull voice.

Doctor Wheelock looked at Trouble, then at Fred, then back again.

"What is this, anyhow, Miss McClurg? Say, I've been looking for you for three days. Do you know this fellow?"

"Yes. He's been drinking." She turned despairingly to Fred. "Will you please get out? Wait for me in the car."

"I'm sorry," Fred repeated.

As soberly as if he had not been a man possessed a few minutes before, he accompanied the orderly out the door.

Doctor Wheelock looked after him for a moment; then he shook his head slowly, astounded and outraged.

"Well, of all the nuts," he muttered. "Come in here. We'll go in a gallery. They'll be cleaned up in a minute and I want to talk to you. Where have you been? Who is this fellow? How's your ankle?"

Trouble couldn't answer his questions all at once. How could she say that the momentary touch of her head against his white gown was the strongest memory she had of the incident, that she had of anything?

"Fired?" he was saying. "Of course, you weren't fired. Why didn't you come to me? I started back two days earlier than I meant to – I got thinking about that crazy ankle of yours – and I heard what happened. It's perfectly all right. I'm sorry that woman ever worried you."

"You mean you fixed it up?" she asked incredulously.

"You bet I did. I said, if you left I left. Mrs Johnston was simply losing her sense of proportion, and a couple of other doctors who had run up against her went to Compson that same week. She thought she was running the hospital. But the difficulty was trying to find you. Where were you?"

"I was in the country."

They had finished cleaning up down below. He called to one of the nurses to wait a minute.

"I want to look at that ankle right now," he said. "Doctor Donowska said you didn't show up."

"Well, after they fired me—"

"Forget it; you're not fired. Come on down here and let me look you over... That's right; take it slow... Where do you pick up these boyfriends who knock you around and try to break into operating rooms? Who is he, anyhow?"

"Oh, he's – nobody," said Trouble. "He's just a crazy boy. I had no idea what he was going to do."

He had helped her onto the table and the nurse was taking off her stocking.

"H'm!" grunted Doctor Wheelock again, after a minute. "Well, young lady, you've played fast and loose with this ankle. I'm going to X-ray you, and then I wouldn't be surprised if we didn't have to go into the joint and replace it."

"Oh, not now," she said quickly.

"We'll take the X-ray now. Then you come back late this afternoon. There's no point in delaying any longer. Maybe you'll only need a cast."

"All right. Late this afternoon then. There's something I've got to do now."

"No walking."

"No, not much. What does it matter, since it's got to be fixed?"

The nurse had gone to the other side of the operating room to throw away the old adhesive tape.

"It matters to me," he said. "It matters more than I can tell you right now."

Then she saw in his eyes the same look that had been in the eyes of the girl who had driven him away from the hospital last week; and simultaneously she realized she had only seen the back of his head and had not known whether he had returned it. Just as she had seen little more than the back of his head the day she fell into his arms.

"Let's have the X-ray," she said quickly.

7

FRED SAT IN THE CAR, leaning forward on the steering wheel. His face was penitent, sobered, boyishly appealing.

"I wasn't sure you'd come," he said humbly.

"Where are we meeting your mother?"

"At Coleman Gardens." And as they started off: "Trouble, I can't begin to tell you about my self-contempt for what I did. For a while when you went in the hospital and didn't come back right away, I hardly knew what I was doing."

"Please don't talk, Fred."

"All right, anything you say. But if I can ever make up to you for this…"

They reached the restaurant, to find Mrs Winslow already there. Looking from one to the other, she guessed something, and when they sat down in the shade of the poplar trees, she caught Trouble's eyes several times, understanding her because she liked her, and each time a deepening expression of apprehension came into her own eyes. Trouble was the first to break the silence.

"Mrs Winslow, you've been awfully good to me," she said, "and it's hard to tell you this. But I don't think I want to give up nursing now."

"Why" – Mrs Winslow looked sharply at her son, the worst of her forebodings justified – "why, then... then you've decided to put things off."

"No," Trouble said, "I want to break everything off definitely."

All in a moment, Mrs Winslow gave up. She loved her son, but she knew in her heart that this girl was worth ten of him and that all their money could not buy her. Her instinct and her sense of justice struggled for a moment, and then she yielded graciously to the inevitable.

"I suppose that hospital life does get in your blood," she said evenly.

"I guess that's it," said Trouble.

She did not dare look at Fred; she did not want to be disturbed by that appeal, childish and false.

"They've X-rayed my ankle and they may have to cut into it this afternoon," she said. "I've let it go too long."

"Oh, that's too bad! I've been worried about it. I suppose you'll be laid up awhile... Please tell me your favourite thing in a garden."

Trouble stood up.

"I'll run you back to the hospital," said Fred in a lost voice.

"No, please. I'd rather not. I'd rather go by myself" – she smiled with an effort – "and get ready for the ordeal."

Out in the street, Trouble waited for a taxi. She was one who never looked backward, and the Winslow family was already behind her. She was thinking that she wanted the X-ray to be bad – so bad that Doctor Wheelock would have to operate, and she would see him every day for a while.

Perhaps it was this wish that made her slip and almost fall as she got into the cab, and feel a keen joy at the throb of pain, thinking, perhaps, that did it.

"Where to, please?"

"Luke Harkless Hospital."

And as Trouble heard her voice saying those familiar words, all the things that made her unique and beloved, a symbol of something greater than herself, came flowing back into her. The rich warm self of Trouble bloomed again – a flower beside the bed of man's distress.

The Guest in Room Nineteen

M R CASS KNEW HE COULDN'T GO TO SLEEP, so he put his tie on again and went back to the lobby. The guests were all gone to bed, but a little aura of activity seemed to linger about a half-finished picture puzzle, and the nightwatchman was putting a big log on the fire.

Mr Cass limped slowly across the soft carpet, stopped behind him and grunted, "Heavy?"

The watchman, a wiry old mountaineer, looked around sharply.

"A hundred pound. It's wet – it'll be one o'clock before it's burning good."

Mr Cass let himself into a chair. Last year he had been active, driving his own car – but he had suffered a stroke before coming south last month, and now life was like waiting for an unwelcome train. He was very lonely.

The watchman built burning chunks about the wet log.

"Thought you was somebody else when you came in," he said.

"Who did you think I was?"

"I thought you was the fella who's always coming in late. First night I was on duty he came in at two without any noise and give me a start. Every night he comes in late."

After a pause Mr Cass asked:

"What's his name?"

"I never did ask him his name."

Another pause. The fire leapt into a premature, short-lived glow.

"How do you know he's a guest here?"

"Oh, he's a guest here." But the watchman considered the matter for the first time. "I hear him go down the corridor and around the corner and then I hear his door shut."

"He may be a burglar," said Mr Cass.

"Oh, he's no burglar. He said he'd been coming here a long time."

"Did he tell you he wasn't a burglar?"

The watchman laughed.

"I never asked him that."

The log slipped and the old man adjusted it; Mr Cass envied his strength. It seemed to him that, if he had strength, he could run out of here, hurry along the roads of the world, the roads that led back, and not sit waiting.

Almost every evening he played bridge with the two clerks, and one night last week he simply passed away during a bridge hand, shrinking up through space, up through the ceilings like a wisp of smoke, looking back, looking down at his body hunched at the table, his white fist clutching the cards. He heard the bids and his own voice speaking – then the two clerks were helping him into his room, and one of them sat with him till the doctor came... After a while Mr Cass had to go to the bathroom, and he decided to go to the public one. It took him some time. When he came back to the lobby the watchman said:

"That fella came in late again. I found out he's in number nineteen."

"What's his name?"

"I didn't like to ask him that – I knew I could find out from his number."

Mr Cass sat down.

"I'm number eighteen," he said. "I thought there were just some women next to me."

The watchman went behind the desk to the mail rack. After a moment he reported.

"Funny thing – his box ain't here. There's number eighteen, that's Mr Cass—"

"That's me."

"—and the next one is twenty, on the second floor. I must've understood him wrong."

"I told you he was a burglar. What did he look like?"

"Well, now, he wasn't an old man and he wasn't a young man. He seemed like he'd been sick and he had little holes all over his face."

Despite its inadequacy, the description somehow conjured up a picture for Mr Cass. His partner, John Canisius, had never looked old or young, and he had little holes in his face.

Suddenly Mr Cass felt the same sensation stealing over him that he had felt the other night. Dimly he was aware that the watchman had gone to the door and dimly he heard his own voice saying: "Leave it open"; then the cold air swept in and his spirit left him and romped around the room with it. He saw John Canisius come in the open door and look at him and advance towards him, and then realized it was the watchman, pouring a paper cup of water into his mouth and spilling it on his collar.

"Thanks."

"Feel all right now?"

"Did I faint?" he muttered.

"You fell over kind of funny. Reckon I better help you get back into your room."

At the door of number eighteen, Mr Cass halted and pointed his cane at the room next door.

"What's that number?"

"Seventeen. And that one without a number is the manager's rooms. There ain't any nineteen."

"Do you think I'd better go in?"

"Sure thing." The watchman lowered his voice. "If you're thinking about that fella, I must've heard him wrong. I can't go looking for him tonight."

"He's in here," said Mr Cass.

"No, he ain't."

"Yes, he is. He's waiting for me."

"Shucks, I'll go in with you."

He opened the door, turned on the light and took a quick look around.

"See – ain't nobody here."

Mr Cass slept well and the next day was full spring, so he decided to go out. It took him a long time to walk down the hill from the hotel, and his progress across the double tracks took a good three minutes and attracted solicitous attention, but it was practically a country stroll compared to his negotiation of the highway, which was accompanied by a great caterwauling of horns and screech of brakes. A welcoming committee waited him on the kerb and helped him into the drugstore, where, exhausted by his adventure, he called a taxi to go home.

Because of this, he fell asleep while undressing and, waking at twelve, felt dismal and oppressed. Finding it difficult to rise, he rang, and the nightwatchman answered the bell.

"Glad to help you, Mr Cass, if you'll wait five minutes. It's turned cold again and I want to get in a big log of wood."

"Oh," said Mr Cass, and then: "Has the guest come in yet?"

"He just got in now."

"Did you ask him if he's a burglar?"

"He's no burglar, Mr Cass. He's a nice fella. He's going to help me with this big log. I'll be right back."

"Did he say what room—" But the watchman was gone, and Mr Cass could only wait.

He waited five minutes, he waited ten. Then he gradually realized that the watchman was not coming back. It was plain that the watchman had been sent for.

Everyone tried to keep distressing things from Mr Cass, and it was not until the following evening that he heard what had happened from some whispering at the desk.

The man had collapsed trying to lift a log too heavy for him. Mr Cass said nothing, because he knew that old people have to be careful what they say. Only he knew the watchman had not been alone.

After Easter, the hotel's short season faded out, and it was not worthwhile to hire a new watchman, but Mr Cass continued to have lonely nights, and often he sat in the lobby after the other guests went to bed. One April night he dozed there for a while, awakening to find that it was after two and he was not alone in the lobby.

The current of cooler air might have roused him, for a man he did not know had just come in the door.

The man was of no special age, but even by the single light left burning Mr Cass could see that he was a pale man, that there were little holes in his face like the ravages of some disease and he did not look like John Canisius, his partner.

"Good evening," said the stranger.

"Hm," said Mr Cass, and then, as the man turned down the corridor, he spoke up in a strong voice:

"You're out late."

"Yes, quite late."

"You a guest here?"

"Yes."

Mr Cass dragged himself to his feet and stood leaning on his cane.

"I suppose you live in room nineteen," he said.

"As it happens, I do."

"You needn't lie to me," said Mr Cass. "I'm not an ignorant mountaineer. Are you a burglar – or did you come for someone?"

The man's face seemed to grow even whiter.

"I don't understand you," he said.

"In any case I want you to get out of here," said Mr Cass. He was growing angry, and it gave him a certain strength. "Otherwise I'm going to arouse the hotel."

The stranger hesitated.

"There's no need of doing that," he said quietly. "That would be…"

Mr Cass raised his cane menacingly, held it up a moment then let it down slowly.

"Wait a minute," he said, "I may want you to do something for me."

"What is it?"

"It's getting cold in here. I want you to help me bring in a log to put on the fire."

The stranger was startled by the request.

"Are you strong enough?" he asked.

"Of course I'm strong enough." Mr Cass stood very upright, throwing back his shoulders.

"I can get it alone."

"No, you can't. You help me or I'll arouse the house."

They went out and down the back steps, Mr Cass refusing the stranger's arm.

He found, in fact, that he could walk much better than he thought, and he left his cane by the stoop so that both hands were free for the log.

It was dark in the woodshed and the stranger lit a match. There was only one log, but it was over a hundred pounds, quite big enough to amply fill the small fireplace.

"Hadn't I better do this?" said the stranger.

Mr Cass did not answer, but bent and put his hands on the rough surface. The touch seemed to stimulate him, he felt no pain or strain in his back at all.

"Catch hold there," he ordered.

"Are you sure—"

"Catch hold!"

Mr Cass took a long breath of cool air into his lungs and shifted his hands on the log. His arms tightened, then his shoulders and the muscles on his back.

"Lift," he grunted. And suddenly the log moved, came up with him as he straightened, and for a triumphant moment he stood there squarely, cradling it against him. Then out into space he went, very slowly, carrying the log, which seemed lighter and lighter, seeming to melt away in his arms. He wanted to call back some word of mockery and derision to the stranger, but he was already too far away, out on the old roads that led back where he wished to be.

Everyone in the hotel was sorry to lose Mr Cass, the manager especially, for he read the open letter on Mr Cass's desk saying that no further money could be remitted that year.

"What a shame. He'd been here so many years that we'd have been glad to carry him a while until he made arrangements."

Mr Cass was the right sort of client – it was because of such guests that the manager had tried to keep his brother out of sight all winter.

The brother, a tough number, was considerably shaken by what had happened.

"That's what I get for trying to be a help," he said. "I should have known better. Both those old guys looked exactly like death itself to me."

In the Holidays

1

THE HOSPITAL WAS THINLY POPULATED, for many convalescents had taken risks to get home for the holidays and
prospective patients were gritting their teeth until vacation was
over. In the private ward, one intern took on the duties of three,
and six nurses the duties of a dozen. After New Year it would be
different – just now the corridors were long and lonely.

Young Dr Kamp came into the room of Mr McKenna, who was
not very ill, and snatched rest in the easy chair.

"How's back feel?" he asked.

"Better, doc. I thought I'd get up and dress tomorrow."

"All right – if you haven't any fever. The X-ray plates didn't
show a thing."

"I've got to be out of here day after tomorrow."

"When you get home you better see your own doctor, though I
never have felt you were seriously ill – in spite of the pain. We've
got a patient downstairs with a dizzy head that we can't find a
thing the matter with – there's probably faulty elimination of
some kind, but he came through every test sound as a dollar."

"What's his name?" McKenna asked.

"Griffin. So you see, sometimes there just isn't any diagnosis to
be made. Say, were you in the war?"

"Me? No, I was too young."

"Did you ever get shot?"

"No."

"That's funny – the X-ray showed a couple of things that looked
like slugs in your buttocks."

"Oh, that was a hunting accident," said McKenna.

When the doctor left, the nurse came in – she was the wrong one: not the beautiful little student nurse, dark and rosy, with eyes as soft as blue oil. Miss Hunter was plain, and talked about the man she was marrying next month.

"That's why I'm here on New Year's Eve. We need the money and a girl gave me five dollars to take her place over the holidays. I can't see him, but I write him a whole book every night."

"It certainly is some life in here," said McKenna. "The food makes me sick."

"Aren't you ashamed – it's better than we get. You ought to see that little student nurse go for the dessert you left today."

He brightened momentarily.

"The pretty one?" Maybe this was an angle.

"Miss Collins." She proffered him a vile liquid. "You can drink her health with this cocktail."

"Oh, skip it. This doctor thinks I'm just bluffing – me and some other fellow that's dizzy in the head. Name's Griffin – do you take care of him?

"He's down on the first floor."

"What does he look like?"

"Well, he wears glasses, about your age."

"Is he handsome like me?"

"He's very pale and he's got a big bald place in his moustache. What's the use of having a moustache if you have a bald place in it?"

He shifted in bed restlessly.

"I think I'd sleep better if I got up for a while – just around the corridors. I could get a paper in the office and all that."

"I'll ask the doctor."

Without waiting for permission, McKenna got up and dressed. He was tying his tie when the nurse returned.

"All right," Miss Hunter said, "but come back soon and wear your overcoat. The corridors are cold. And would you please drop this letter in the box for me?"

McKenna went out and downstairs and through many halls to the main office. He stopped at the registry desk and asked a question, afterwards writing down something on the back of an envelope.

Out in the damp, snowless night, he enquired the way to a drug-store; he went directly to the phone booth and closeted himself for some minutes. Then he bought a movie magazine and a hip flask of port, and asked for a glass at the fountain.

All around the hospital the streets were quiet, and the houses, largely occupied by medical people, were dark and deserted. Across the street, the dark fortress of the hospital was blocked out against a pink blur in the downtown sky. There was a mailbox on the corner, and after a moment he took out the nurse's letter, tore it slowly into four pieces and dropped it in the slot. Then he began thinking of the little student nurse, Miss Collins. He had a vague idea about Miss Collins. She had told him yesterday that she was sure to be flunked from her class in February. Why? Because she had stayed out too late with boyfriends. Now, if that wasn't a sort of come-on – especially when she added that she wasn't going back to the old homestead and had no plans at all. Tomorrow McKenna was leaving town, but in a couple of weeks he could ride down again and keep her out late in a big way, and – if he liked her – get her some clothes and set her up in Jersey City, where he owned an apartment house. She was the double for a girl he once went with at Ohio State.

He looked at his watch – an hour and a half till midnight. Save for several occasions when he had been deterred for reasons contingent on his profession, all his New Years were opaque memories of whoopee. He never made resolves or thought of the past with nostalgia or regret – he was joyless and fearless, one of the stillborn who manage to use death as a mainspring. When he caused suffering it made his neck swell and glow, and yet he had a feeling for it that was akin to sympathy. "Does it hurt, fella?" he had asked once. "Where does it hurt most? Cheer up – you're almost out."

McKenna had intended to leave the hospital before the thing came off, but the intern and nurse had only just spilt what he wanted to know into his lap, and it was too late at night to leave without attracting attention. He crossed the street in order to re-enter the hospital by the door of the dispensary.

On the sidewalk, a man and a woman, young and poorly dressed, stood hesitating.

"Say, mister," the man said, "can you tell us something – if doctors look to see what's wrong with you, is it free? Somebody told me they sting you."

McKenna paused in the doorway and regarded them – the woman watched him breathlessly.

"Sure they sting you," McKenna said. "They charge you twenty bucks or they take it out on your hide."

He went on in, past the screen door of the dispensary, past the entrance to the surgical unit where men made repairs that would not wait for the year to turn, past the children's clinic where a single sharp cry of distress came through an open door, past the psychiatric wards, exuding a haunted darkness. A group of probationers in street clothes chattered by him, an orderly with a wheelchair, an old Negress leaning on a grizzled man, a young woman weeping between a doctor and a nurse. Through all that life, protesting but clinging, through all that hope of a better year, moved McKenna, the murderer, looking straight ahead lest they see death in his eyes.

2

I N HIS ROOM HE RANG FOR THE NURSE, had a quick drink and rang again. This time it was Miss Collins.

"It took you long enough," he said. "Say, I don't think I'll go to bed yet. It's so near twelve I think I'll stay up and see the New Year in and all that stuff; maybe go out on the porch and hear the noise."

"I suppose it's all right."

"You'll stick with me, won't you? Want a little port wine?"

Miss Collins wouldn't dare do that, but she'd be back presently. She was the prettiest twitch he had seen in a year.

After another glass of port, he felt a growing excitement. He pictured "Mr Griffin" on the floor below, feeling so hidden and secure, possibly asleep. He pictured Oaky and Flute Cuneo and Vandervere strapping on the arsenal; he wished he could be in on the finish, but that was no play for a front man.

At a quarter of twelve, Miss Collins came back and they went down the corridor to a glassed-in porch overlooking the city.

"I'm afraid this is my last New Year's here," she said.

"What do you care? You've got too much on the ball to go around washing mummies."

At a minute before twelve, a din started – first thin and far away, then rolling towards the hospital – a discord of whistles, bells, firecrackers and shots. Once, after a few minutes, McKenna thought he heard the pump sound of a silencer, once and again, but he could not be sure. From time to time, Miss Collins darted in to the desk to see if there was a call for her, and each time he kept carefully in her sight.

After fifteen minutes the cacophony died away.

"My back hurts," McKenna said. "I wish you'd help me off with my clothes and then rub me."

"Certainly."

On the way to his room, he listened carefully for the sounds of commotion, but there was nothing. Therefore, barring the unforeseen, all had gone off as planned – the State of New York's intended witness was now with his fathers.

She bent over the bed, rubbing his back with alcohol.

"Sit down," he ordered. "Just sit on the bed."

He had almost finished the flask of port and he felt fine. There were worse ways to spend New Year's – a job all mopped up, the good warming wine and a swell girl to rub his back.

"You certainly are something to look at."

Two minutes later she tugged his hand from her rumpled belt.

"You're crazy," she exclaimed, panting.

"Oh, don't get sore. I thought you kind of liked me."

"Liked you! You! Why, your room smells like a dog's room. I hate to touch you!"

Then was a small knock, and the night superintendent called Miss Collins, who went into the hall, hastily smoothing her apron. McKenna got out of bed, tiptoed to the door and listened – in a minute he heard Miss Collins's voice:

"But I don't know how to do it, Miss Gleason... You say the patient was shot..."

And then the other nurse:

"...then you simply tie the hands and feet together and..." McKenna got back into bed cautiously.

"Last rites for Mr Griffin," he thought. "That's fine. It'll take her mind off being sore."

3

HE HAD DECIDED TO LEAVE NEXT AFTERNOON, when the winter dusk was closing down outside. The intern was uncertain and called the resident, just back from vacation. The latter came in after lunch when the orderly was helping McKenna pack.

"Don't you want to see your doctor tomorrow?" he asked.

He was big and informal, more competent-looking than the intern.

"He's just a doctor I got at the hotel. He doesn't know anything about it."

"Well, we've got one more test to hear from."

"I haven't got any fever," said McKenna. "It must have been just a false alarm."

The resident yawned.

"Excuse me," he said – "they called me at two o'clock last night."

"Somebody die?"

The resident nodded.

"Very suddenly. Somebody shot and killed a patient on the floor below."

"Go on! You're not safe anywhere now, are you?"

"Seems not."

McKenna rang the bell at the head of the bed.

"I can't find my hat, and none of those nurses have been in here all day – only the maid." He turned to the orderly. "Go find a nurse and see if they know where my hat is."

"And oh…" the resident added, "tell them, if they have that test ready, to send it in."

"What test?" McKenna asked.

"Just a routine business. Just a part of your body."

"What part?"

"It ought to be here now. It's hard to get these laboratory tests on a holiday."

Miss Hunter's face appeared in the doorway, but she did not look towards McKenna.

"The message came," she said. "It was just to tell you that the test was positive. And to give you this paper."

The resident read it with interest.

"What is it?" demanded McKenna. "Say, I haven't got—"

"You haven't got anything," said the resident, "not even a leg to stand on. In fact, I'd be sorry for you – if you hadn't torn up that nurse's letter."

"What nurse's letter?"

"The one the postman put together and brought in this morning."

"I don't know anything about it."

"We do. You left your finger prints on it – and they seem to belong to a man named Joe Kinney, who got three slugs in his bottom in New York last June."

"You got nothing on me – what do you think you are, a tec?"

"That's just what I am. And I know now that you work out of Jersey City, and so did Griffin."

"I was with Miss Collins when that happened."

"What time?"

Catching his mistake, McKenna hesitated.

"I was with her all evening – till one o'clock."

"Miss Collins says she left you after five minutes because you got tough with her. Say, why did you have to pick a hospital? These girls have work to do – they can't play with animals."

"You got nothing at all on me – not even a gun."

"Maybe you'll wish you had one when I get done with you down at the station. Miss Hunter and I are engaged to be married, and that letter was to me."

By nightfall the hospital showed signs of increasing life – the doctors and nurses back early to go to work in the morning, and casualties of riot and diet, victims of colds, aches and infections saved since Christmas. Even the recently vacated beds of Messrs Griffin and McKenna would be occupied by tomorrow. Both of them had better have celebrated the holidays outside.

The End of Hate

THE BUGGY PROGRESSED at a tired trot and the two occu-
pants were as warm and weary as the horses. The girl's hair
was a crackly yellow and she wore a dress of light blue bombazine
– the first really grown-up dress she had ever known. She was going
to be a nurse in a wartime hospital, and her brother complained
that she was arrayed like a woman of the world.

"We're now almost in the District of Columbia," said Captain
Doctor Pilgrim. "We will stop and get water at the next farmhouse."

The two Pilgrims were probably the only adults thereabout
who did not know that Southern Maryland was suddenly and
surprisingly in Confederate hands. To ease the pressure on Lee
at Petersburg, General Jubal Early had marched his corps up the
valley in a desperate threat at the capital, had thrown shells into
the suburbs and then unwillingly turned back towards the west.*
His last infantry columns had scarcely slogged along this road,
leaving a stubborn dust behind.

The Pilgrims, who had driven down from Ohio, were unaware
of the situation, and as the buggy turned into the Washington
Pike, Josie was puzzled by a number of what seemed to be armed
tramps who limped past. And there was something about two
men who galloped towards the buggy from the farmhouse that
made her ask alertly, "What are those people, Brother? Secesh?"*

To anyone who had not been at the front, it would have been
hard to place the men as soldiers – Tib Dulany, who had once
written verse for the *Lynchburg Courier*, wore a planter's hat,
a rag of a coat, blue pants originally issued to a Union trooper,
and a cartridge belt stamped CSA.* The riders drew up beside
the buggy and Tib saluted Pilgrim.

"Hi there, Yank!"

"Tell us where we can get water..." began Josie haughtily. Suddenly she saw that Captain Doctor Pilgrim's hand was at his holster – but it stayed there – the second rider held a carbine at his heart.

Captain Pilgrim raised his hands.

"Is this a raid?" he demanded. "Are you guerrillas?"

"Turn in yonder at the farmhouse," said Tib politely. "You can get water there."

He addressed Josie, who was driving. He observed that her skin had a peculiar radiance, as if phosphorus had touched it, and around her eyes was that veiled expression sometimes described as starry.

"Nobody's going to hurt you," he said. "You're inside Lee's lines."

"Lee's lines!" Captain Pilgrim cried indignantly as he turned the carriage. "Every time you Mosby* cut-throats come out of your hills and cut a telegraph—"

The team jolted to a stop – the second trooper had grabbed the reins, and turned white eyes upon the doctor.

"One more peep about Mosby—"

"He just doesn't know the news, Wash," said Tib. "He doesn't recognize the Army of Northern Virginia."

Wash released the reins, and the buggy drove up to the farmhouse. Only as the doctor saw a dozen horses tied by the porch did he realize that he was several days behind the times.

"Right now," continued Tib, "Grant is washing the dishes and Old Abe* is upstairs making the beds." He turned to Wash: "I sure would like to be in Washington tonight when Mr Davis rides in. That Yankee rebellion didn't last long, did it?"

Josie suddenly believed it, and her world crashed around her – the Boys in Blue – the Union for ever – 'Mine Eyes Have Seen the Glory'...

"You can't take my brother prisoner – he's not really an officer: he's a doctor."

"Doctor, eh? Don't know about teeth, does he?" asked Tib, dismounting at the porch.

"That's his specialty."

"He's just what we're looking for. Doctor, if you'll be so kind as to come in, you can pull a tooth of a Bonaparte, a cousin of Napoleon the Third. He's attached to General Early's staff and he's been carrying on for an hour, but the ambulances have gone on."

An officer came out on the porch, gave a nervous ear to a crackling of rifles in the distance and bent an eye upon the buggy.

"We found a tooth specialist, Lieutenant," said Tib. "The Lord sent him into our lines, and if Napoleon still needs help—"

"Bring him in," the officer exclaimed. "We didn't know whether to take the prince along or leave him."

Suddenly Josie had a glimpse at the Confederacy on the vine-covered veranda. There was an egress from the house: a spidery man in a shabby riding coat adorned with faded stars, followed by two younger men cramming papers into a canvas sack. Then a miscellany of officers, one on a crutch, one stripped to his under-shirt with the gold star of a general pinned to a bandage on his shoulder. There was disappointment in their tired eyes. Seeing Josie, they made a single gesture: their dozen right hands rose to their dozen hats, and they bowed in her direction.

Josie bowed back stiffly. In a moment they swung into their saddles and General Early looked for a moment towards the city he had not taken. Then he spoke to the aide at his stirrup: "I want couriers from Colonel Mosby every half hour till we reach White's Ford."

"Yes, sir."

The general's sun-strained eyes focused on Dr Pilgrim in the buggy.

"I understand you're a dentist," he said. "Pull out Prince Napoleon's tooth or whatever he needs. Do well by him and these troopers will let you go without parole."

The clop and crunch of mounted men moved down the lane, and in a minute the last sally of the Army of Northern Virginia faded into the distance. A French aide-de-camp came out of the farmhouse.

"The prince is still in agony," he announced.

"This Yank is a doctor." Tib said. "One of us'll go along while he's operating."

The stout invalid in the kitchen, a gross miniature of his world-shaking uncle, tore his hand from his mouth and sat upright.

"*Opération!*" he cried. "*Quelle horreur!*"*

Dr Pilgrim looked suspicious.

"My sister – where will she be?"

"In the parlour, Doctor. Wash, you stay here."

Prince Napoleon groaned again.

"I am a trained surgeon," Pilgrim reassured him stiffly. "Now, sir, will you take off that hat?"

The prince removed the white Cordoba which topped a costume of red tailcoat, French uniform breeches and dragoon boots.

"Prince, if he doesn't do well we got some apple trees outside and plenty rope."

Tib went into the parlour, where Miss Josie sat on the edge of a sofa.

"The general said not to harm my brother," she reminded him.

"I'm more worried about what he's about to do to the prince," said Tib, sorry for her lovely, anxious face.

An animal howl arose from the library.

"You hear that?" Tib said. "Napoleon's the one to worry about. And then, after our cavalry pickets pass, you and your brother can resume your journey."

Josie relaxed and looked at him with a certain human interest.

"What did my brother mean when he said you were a gorilla?"

"It's '*guer*rilla', not '*go*rilla'," he objected. "When a Yankee's on detached service they call him a scout, but they pretended we're only part-time soldiers so they can hang us."

"A soldier not in uniform is a spy, isn't he?"

"I *am* in uniform – look at my buckle. And, believe it or not, Miss Pilgrim, I was a smart-looking trooper when I rode out of Lynchburg four years ago."

He told her how he had been dressed that day, and Josie listened – it wasn't unlike the first volunteers leaving Youngstown, Ohio.

"…with a big red sash that belonged to my mother. One of the girls stood in front of the troop and read a poem I had published."

"Say the poem," Josie urged him. "I would so enjoy hearing it."

Tib considered. "All I remember is: 'Lynchburg, thy guardsmen bid thy hills farewell.' I—"

Came a scream from across the hall and a medley of French. Wash appeared in the door.

"Say, Tib – the Yank got the tooth."

"Fine," said Tib. He turned back to Josie.

"I certainly would like to write a few lines sometime to express my admiration of you."

"This is so sudden," she said lightly.

She might have spoken for herself too.

Presently, Wash turned from the window:

"Tib, the patrols have started shootin' back from the saddle."

"Will you leave without *us*?" the French aide demanded suspiciously.

"We sure will," said Tib. "The prince can observe the war from the Yankee side for a while. Miss Pilgrim, I bid you a most unwilling goodbye."

Peering hastily into the kitchen, Tib saw the prince so far recovered as to be sitting upright.

Now Wash called from outside:

"Hey, Tib!"

There were shots very near. The two scouts were unhitching their horses when Wash muttered, "Hell's fire!" and pointed down the drive where five Federal troopers were in view at the far gate. Wash swung his carbine one-handed to his right shoulder.

"I'll take the two on the left."

"Maybe we could run for it," Tib suggested.

"They got seven-rail fences."

Leisurely the file of cavalry trotted up the drive. Even after four years, Tib hated to shoot from ambush, but he had no choice.

"Get your mark, Wash. When they break we'll ride through 'em."

But the ill luck of southern arms that day was with them. Before they could loose a shot, a man's body flung against Tib and pinioned him – a voice shouted beside his ear:

"Men! There're rebels here!"

As Tib wrestled desperately with Pilgrim, the northern patrol stopped, drew pistols. Wash was bobbing from side to side trying to get a shot at Pilgrim, but the doctor manoeuvred Tib's body in between.

In a few seconds it was over. Wash fired once, but the Federals were around them before he was in his saddle. Panting, the two young men faced the Federals. Dr Pilgrim spoke sharply to their corporal:

"These are Mosby's men."

Those years were bitter on the border. And nothing was more bitter than Mosby's name. Wash dodged suddenly, ran and sprawled dead on the grass in a last attempt to get away. Tib, still struggling, was trussed up at the porch rail.

"There's a good tree," said a soldier.

The corporal glanced at Dr Pilgrim.

"You know he's one of Mosby's men?"

"I'm in the Seventh Virginia Cavalry," said Tib.

"Are you one of Mosby's men?"

Tib didn't answer.

"All right, boys, get the rope."

Dr Pilgrim's austere presence asserted itself again.

"I don't want to hang him, but this type of irregular must be discouraged."

"We string 'em up by their thumbs sometimes," suggested the corporal.

"Then do that," said Dr Pilgrim.

By seven that evening, the road outside was busy again. Mail and fresh vegetables were moving towards the capital – the diversion was over, except for the stragglers along the Pike.

In the farmhouse it was quiet. Prince Napoleon was waiting for an ambulance from Washington. There was no sound – except from Tib, who, as his skin slipped off his thumbs, repeated aloud to himself fragments of his own political verses.

When it was late and the provost guard was dozing on the porch, someone came who knew where the stepladder was – she had heard them dump it after they strung up Tib. When she had half-sawed through the rope, she went back to her room for pillows and moved the table under him and laid the pillows on it. She did not need any precedent for what she was doing. When Tib fell with a grunting gasp, murmuring deliriously, "Nothing to be ashamed of," she poured a bottle of sherry over his hands.

It was a hot, sultry morning, with sleeping dust from the fields and leaves. Since midnight, Josie had been driving in the direction that Tib indicated before he lapsed into a broken sleep beside her; but as they approached the village she reined in and woke him gently.

Tib sat up with a jerk, stared at his hands wrapped in the tearings of a petticoat and remembered.

"We've got to find a doctor," Josie said. "I think we're in Virginia."

Tib stared around. "It looks like Louden County. Leave me anywhere."

"Not before we find a doctor."

That was the last thing he heard as his tired heart tried once more to leap out of his body. His knees buckled…

When he awoke hours later, everything was changed – they were in a glade of trees, with the horses hitched and standing. His hands burnt like fire.

"I know a doctor…" he murmured.

"We found a doctor and he fixed your hands. I wanted him to put you to bed – it seems that our cavalry… the Union cavalry are all over here. He didn't dare hide one of Mosby's men."

Her hand touched his hot forehead.

"You're exactly like an angel," he whispered drunkenly. "That's a fact."

"You don't know me," said Josie, but her fingers stayed on his forehead, pushed back the damp strands.

"If I could just get to one of our houses..." Tib fretted indiscreetly. "We have a chain of sympathizers' houses right through the Yankee lines. Or else I could go due east to Georgetown."

"Georgetown!" Josie exclaimed. "That's part of Washington."

"If you think I haven't been in Washington often enough..." He stopped himself and added cryptically. "Not as a spy, mind you – as a dispatch carrier."

"It seems too risky to go there."

"Longest way around, shortest way home."

He closed his eyes – then surprisingly he added: "We can get married in Lynchburg."

In the dim world of the journey it seemed to him that he had proposed to Josie somewhere and she had accepted.

"Try to sleep until it's dark," she whispered.

As he slept, she watched him. Then, exhausted herself, she lay down beside him, moving his head till it rested on her shoulder.

When she awoke it was dark; she felt that he was awake too, but she did not speak. Why not wait a while – wait like this – alive through the very recklessness of her protest and its unknown consequence. Who was she now? What had she done with herself in twenty hours?

After an hour a faint chill from the uplands sifted through the glade.

"What are you?" he demanded suddenly. "You're a good girl, I know—"

"Just another human being."

He considered for a moment. "You're coming on South with me. When we get to our lines we can be married."

"That's not a good idea. I must go to Washington. My brother'll understand – in his own way."

They got up and walked to where the horses had stood patiently through the hours. Before they got into the buggy, Josie turned to him suddenly, and for a moment they faded into the sweet darkness, so deep that they were darker than the darkness – darker than the black trees – then so dark that when she tried to look up at him she could but look at the black waves of the universe over his shoulder and say, "Yes, I'll go with you if you want – anywhere. I love you too."

It was a long night. Somewhere outside the first ring of Washington forts they stopped the horses; Tib went into a farmhouse he knew and came out in civilian clothes with the papers of a Kentucky deserter. Josie gave her own name at the barriers and showed a letter from the hospital where she was to nurse.

Then along the sleeping streets of Georgetown with the horses nodding and drowsing in their traces.

"That house on the corner," he said. "This is the only possible danger. Sometimes they get on to the southern stations and set traps. I'll go in alone first…"

He pulled with his teeth at the bandage on one hand and she cried out in protest.

"I'll just free this one. In case of any trouble I'd like to be able to use one hand. It won't hurt."

"It will!" she said in agony. "I wanted to wait till you were safe before I told you – the doctor had to amputate your thumbs."

"Oh."

With an odd expression, Tib stared down at the bandages.

"In order to save your hands."

"I can feel my thumbs."

"It's the nerves you feel."

Tib was out of the buggy like a flash – stood beside it trembling.

"Drive on," he said in a strange voice.

"What?"

"You were trying to pay for what your brother did. Drive on!"

In the brightening dawn she looked at him once more, all other feeling washed by a great surge of compassion. Then he was no longer there – and a sense of utter ruin crept slowly over her. She slapped the reins on the horses and drove down the street, aghast and alone.

April 1865. And Tib Dulany – by two days an ex-trooper of Confederate cavalry – looking into the bar of the Willard Hotel – in Washington, now a busy, noisy world. He had come on a desperate chance – turned his back on the dark years – to get a job in the West. It was for a test of his ability to forget the past that he had ridden penniless into the capital – the day after Lee's surrender. His story was the story of men who have fought in wars – at the newspaper offices:

"We're saving our jobs for our own men." In the printing shops they stared at his thumbs: "How do you set type with a mutilation?"

Tib went into a shop and bought gloves, as a sort of disguise; he got a trial at one place – but he was no good now as a journeyman printer. No good as a printer – no good now.

The atmosphere of the Willard bar – a boom-town atmosphere – depressed him. Upstairs, in the plush corridors, he quivered at the sight of women in fine clothes; he became conscious of his hand-me-down suit, bought in Alexandria, Virginia, that morning.

Then he saw Josie Pilgrim coming out of a dining room on the arms of two officers – more beautiful than he had remembered. She was a ripe grape; she was ready to fall for the shaking of a vine…

But it wasn't quite this that made him turn around and walk blindly in the other direction – it was rather that she was the same: she was the girl of those old nightmare hours, the girl whose brother's face he had conjured up in the last cavalry action.

And this had made her beauty a reminder of cruelty and pain.

In the past months, Tib had been trying to belittle her into a species of impressionable gamin – a girl who might have ridden off with *any* man. To certain people, the symbolism of women is intolerable. Because Josie's face represented a dream and a desire, it took him back to the very hour of his torture…

Later, when a fellow boarder in Georgetown buttonholed him on the stairs, he shook him off.

"Mr Dulany, I ask only a little of your time," the man said. "I know you were one of Mosby's men – a true Southerner – that you came to this house several times during the war…"

"Very busy," Tib said.

They were a ruined lot – Tib hadn't liked the spies with whom he had been in contact during the war – now, anyhow, he was absorbed in an idea of his own.

To get a fresh start, one had to even things up. Spew forth in a gesture the hate and resentment that made life into a choking muddle. He went upstairs and took a derringer out of his haversack.

An hour later Josie Pilgrim's carriage drew up in front of the boarding house. A woman held the front door half-open and looked at her suspiciously.

"I saw a friend, Mr Tib Dulany, in the Willard," she said.

She kept looking at the flounce on her French skirt.

"You want to see him?" the woman asked. "Please step inside." She took Josie by the arm like a doll, spinning her into the hall.

"Wait," she said.

As Josie waited obediently she was conscious of a scrutiny from the parted double doors of a parlour – first one pair of eyes, then another.

The woman came down the stairs.

"He's gone," she said. "Maybe he's gone for good."

Josie went back to her carriage – back to the state of mind where she lived between two worlds. Her beauty had not gone unnoticed in Washington. She had danced at balls with young men on government pay, and now in this time of victory she should be rejoicing – but she had seen the Glory of the Lord hung up by the thumbs – and then left her heart in the street in front of this house eight months ago.

Dr Pilgrim was busy packing when the housekeeper told him he had a patient below.

"Tell him I'm busy. Tell him I'm leaving the city – tell him it's nine o'clock at night."

"I did tell him. He said he was from another town – that you once operated on him."

The word operate aroused Pilgrim's curiosity. Patients seldom spoke of the new dental work as "operating".

"Tell him I'll be right down."

He did not recognize the young man wearing black gloves who sat in his parlour. He did not remember any previous transaction – moreover, he didn't like the young man – who took some time getting to the point.

The doctor was starting next day for France, on a special invitation from a cousin of Napoleon the Third, to take up plutocratic practice in Paris.

"You're a Southerner," he said, "and I have never practised my profession in the South."

"Yes, you have," Tib reminded him. "Once you practised within the Southern lines."

"That's true! I did. Thanks to that I am going to France…" He broke off suddenly – he knew who Tib was – he saw death looking at him from across the room.

"Why – it's you!" he said. "You're that rebel."

Tib held his pistol loosely in his hand, pointing at the floor. He slipped off his right-hand glove.

"There are servants in the house – and my sister—"

"She's at the theatre."

"What are you going to do?"

With a sudden surge of hate up into his throat:

"I'm going to shoot your thumbs off. You won't be much use in your profession, but you may find something else to do."

"They'll hang you – whatever I did to you was in discharge of my duty. Why – the war's practically over—"

"Nothing's over. Things won't begin till you and I start life on the same terms. Even this won't be as bad as what you did to me… I think we'll close the windows."

He got up without taking his eyes off Pilgrim. There were loud voices in the street now, but in his preoccupation Tib did not at first hear what they were calling. A window was flung up across the street and someone shouted from a passing carriage.

"The President's been shot! Lincoln's been shot!"

The carriage went on – the shouting voices multiplied – the quality of panic in them chilled Tib before he realized the import of the words.

"Abe Lincoln has been shot," he repeated aloud. Automatically he pulled down the last window.

"Oh!" groaned Pilgrim. "You people allowed to run loose in Washington!"

Into Tib's bedevilled head came the thought that the plot had been formed in the boarding house where he had laid his head last night – half-heard conversations became plain to him – that must have been the private business of the man who tried to speak to him on the stairs.

On the porch outside there were footsteps – Tib had scarcely put away his gun when Josie Pilgrim, a young officer by her side, hurried into the room.

"Brother, have you heard?" Seeing Tib, Josie's voice looped down: "The President was shot and killed in the theatre…" Now her voice was high, flicking at the lower edge of panic.

Dr Pilgrim stood up, trembling with relief at the interruption.

"It's a reign of terror!" he said. "This man…"

Josie crossed the room and stood beside Tib.

"So glad you're here," she said.

"So am I," Dr Pilgrim said. "Perhaps Captain Taswell will put him under arrest."

Confused, the officer hesitated.

"Captain Taswell," Josie said, "when you asked me to marry you, I told you there was someone else, didn't I?"

He nodded.

"This is the man. He and my brother have quarrelled. Nothing that my brother says about him can be believed."

"He came here to kill me!" Pilgrim announced with certain civility – sobered way down. He walked to the window, came back, sat down and listened to Tib's voice speaking loud and fierce:

"No. Not to kill you."

"My brother is afraid," Josie said, with calculated scorn. "He's bothered by something he did months ago."

Dr Pilgrim made himself speak coolly:

"This man happens to be a Mosby guerrilla."

As Captain Taswell's belief wavered between brother and sister, Josie did something irrevocable, crossed a bridge as definite as the rivers that mark the Virginia border.

"We ran away together," she said to Captain Taswell. "We were going to get married, but it seemed better to wait till the war was over."

Captain Taswell nodded.

"In that case, I'm afraid I'm in the way."

As he went out, Dr Pilgrim started to call after him, but his lips closed without sound. Josie looked earnestly at Tib. "I guess now you've *got* to marry me."

"You seem to be doing things for me always," Tib answered.

It has been whispered that there are only two kinds of women – those who take and those who give – and it was plain which kind Josie was. Even though his country was a desert of hate, Tib was no longer a soul lost by wandering in it.

The shocking news of the evening – still only faintly appreciated – had made a sea change. The strongest man had taken the burden upon his great shoulders, given life its impetus again, even in the accident of his death.

Dr Pilgrim realized something of the sort, for in the silence that ensued he made no comment; nor did he voice any objection when Josie made another decision:

"Tib, dear, I don't know where you're going – I don't know where we're going, but Brother and I would be awfully happy if you'd sleep in this house tonight."

On an Ocean Wave*

1

G ASTON T. SCHEER – the man, the company, the idea – five feet eight, carrying himself with dash and pride, walking the deck of the ocean liner like a conqueror. This was when it was something to be an American – spring of 1929.

O'Kane, his confidential secretary, met him in the morning on the open front of the promenade deck.

"See her?" Scheer asked.

"Yes – sure. She's all right."

"Why shouldn't she be all right?"

O'Kane hesitated.

"Some of her baggage is marked with her real initials – and the stewardess said—"

"Oh, hell!" said Scheer. "She should have had that fixed up in New York. It's the same old story – girl's not your wife, she's always sensitive, always complaining about slights and injuries. Oh, hell."

"She was all right."

"Women are small potatoes," said Scheer disgustedly. "Did you see that cable from Claud Hanson today that said he'd gladly die for me?"

"I saw it, Mr Scheer."

"I liked it," Scheer said defiantly. "I think Claud meant it. I think he'd gladly die for me."

Claud Hanson was Mr Scheer's other secretary. O'Kane let his natural cynicism run riot in silence.

"I think many people would, Mr Scheer," he said without vomiting. Gosh, it was probably true. Mr Scheer did a lot for a lot of people – kept them alive, gave them work.

"I liked the sentiment," said Scheer gazing gravely out to sea. "Anyhow, Miss Denzer oughtn't to grouse – it's just four days and twelve hours. She doesn't have to stay in her cabin just so she doesn't make herself conspicuous or talk to me – just in case."

Just in case anyone had seen them together in New York.

"Anyhow…" he concluded. "My wife's never seen her or heard of her."

Mr O'Kane had concluded that he himself would possibly die for Mr Scheer if Mr Scheer kept on giving him market tips for ten years more. He would die at the end of the ten – you could cram a lot into ten years. By that time he himself might be able to bring two women abroad in the same load – in separate crates, so to speak.

Alone, Gaston T. Scheer faced a strong west wind with a little spray in it. He was not afraid of the situation he had created – he had never been afraid since the day he had forced himself to lay out a foreman with a section of pitch chain.

It just felt a little strange when he walked with Minna and the children to think that Catherine Denzer might be watching them. So when he was on deck with Minna he kept his face impassive and aloof, appearing not to have a good time. This was false. He liked Minna – she said nice things.

In Europe this summer it would be easier. Minna and the children would be parked here and there, in Paris and on the Riviera, and he would make business trips with Catherine. It was a wilful, daring arrangement, but he was twice a man in every way. Life certainly owed him two women.

The day passed – once he saw Catherine Denzer, passing her in an empty corridor. She kept her bargain, all except for her lovely pale head, which yearned towards him momentarily as they passed and made his throat warm, made him want to turn and go after her. But he kept himself in control – they would be in Cherbourg in fifty hours.

Another day passed – there was a brokerage office on board and he spent the time there, putting in a few orders, using the ship-to-shore telephone once, sending a few code wires.

That evening he left Minna talking to the college professor in the adjoining deckchair, and strolled restlessly around the ship, continually playing with the idea of going to Catherine Denzer, but only as a form of mental indulgence, because it was twenty-four hours now to Paris and the situation was well in hand.

But he walked the halls of her deck, sometimes glancing casually down the little branch corridors to the staterooms. And, so entirely by accident, in one of these corridors he saw his wife Minna and the professor. They were in each other's arms, embracing, with all abandon. No mistake.

2

CAUTIOUSLY, SCHEER BACKED away from the corridor. His first thought was very simple: it jumped over several steps – over fury, hot jealousy and amazement – it was that his entire plan for the summer was ruined. His next thought was that Minna must sweat blood for this, and then he jumped a few more steps. He was what is known medically as a "schizoid" – in his business dealings too, he left out intermediate steps, surprising competitors by arriving quickly at an extreme position without any discoverable logic. He had arrived at one of these extreme positions now and was not even surprised to find himself there.

An hour later, there was a knock on the door of Mr O'Kane's cabin, and Professor Dollard of the faculty of Weston Technical College came into the room. He was a thin quiet man of forty, wearing a loose tweed suit.

"Oh yes," said O'Kane. "Come in. Sit down."

"Thank you," said Dollard. "What do you want to see me about?"

"Have a cigarette."

"No thanks. I'm on my way to bed, but tell me, what's it about?"

O'Kane coughed pointedly – whereupon Cates, the swimming-pool steward, came out of the private bathroom behind Dollard and went to the corridor door, locking it and standing in front of it. At the same time Gaston T. Scheer came out of the bathroom and Dollard stood up, blushing suddenly dark as he recognized him.

"Oh, hello..." he said. "Mr Scheer. What's the idea of this?" He took off his glasses with the thought that Scheer was going to hit him.

"What are you a professor of, Professor?"

"Mathematics, Mr Scheer – I told you that. What's the idea of asking me down here?"

"You ought to stick to your job," said Scheer. "You ought to stick there in the college and teach it, and not mess around with decent people."

"I'm not messing around with anybody."

"You oughtn't to fool around with people that could buy you out ten thousand times – and not know they spent a nickel."

Dollard stood up.

"You're out of your class," said Scheer. "You're a schoolteacher that's promoted himself out of his class."

Cates, the steward, stirred impatiently. He had left the two hundred pounds in cash in his locker, and he wanted to have this over with and get back and hide it better.

"I don't know yet what I've done," Dollard said. But he knew all right. It was too bad. A long time ago he had decided to avoid rich people, and here he was tangled up with the very worst type.

"You stepped out of your class," said Scheer thickly, "but you're not going to do it any more. You're going to feed the fishes out there, see?"

Mr O'Kane, who had bucked himself with whisky, kept imagining that it was Claud Hanson who was about to die for Mr Scheer – instead of Professor Dollard, who had not offered himself for a sacrifice. There was still a moment when Dollard could have cried out for help, but because he was guilty he could not bring himself to cry out. Then he was engrossed in a struggle to keep breathing, a struggle that he lost without a sigh.

3

M INNA SCHEER WAITED on the front of the promenade deck, walking in the chalked numbers of the shuffleboard game. She was excited and happy. Her feet as she placed them in the squares felt young and barefoot and desperate. She could play too – whatever it was they played. She had been a good girl so long, but now almost everybody she knew was raising the devil, and it was a thrilling discovery to find that she could join in with such pleasure. The man was late, but that made it all the more tense and unbearably lovely, and from time to time she raised her eyes in delight and looked off into the white-hot wake of the steamer.

The Woman from Twenty-One

A H, WHAT A DAY for Raymond Torrence! Once you knew that your roots were safely planted outside megalopolitanism, what fun it was to come back – every five years. He and Elizabeth woke up to the frozen music of Fifth Avenue and 59th Street, and first thing went down to his publishers on Fifth Avenue. Elizabeth, who was half Javanese and had never been in America before, liked it best of all there, because her husband's book was on multiple display in the window. She liked it in the store, where she squeezed Ray's hand tensely when people asked for it, and again when they bought it.

They lunched at the Stork Club with Hat Milbank, a pal of Ray's at college and in the war. Of course no one there recognized Ray after these years, but a man came in with the Book in his hands, crumpling up the jacket. Afterwards Hat asked them down to old Westbury to see the polo in which he still performed, but they went to the hotel and rested, as they did in Java. Otherwise it would all be a little too much. Elizabeth wrote a letter to the children in Suva and told them "everyone in New York" was reading father's book, and admired the photograph which Janice had taken of a girl sick with yaws.

They went alone to a play by William Saroyan.* After the curtain had been up five minutes, the woman from Twenty-One came in.

She was in the mid-thirties, dark and pretty. As she took her seat beside Ray Torrence, she continued her conversation in a voice that was for outside and Elizabeth was a little sorry for her, because obviously she did not know she was making herself a nuisance. They were a quartet – two in front. The girl's escort was a tall and good-looking man. The woman, leaning forward in her seat and talking to her friend in front, distracted Ray a little, but not overwhelmingly, until she said in a conversational voice that must have reached the actors on the stage:

"Let's all go back to Twenty-One."

Her escort replied in a whisper and there was quiet for a moment. Then the woman drew a long, long sigh, culminating in an exhausted groan, in which could be distinguished the words "Oh, my God".

Her friend in front turned around so sweetly that Ray thought the woman next to him must be someone very prominent and powerful – an Astor or a Vanderbilt or a Roosevelt.

"See a little bit of it," suggested her friend.

The woman from Twenty-One flopped forward with a dynamic movement and began an audible but indecipherable conversation in which the number of the restaurant occurred again and again. When she shifted restlessly back into her chair with another groaning "My God!" – this time directed towards the play – Raymond turned his head sideways and uttered a prayer to her aloud:

"Please."

If Ray had muttered a four-letter word, the effect could not have been more catalytic. The woman flashed about and regarded him – her eyes ablaze with the gastric hatred of many dying Martinis and with something more. These were the unmistakable eyes of Mrs Richbitch, that leftist creation as devoid of nuance as Mrs Jiggs.* As they burned with scalding arrogance – the very eyes of the Russian lady who let her coachman freeze outside while she wept at poverty in a play – at this moment Ray recognized a girl with whom he had played run sheep run in Pittsburgh twenty years ago.

The woman did not, after all, excoriate him, but this time her flop forward was so violent that it rocked the row ahead.

"Can you bel*ieve*… can you imagine…"

Her voice raced along in a hoarse whisper. Presently she lunged sideways towards her escort and told him of the outrage. His eye caught Ray's in a flickering embarrassed glance. On the other side of Ray, Elizabeth became disturbed and alarmed.

Ray did not remember the last five minutes of the act – beside him smouldered fury, and he knew its name and the shape of its legs. Wanting nothing less than to kill, he hoped her man would speak to him or even look at him in a certain way during the entr'acte – but when it came the party stood up quickly, and the woman said: "We'll go to Twenty-One."

On the crowded sidewalk between the acts, Elizabeth talked softly to Ray. She did not seem to think it was of any great importance except for the effect on him. He agreed in theory – but when they went inside again the woman from Twenty-One was already in her place, smoking and waving a cigarette.

"I could speak to the usher," Ray muttered.

"Never mind," said Elizabeth quickly. "In France you smoke in the music halls."

"But you have some place to put the butt. She's going to crush it out in my lap!"

In the sequel she spread the butt on the carpet and kept rubbing it in. Since a lady lush moves in mutually exclusive preoccupations just as a gent does, and the woman had passed beyond her preoccupation with Ray, things were tensely quiet.

When the lights went on after the second act, a voice called to Ray from the aisle. It was Hat Milbank.

"Hello, hello there, Ray! Hello, Mrs Torrence. Do you want to go to Twenty-One after the theatre?"

His glance fell upon the people in between.

"Hello, Jidge," he said to the woman's escort; to the other three, who called him eagerly by name, he answered with an inclusive nod. Ray and Elizabeth crawled out over them. Ray told the story to Hat, who seemed to ascribe as little importance to it as Elizabeth did, and wanted to know if he could come out to Fiji this spring.

But the effect upon Ray had been profound. It made him remember why he had left New York in the first place. This woman was what everything was for. She should have been humble, not awful, but she had become confused and thought she should be awful.

So Ray and Elizabeth would go back to Java, unmounted by anyone except Hat. Elizabeth would be a little disappointed at not seeing any more plays and not going to Palm Beach, and wouldn't like having to pack so late at night. But in a silently communicable way, she would understand. In a sense she would be glad. She even guessed that it was the children Ray was running to – to save them and shield them from all the walking dead.

When they went back to their seats for the third act, the party from Twenty-One were no longer there – nor did they come in later. It had clearly been another game of run sheep run.

Discard (Director's Special)

T HE MAN AND THE BOY TALKED intermittently as they drove down Ventura Boulevard in the cool of the morning. The boy, George Baker, was dressed in the austere grey of a military school.

"This is very nice of you, Mr Jerome."

"Not at all. Glad I happened by. I have to pass your school going to the studio every morning."

"What a school!" George volunteered emphatically. "All I do is teach peewees the drill I learnt last year. Anyhow I wouldn't go to any war – unless it was in the Sahara or Morocco or the Afghan post."

James Jerome, who was casting a difficult part in his mind, answered with "Hm!" Then, feeling inadequate, he added:

"But you told me you're learning math – and French."

"What good is French?"

"What good – say, I wouldn't take *any*thing for the French I learnt in the war and just after."

That was a long speech for Jerome; he did not guess that presently he would make a longer one.

"That's just it," George said eagerly. "When you were young, it was the war, but now it's pictures. I could be getting a start in pictures, but Dolly is narrow-minded." Hastily he added, "I know you like her; I know everybody does, and I'm lucky to be her nephew, but..." he resumed his brooding, "but I'm sixteen, and if I was in pictures I could go around more like Mickey Rooney and the Dead-Ends – or even Freddie Bartholomew."*

"You mean act in pictures?"

George laughed modestly.

"Not with these ears; but there's a lot of other angles. You're a director; you know. And Dolly could get me a start."

The mountains were dear as bells when they twisted west into the traffic of Studio City.

"Dolly's been wonderful," conceded George, "but gee whizz, she's arrived. She's got everything – the best house in the valley, and the Academy award, and being a countess if she wanted to call herself by it. I can't imagine why she wants to go on the stage, but if she does, I'd like to get started while she's still here. She needn't be small about that."

"There's nothing small about your aunt – except her person," said Jim Jerome grimly. "She's a *grande cliente*."*

"A what?"

Thought you studied French."

"We didn't have that."

"Look it up," said Jerome briefly. He was used to an hour of quiet before getting to the studio – even with a nephew of Dolly Bordon. They turned into Hollywood, crossed Sunset Boulevard.

"How do you say that?" George asked.

"*Une grande cliente*," Jerome repeated. 'It's hard to translate exactly, but I'm sure your aunt was just that even before she became famous."

George repeated the French words aloud.

"There aren't very many of them," Jerome said. "The term's misused even in France; on the other hand it *is* something to be."

Following Cahuenga, they approached George's school. As Jerome heard the boy murmur the words to himself once more, he looked at his watch and stopped the car.

"Both of us are a few minutes early," he said. "Just so the words won't haunt you, I'll give you an example. Suppose you run up a big bill at a store, *and* pay it; you become a *grand client*. But it's more than just a commercial phrase. Once, years ago, I was at a table with some people in the Summer Casino at Cannes, in France. I happened to look at the crowd trying to get tables, and there was Irving Berlin with his wife. You've seen him…"

"Oh, sure, I've met him," said George.

"Well, you know he's not the conspicuous type. And he was getting no attention whatever and even being told to stand aside."

"Why didn't he tell who he was?" demanded George.

"Not Irving Berlin. Well, I got a waiter, and he didn't recognize the name; nothing was done and other people who came later were getting tables. And suddenly a Russian in our party grabbed the head waiter as he went by and said, 'Listen!' – and pointed: 'Listen! Seat that man immediately. *Il est un grand client – vous comprenez? – un grand client!'"*

"Did he get a seat?" asked George.

The car started moving again; Jerome stretched out his legs as he drove, and nodded.

"I'd just have busted right in," said George. "Just grabbed a table."

"That's one way. But it may be better to be like Irving Berlin – and your Aunt Dolly. Here's the school."

"This certainly was nice of you, Mr Jerome – and I'll look up those words."

That night George tried them on the young leading woman he sat next to at his aunt's table. Most of the time she talked to the actor on the other side, but George managed it finally.

"My aunt," he remarked, "is a typical *grande cliente*."

"I can't speak French," Phyllis said. "I took Spanish."

"I take French."

"I took Spanish."

The conversation anchored there a moment. Phyllis Burns was twenty-one, four years younger than Dolly – and, to his nervous system, the oomphiest personality on the screen.

"What does it mean?" she enquired.

"It isn't because she *has* everything," he said, "the Academy Award and this house and being Countess de Lanclerc and all that…"

"I think that's quite a bit," laughed Phyllis. "Goodness, I wish *I* had it. I know and admire your aunt more than anybody I know."

Two hours later, down by the great pool that changed colours with the fickle lights, George had his great break. His Aunt Dolly took him aside.

"You did get your driver's licence, George?"

"Of course."

"Well, I'm glad, because you can be the greatest help. When things break up will you drive Phyllis Burns home?"

"Sure I will, Dolly."

"Slowly, I mean. I mean she wouldn't be a *bit* impressed if you stepped on it. Besides, I happen to be fond of her."

There were men around her suddenly – her husband, Count Hennen de Lanclerc, and several others who loved her tenderly, hopelessly – and as George backed away, glowing, one of the lights playing delicately on her made him stand still, almost shocked. For almost the first time he saw her not as Aunt Dolly, whom he had always known as generous and kind, but as a tongue of fire, so vivid in the night, so fearless and stabbing sharp – so apt at spreading an infection of whatever she laughed at or grieved over, loved or despised – that he understood why the world forgave her for not being a really great beauty.

"I haven't signed anything," she said explaining, "east or west. But out here I'm in a mist at present. If I were only *sure* they were going to make *Sense and Sensibility*, and meant it for me. In New York I know at least what play I'll do – and I know it will be fun."

Later, in the car with Phyllis, George started to tell her about Dolly – but Phyllis anticipated him, surprisingly going back to what they had talked of at dinner.

"What was that about a *cliente*?"

A miracle – her hand touched his shoulder, or was it the dew falling early?

"When we get to my house I'll make you a special drink for taking me home."

"I don't exactly drink as yet," he said.

"You've never answered my question." Phyllis's hand was still on his shoulder. "Is Dolly dissatisfied with who she's... with what she's got?"

Then it happened – one of those four-second earthquakes, afterwards reported to have occurred "within a twenty-mile radius of this station". The instruments on the dashboard trembled; another car coming in their direction wavered and shimmied, sideswiped the rear fender of George's car, passed on nameless into the night, leaving them unharmed but shaken.

When George stopped the car, they both looked to see if Phyllis was damaged; only then George gasped: "It was the earthquake!"

"I suppose it was the earthquake," said Phyllis evenly. "Will the car still run?"

"Oh, yes." And he repeated hoarsely, "It was the earthquake – *I* held the road all right."

"Let's not discuss it," Phyllis interrupted. "I've got to be on the lot at eight and I want to sleep. What were we talking about?"

"That earth..." He controlled himself as they drove off, and tried to remember what he had said about Dolly. "She's just worried about whether they are going to do *Sense and Sensibility*. If they're not, she'll close the house and sign up for some play—"

"I could have told her about that," said Phyllis. "They're probably not doing it – and if they do, Bette Davis* has a signed contract."

Recovering his self-respect about the earthquake, George returned to his obsession of the day.

"She'd be a *grande cliente*," he said, "even if she went on the stage."

"Well, I don't know the role," said Phyllis, "but she'd be unwise to go on the stage, and you can tell her that for me."

George was tired of discussing Dolly; things had been so amazingly pleasant just ten minutes before. Already they were on Phyllis's street.

"I would like that drink," he remarked with a deprecatory little laugh. "I've had a glass of beer a couple of times, and after that earthquake – well, I've got to be at school at half-past eight in the morning."

When they stopped in front of her house there was a smile with all heaven in it – but she shook her head.

"Afraid the earthquake came between us," she said gently. "I want to hide my head right under a big pillow."

George drove several blocks and parked at a corner where two mysterious men swung a huge drum light in pointless arcs over paradise. It was not Dolly who "had everything" – it was Phyllis. Dolly was made, her private life arranged. Phyllis, on the contrary, had everything to look forward to – the whole world that in some obscure way was represented more by the drum light and the red and white gleams of neon signs on cocktail bars than by the changing colours of Dolly's pool. He knew how the latter worked – why, he had seen it installed in broad daylight. But he did not know how the world worked, and he felt that Phyllis lived in the same delicious oblivion.

After that fall, things were different. George stayed on at school, but this time as a boarder, and visited Dolly in New York on Christmas and Easter. The following summer she came back to the Coast and opened up the house for a month's rest, but she was committed to another season in the East, and George went back with her to attend a tutoring school for Yale.

Sense and Sensibility was made after all, but with Phyllis, not Bette Davis, in the part of Marianne. George saw Phyllis only once during that year – when Jim Jerome, who sometimes took him to his ranch for weekends, told him one Sunday they'd do anything George wanted. George suggested a call on Phyllis.

"Do you remember when you told me about *une grande cliente*?"

"You mean I said that about Phyllis?"

"No, about Dolly."

Phyllis was no fun that day, surrounded and engulfed by men; after his departure for the East, George found other girls, and was a personage for having known Phyllis and for what was, in his honest recollection, a superflirtation.

The next June, after examinations, Dolly came down to the liner to see Hennen and George off to Europe; she was coming herself when the show closed – and by transatlantic plane.

"I'd like to wait and do that with you," George offered.

"You're eighteen – you have a long and questionable life before you."

"You're just twenty-seven."

"You've got to stick to the boys you're travelling with."

Hennen was going first-class; George was going tourist. At the tourist gangplank there were so many girls from Bryn Mawr and Smith and the finishing schools that Dolly warned him.

"Don't sit up all night drinking beer with them. And if the pressure gets too bad, slip over into first-class, and let Hennen calm you."

Hennen was very calm and depressed about the parting.

"I shall go down to tourist," he said desperately. "And meet those beautiful girls."

"It would make you a heavy," she warned him, "like Ivan Lebedeff* in a picture."

Hennen and George talked between upper and lower deck as the ship steamed through the narrows.

"I feel great contempt for you down in the slums," said Hennen. "I hope no one sees me speaking to you."

"This is the cream of the passenger list. They call us tycoon skins. Speaking of furs, are you going after one of those barges in a mink coat?"

"No – I still expect Dolly to turn up in my stateroom. And, actually, I have cabled her *not* to cross by plane."

"She'll do what she likes."

"Will you come up and dine with me tonight – after washing your ears?"

There was only one girl of George's tone of voice on the boat and someone wolfed her away – so he wished Hennen would invite him up to dinner every night, but after the first time it was only for luncheon, and Hennen mooned and moped.

"I go to my cabin every night at six," he said, "and have dinner in bed. I cable Dolly and I think her press agent answers."

The day before arriving at Southampton, the girl whom George liked quarrelled with her admirer over the length of her fingernails or the Munich Pact* or both – and George stepped out, once more, into tourist-class society.

He began, as was fitting, with the ironic touch.

"You and Princeton amused yourself pretty well," he remarked. "Now you come back to me."

"It was this way," explained Martha. "I thought you were conceited about your aunt being Dolly Bordan and having lived in Hollywood—"

"Where did you two disappear to?" he interrupted. "It was a great act while it lasted."

"Nothing to it," Martha said briskly. "And if you're going to be like that…"

Resigning himself to the past, George was presently rewarded.

"As a matter of fact I'll show you," she said. "We'll do what we used to do – before he criticized me as an ignoramus. Good gracious! As if going to Princeton meant anything! My *own* father went there!"

George followed her, rather excited, through an iron door marked "Private", upstairs, along a corridor and up to another door that said "First-Class Passengers Only".

He was disappointed.

"Is *this* all? I've been up in first-class before."

"Wait!"

She opened the door cautiously, and they rounded a lifeboat overlooking a fenced-in square of deck.

There was nothing to see – the flash of an officer's face glancing seaward over a still higher deck, another mink coat in a deck chair; he even peered into the lifeboat to see if they had discovered a stowaway.

"And I found out things that are going to help me later," Martha muttered as if to herself. "How they work it – if I ever go in for it I'll certainly know the technique."

"Of what?"

"Look at the deckchair, stupe."

Even as George gazed, a long-remembered face emerged in its individuality from behind the huge dark of the figure in the mink coat. And at the moment he recognized Phyllis Burns he saw that Hennen was sitting beside her.

"Watch how she works," Martha murmured. "Even if you can't hear, you'll realize you're looking at a preview."

George had not been seasick so far, but now only the fear of being seen made him control his impulse as Hennen shifted from his chair to the foot of hers and took her hand. After a moment, Phyllis leant forward, touching his arm gently in exactly the way George remembered; in her eyes was an ineffable sympathy.

From somewhere the mess call shrilled from a bugle – George seized Martha's hand and pulled her back along the way they had come.

"But they *like* it!" Martha protested. "She lives in the public eye. I'd like to cable Winchell right away."

All George heard was the word "cable". Within half an hour he had written in an indecipherable code:

HE DIDN'T COME DOWN TOURIST AS DIDN'T NEED TO BECAUSE
SENSE AND SENSIBILITY STOP ADVISE SAIL IMMEDIATELY
GEORGE
(COLLECT)

Either Dolly didn't understand or just waited for the clipper anyhow, while George bicycled uneasily through Belgium, timing his arrival in Paris to coincide with hers. She must have been fore-warned by his letter, but there was nothing to prove it, as she and Hennen and George rode from Le Bourget into Paris. It was the next morning before the cat jumped nimbly out of the bag, and it had become a sizeable cat by afternoon, when George walked into the situation. To get there he had to pass a stringy crowd extending from one hotel to another, for word had drifted about that *two* big stars were in the neighbourhood.

"Come in, George," Dolly called. "You know Phyllis – she's just leaving for Aix-les-Bains. She's lucky – either Hennen or I will have to take up residence, depending on who's going to sue whom. I suggest Hennen sues me – on the charge I made him a poodle dog."

She was in a reckless mood, for there were secretaries within hearing – and press agents outside and waiters who dashed in from time to time. Phyllis was very composed behind the attitude of "please leave me out of it". George was damp, bewildered, sad.

"Shall I be difficult, George?" Dolly asked him. "Or shall I play it like a character part – just suited to my sweet nature. Or shall I be primitive? Jim Jerome or Frank Capra* could tell me. Have you got good judgement, George, or don't they teach that till college?"

"Frankly…" said Phyllis getting up, "frankly, it's as much a surprise to me as it is to you. I didn't know Hennen would be on the boat any more than he did me."

At least George had learnt at tutoring school how to be rude. He made noxious sounds – and faced Hennen, who got to his feet.

"Don't irritate me!" George was trembling a little with anger. "You've always been nice till now, but you're twice my age and I don't want to tear you in two."

Dolly sat him down; Phyllis went out and they heard her emphatic "Not now! Not now!" echo in the corridor.

"You and I could take a trip somewhere," said Hennen unhappily.

Dolly shook her head.

"I know about those solutions. I've been confidential friend in some of these things. You go away and take it with you. Silence falls – nobody has any lines. Silence – trying to guess behind the silence – then imitating how it was – and more silence – and great wrinkles in the heart."

"I can only say I am very sorry," said Hennen.

"Don't be. I'll go along on George's bicycle trip if he'll have me. And you take your new chippie up to Pont-à-Dieu to meet your family. I'm alive, Hennen – though I admit I'm not enjoying it. Evidently you've been dead some time and I didn't know it."

She told George afterwards that she was grateful to Hennen for not appealing to the maternal instinct. She had done all her violent suffering on the plane, in an economical way she had. Even being a saint requires a certain power of organization, and Dolly was pretty near to a saint to those close to her – even to the occasional loss of temper.

But all the next two months George never saw Dolly's eyes gleam silvery blue in the morning; and often, when his hotel room was near hers, he would lie awake and listen while she moved about whimpering softly in the night.

But by breakfast time she was always a *grande cliente*. George knew exactly what that meant now.

In September, Dolly, her secretary and her maid and George moved into a bungalow of a Beverly Hills hotel – a bungalow crowded with flowers that went to the hospitals almost as fast as they came in. Around them again was the twilight privacy of pictures against a jealous and intrusive world; inside, the telephones, agent, producers and friends.

Dolly went about, talking possibilities, turning down offers, encouraging others – considered, or pretended to consider, a return to the stage.

"You *dar*ling! Everybody's *so* glad you're back."

She gave them background; for their own dignity they wanted her in pictures again. There was scarcely any other actress of whom that could have been said.

"Now, *I've* got to give a party," she told George.

"But you *have*. Your being anywhere *makes* it a party."

George was growing up – entering Yale in a week. But he meant it too.

"Either very small or very large," she pondered, "…or else I'll hurt people's feelings. And this is not the time, at the very start of a career."

"You ought to worry, with people breaking veins to get you."

She hesitated – then brought him a two-page list.

"Here are the broken veins," she said. "Notice that there's something the matter with every offer – a condition or a catch. Look at this character part; a fascinating older woman – and me not thirty. It's either money – lots of money tied to a fatal part, or else a nice part with no money. I'll open up the house."

With her entourage and some scrubbers, Dolly went out next day and made ready as much of the house as she would need.

"Candles everywhere," George exclaimed, the afternoon of the event. "A fortune in candles."

"Aren't they nice! And once I was ungrateful when people gave them to me."

"It's magnificent. I'm going into the garden and rehearse the pool lights – for old times' sake."

"They don't work," said Dolly cheerfully. "No electricity works – a flood got in the cellar."

"Get it fixed."

"Oh, no – I'm dead broke. Oh yes – I am. The banks are positive. And the house is thoroughly mortgaged and I'm trying to sell it."

He sat in a dusty chair.

"But how?"

"Well – it began when I promised the cast to go on tour, and it turned hot. Then the treasurer ran away to Canada. George, we have guests coming in two hours. Can't you put candles around the pool?"

"Nobody sent you pool candlesticks. How about calling in the money you've loaned people?"

"What? A little glamour girl like me! Besides, now they're poorer still, probably. Besides, Hennen kept the accounts, except he never put things down. If you look so blue I'll go over you with this dustcloth. Your tuition is paid for a year…"

"You think I'd go?"

Through the big room, a man George had never seen was advancing towards them.

"I didn't see any lights, Miss Bordon. I didn't dream you were here; I'm from Ridgeway Real Estate…"

He broke off in profound embarrassment. It was unnecessary to explain that he had brought a client – for the client stood directly behind him.

"Oh," said Dolly. She looked at Phyllis, smiled – then she sat down on the sofa, laughing. "*You're* the client; you want my house, do you?"

"Frankly, I heard you wanted to sell it," said Phyllis.

Dolly's answer was muffled in laughter, but George thought he heard: "It would save time if I just sent you all my pawn checks."

"What's so very funny?" Phyllis enquired.

"Will your… family move in too? Excuse me; that's not my business." Dolly turned to Ridgeway Real Estate. "Show the Countess around – here's a candlestick. The lights are out of commission."

"I know the house," said Phyllis. "I only wanted to get a general impression."

"Everything goes with it," said Dolly, adding irresistibly, "…as you know. Except George. I want to keep George."

"I own the mortgage," said Phyllis absently.

George had an impulse to walk her from the room by the seat of her sea-green slacks.

"Now *Phyl*lis!" Dolly reproved her gently. "You know you can't use that without a riding crop and a black moustache. You have to get a Guild permit. Your proper line is 'I don't have to listen to this'."

"Well, I *don't* have to listen to this," said Phyllis.

When she had gone, Dolly said, "They asked *me* to play heavies."

"Why, four years ago," began George, "Phyllis was—"

"Shut up, George. This is Hollywood and you play by the rules. There'll be people coming here tonight who've committed first-degree murder."

When they came, she was her charming self, and she made everyone kind and charming so that George even failed to identify the killers. Only in a washroom did he hear a whisper of conversation that told him all was guessed at about her hard times. The surface, though, was unbroken. Even Hymie Fink roamed around the rooms, the white blink of his camera when he pointed it or his alternate grin when he passed by dividing those who were up from those coming down.

He pointed it at Dolly, on the porch. She was an old friend and he took her from all angles. Judging by the man she was sitting beside, it wouldn't be long now before she was back in the big time.

"Aren't you going to snap Mr Jim Jerome?" Dolly asked him. "He's just back in Hollywood today – from England. He says they're making better pictures; he's convinced them not to take out time for tea in the middle of the big emotional scenes."

George saw them there together, and he had a feeling of great relief – that everything was coming out all right. But after the party, when the candles had squatted down into little tallow drips, he detected a look of uncertainty in Dolly's face – the first he had ever seen there. In the car going back to the hotel bungalow, she told him what had happened.

"He wants me to give up pictures and marry him. Oh, he's set on it. The old business of *two* careers and so forth. I wonder…"

"Yes?"

"I don't wonder. He thinks I'm through. That's part of it."

"Could you fall in love with him?"

She looked at George – laughed.

"Could I? Let me see…"

"He's always loved you. He almost told me once."

"I know. But it would be a strange business; I'd have nothing to do – just like Hennen."

"Then don't marry him; wait it out. I've thought of a dozen ideas to make money."

"George, you terrify me," she said lightly. "Next thing I'll find racing forms in your pocket, or see you down on Hollywood

Boulevard with an oil-well angle – and your hat pulled down over your eyes."

"I mean honest money," he said defiantly.

"You could go on the stage like Freddie and I'll be your Aunt Prissy."

"Well, don't marry him unless you want to."

"I wouldn't mind – if he was just passing through; after all, every woman needs a man. But he's so *set* about everything. Mrs James Jerome. No! That isn't the way I grew to be, and you can't help the way you grow to be, can you? Remind me to wire him tonight – because tomorrow he's going East to pick up talent for *Portrait of a Woman*."

George wrote out and telephoned the wire, and three days later went once more to the big house in the valley to pick up a scattering of personal things that Dolly wanted.

Phyllis was there – the deal for the house was closed, but she made no objections, trying to get him to take more and winning a little of his sympathy again, or at least bringing back his young assurance that there's good in everyone. They walked in the garden, where already workmen had repaired the cables and were testing the many-coloured bulbs around the pool.

"Anything in the house she wants," Phyllis said. "I'll never forget that she was my inspiration and ideal, and frankly, what's happened to her might happen to any of us."

"Not exactly," objected George. "She has special things happen because she's a *grande cliente*."

"I never knew what that meant," laughed Phyllis. "But I hope it's a consolation if she begins brooding."

"Oh, she's too busy to brood. She started work on *Portrait of a Woman* this morning."

Phyllis stopped in her promenade.

"She did! Why, that was for Katharine Cornell,* if they could persuade her! Why, they swore to me—"

"They didn't try to persuade Cornell or anyone else. Dolly just walked into the test – and I never saw so many people crying in a projection room at once. One guy had to leave the room – and the test was just three minutes long."

He caught Phyllis's arm to keep her from tripping over the board into the pool. He changed the subject quickly.

"When are you… when are you two moving in?"

"I don't know," said Phyllis. Her voice rose. "I don't like the place! She can have it all – with my compliments."

But George knew that Dolly didn't want it. She was in another street now, opening another big charge account with life. Which is what we all do after a fashion – open an account and then pay.

Note on the Texts

The text of 'Zone of Accident' is based on the version published in the *Saturday Evening Post* (13th July 1935). The text of 'Fate in Her Hands' is based on the version published in the *American Magazine* (April 1936). The text of 'Image on the Heart' is based on the version published in *McCall's* (April 1936). The text of 'Too Cute for Words' is based on the version published in the *Saturday Evening Post* (18th April 1936). The text of 'Three Acts of Music' is based on the version published in *Esquire* (May 1936). The text of 'An Author's Mother' is based on the version published in *Esquire* (September 1936). The text of '"Trouble"' is based on the version published in the *Saturday Evening Post* (6th March 1937). The text of 'The Guest in Room Nineteen' is based on the version published in *Esquire* (October 1937). The text of 'In the Holidays' is based on the version published in *Esquire* (December 1937). The text of 'The End of Hate' is based on the version published in *Collier's* (22nd June 1940). The text of 'On an Ocean Wave' is based on the version published in *Esquire* (February 1941). The text of 'The Woman from Twenty-One' is based on the version published in *Esquire* (June 1941). The text of 'Discard (Director's Special)' is based on the version published in *Harper's Bazaar* (January 1948). The spelling and punctuation have been Anglicized, standardized, modernized and made consistent throughout.

Notes

p. 5, *a negotio perambulante in tenebris*: "Of the pestilence that stalks in the darkness" (Latin), from Psalm 91:6.

p. 6, *John D. Rockefeller*: John D. Rockefeller Sr (1839–1937) was a an American oil tycoon.

p. 11, *Shirley Temple*: Shirley Temple (1928– 2014) was a hugely successful child actress.

p. 15, *Clark Gable*: Clark Gable (1901–60) was one of Hollywood's leading stars.

p. 19, *Will Hays*: Will H. Hays (1879–1954) was the president of the Motion Picture Producers and Distributors of America. He famously imposed a code of censorship on the studios.

p. 21, *Lillian Gish*: Lillian Gish (1893–1993) was a major Hollywood actress whose career spanned seventy-five years.

p. 25, *The Breakaway*: A reference to 'Breakaway', a 1929 song by Jack Hylton (1892–1969) and his orchestra.

p. 31, *Your words is your bond – Portia*: In order to outwit Shylock, Portia, the heroine of Shakespeare's *The Merchant of Venice*, uses loopholes in the exact phrasing of contracts.

p. 38, *Federal Period*: The classical style of architecture in vogue in the US in the late eighteenth and early nineteenth centuries.

p. 45, *magasin de tabac*: "Tobacco shop" (French).

p. 47, *—soir... —chantée*: Shortened forms of "Bonsoir" and "Enchantée" – "Good evening" and "Pleased to meet you" respectively (French).

p. 52, *Carmagnole*: A song and dance, originally from Italy, which became popular during the French Revolution.

p. 57, *l'heure bleue*: "The blue hour" (French).

p. 61, *wagon-lit*: "Sleeping car" (French).

p. 63, *PLM*: A reference to the Compagnie des Chemins de Fer de Paris à Lyon et à la Méditerranée, a railway company which connected Paris to the French Riviera.

p. 66, *Top Hat*: A 1935 musical film directed Mark Sandrich (1900–1945) and starring Fred Astaire (1899–1987) and Ginger Rogers (1911–95).

p. 67, *Eliza on the ice*: A reference to an episode in *Uncle Tom's Cabin* (1852) by Harriet Beecher Stowe (1811–96), in which the runaway slave Eliza escapes over a frozen river.

p. 69, *Cheek to Cheek*: One of the most famous songs in *Top Hat*, written by Irving Berlin (1888–1989).

p. 72, *Una Merkel*: Una Merkel (1903–86) was a prominent Hollywood actress.

p. 104, *No, No, Nanette… Vincent Youmans*: *No, No, Nanette* was a 1925 musical comedy with music by Vincent Youmans (1898–1946) and lyrics by Irving Caesar (1895–1996) and Otto Harbach (1873–1963).

p. 105, *All Alone… How about Me*: All famous songs by Irving Berlin (see note to p. 69).

p. 106, *Berlin*: Irving Berlin (see note to p. 69).

p. 106, *this Mackay girl*: A reference to Berlin's wife, the novelist Ellin Mackay (1903–88).

p. 108, *Lovely… to know*: Misquoted lyrics from 'Lovely to Look At' (1933) composed by Jerome Kern (1885–1945) with lyrics by Otto Harbach (1873–1963).

p. 109, *Jerome Kern*: See note to p. 108.

p. 111, *Longfellow, or Alice and Phoebe Cary*: Henry Wadsworth Longfellow (1807–82) was an influential American poet. Alice (1820–71) and Phoebe Cary (1824–71) were sisters who published joint poetry collections.

p. 111, *Mrs Humphry Ward… Edna Ferber*: Mary Augusta Ward (1851–1920), who wrote under the name Mrs Humphry Ward, was a British novelist who enjoyed great success with novels like *Robert Elsmere* (1888). Edna Ferber (1885–1968) was a popular American novelist.

p. 115, *the Spirit of Seventy-Six, Haile Selassie*: References to the American War of Independence and Haile Selassie (1892–1975), Emperor of Ethiopia from 1930 to 1974.

p. 154, *To ease the pressure… back towards the west*: During the 1864–65 siege of Petersburg, Virginia, which ultimately led to a defeat of the Confederate troops led by Robert E. Lee (1807–70), the commander Jubal Early (1816–94) marched his troops through the Shenandoah Valley towards Washington, DC, but was forced to withdrew after the Union brought in reinforcements.

p. 154, *Secesh*: Secessionists.

p. 154, *CSA*: Confederate States of America.

p. 155, *Mosby*: John S. Mosby (1833–1916) was a Confederate cavalry commander who operated in northern Virginia during the American Civil War and was known for his adeptness at eluding Union troops in between his raids.

p. 155, *Grant... Old Abe*: A reference to the commanding general of the Union Army (and future President of the United States) Ulysses S. Grant (1822–85) and the President of the United States during the Civil War, Abraham Lincoln (1809–65).

p. 157, *Opération... Quelle horreur*: "Operation!... How dreadful!" (French).

p. 168, *On an Ocean Wave*: Originally published under the pseudonym Paul Elgin.

p. 173, *William Saroyan*: William Saroyan (1908–81) was a playwright and writer of short stories who specialized in depictions of immigrant life in California.

p. 174, *Mrs Jiggs*: The stereotypical harridan Mrs Jiggs, also known as Maggie, was one of the main characters of the popular comic strip *Bringing up Father* by George McManus (1884–1954).

p. 177, *Mickey Rooney... Freddie Bartholomew*: The actor Mickey Rooney (1920–2014) was a highly successful child star in the 1930s, as was Freddie Bartholomew (1924–92).

p. 178, *grande cliente*: "Important customer" (French).

p. 179, *Il est un grand client... un grand client*': "He is an important customer – you understand? – an important customer!" (French).

p. 181, *Bette Davis*: Bette Davis (1908–89) was considered one of the greatest Hollywood actress of her time.

p. 183, *Ivan Lebedeff*: Ivan Lebedeff (1894–1953) was a Russian actor who moved to the USA in the 1920s.

p. 184, *Munich Pact*: The Munich Pact, or Munich Agreement, was an international treaty signed between Germany, France, the United Kingdom and Italy, which recognized Germany's annexation of a German-speaking part of Czechoslovakia.

p. 186, *Frank Capra*: Frank Capra (1897–1991) was one of the most successful Hollywood directors of the 1930s and 1940s.

p. 191, *Katharine Cornell*: Katharine Cornell (1893–1974) was a famous American stage actress, who only ever appeared in one Hollywood film.

Extra Material

on

F. Scott Fitzgerald's

Image on the Heart
and
Other Stories

F. Scott Fitzgerald's Life

Francis Scott Key Fitzgerald was born on 24th September 1896 at 481 Laurel Avenue in St Paul, Minnesota. Fitzgerald, who would always be known as "Scott", was named after Francis Scott Key, the author of 'The Star-Spangled Banner' and his father's second cousin three times removed. His mother, Mary "Mollie" McQuillan, was born in 1860 in one of St Paul's wealthier streets, and would come into a modest inheritance at the death of her father in 1877. His father, Edward Fitzgerald, was born in 1853 near Rockville, Maryland. A wicker-furniture manufacturer at the time of Fitzgerald's birth, his business would collapse in 1898 and he would then take to the road as a wholesale grocery salesman for Procter & Gamble. This change of job necessitated various moves of home and the family initially shifted east to Buffalo, New York, in 1898, and then on to Syracuse, New York, in 1901. By 1903 they were back in Buffalo and in March 1908 they were in St Paul again after Edward lost his job at Procter & Gamble. The *déclassé* Fitzgeralds would initially live with the McQuillans and then moved into a series of rented houses, settling down at 599 Summit Avenue.

Early Life

This itinerancy would disrupt Fitzgerald's early schooling, isolating him and making it difficult to make many friends at his various schools in Buffalo, Syracuse and St Paul. The first one at which Fitzgerald would settle for a prolonged period was the St Paul Academy, which he entered in September 1908. It was here that Fitzgerald would achieve his first appearance in print, 'The Mystery of the Raymond Mortgage', which appeared in the St Paul Academy school magazine *Now and Then* in October 1909. 'Reade, Substitute Right Half' and 'A Debt of Honor' would follow in the February and March 1910 numbers, and 'The Room with the Green Blinds' in the June 1911 number. His reading at this time was dominated by adventure stories and the other typical literary interests of a turn-of-the-century American teen, with the novels of G.A. Henty, Walter Scott's *Ivanhoe* and Jane Porter's *The Scottish Chiefs* among his favourites; their influence was apparent in the floridly melodramatic tone of his early pieces, though themes that would recur throughout Fitzgerald's mature fiction, such as the social difficulties of the outsider, would be

Schooling and Early Writings

introduced in these stories. An interest in the theatre also surfaced at this time, with Fitzgerald writing and taking the lead role in *The Girl from Lazy J*, a play that would be performed with a local amateur-dramatic group, the Elizabethan Drama Club, in August 1911. The group would also produce *The Captured Shadow* in 1912, *The Coward* in 1913 and *Assorted Spirits* in 1914.

At the end of the summer of 1911, Fitzgerald was once again uprooted (in response to poor academic achievements) and moved to the Newman School, a private Catholic school in Hackensack, New Jersey. He was singularly unpopular with the other boys, who considered him aloof and overbearing. This period as a social pariah at Newman was a defining time for Fitzgerald, one that would be echoed repeatedly in his fiction, most straightforwardly in the "Basil" stories, the most famous of which, 'The Freshest Boy', would appear in *The Saturday Evening Post* in July 1928 and is clearly autobiographical in its depiction of a boastful schoolboy's social exclusion.

Hackensack had, however, the advantage of proximity to New York City, and Fitzgerald began to get to know Manhattan, visiting a series of shows, including *The Quaker Girl* and *Little Boy Blue*. His first publication in Newman's school magazine, *The Newman News*, was 'Football', a poem written in an attempt to appease his peers following a traumatic incident on the football field that led to widespread accusation of cowardice, compounding the young writer's isolation. In his last year at Newman he would publish three stories in *The Newman News*.

Father Fay and the Catholic Influence

Also in that last academic year Fitzgerald would encounter the prominent Catholic priest Father Cyril Sigourney Webster Fay, a lasting and formative connection that would influence the author's character, oeuvre and career. Father Fay introduced Fitzgerald to such figures as Henry Adams and encouraged the young writer towards the aesthetic and moral understanding that underpins all of his work. In spite of the licence and debauchery for which Fitzgerald's life and work are often read, a strong moral sense informs all of his fiction – a sense that can be readily traced to Fay and the author's Catholic schooling at Newman. Fay would later appear in thinly disguised form as Amory Blaine's spiritual mentor, and man of the world, Monsignor Darcy, in *This Side of Paradise*.

Princeton

Fitzgerald's academic performance was little improved at Newman, and he would fail four courses in his two years there. In spite of this, in May 1913 Fitzgerald took the entrance exams for Princeton, the preferred destination for Catholic undergraduates in New Jersey. He would go up in September 1913, his fees paid for through a legacy left by his grandmother Louisa McQuillan, who had died in August.

At Princeton Fitzgerald would begin to work in earnest on the process of turning himself into an author: in his first year he met confrères and future collaborators John Peale Bishop and Edmund Wilson. During his freshman year Fitzgerald won a competition to write the book and lyrics for the 1914–15 Triangle Club (the Princeton dramatic society) production *Fie! Fie! Fi-Fi!* He would also co-author, with Wilson, the 1915–16 production, *The Evil Eye*, and the lyrics for *Safety First*, the 1916–17 offering. He also quickly began to contribute to the Princeton humour magazine *The Princeton Tiger*, while his reading tastes had moved on to the social concerns of George Bernard Shaw, Compton Mackenzie and H.G. Wells. His social progress at Princeton also seemed assured as Fitzgerald was approached by the Cottage Club (one of Princeton's exclusive eating clubs) and prominence in the Triangle Club seemed inevitable.

September 1914 and the beginning of Fitzgerald's sophomore year would mark the great calamity of his Princeton education, causing a trauma that Fitzgerald would approach variously in his writing (notably in *This Side of Paradise* and Gatsby's abortive "Oxford" career in *The Great Gatsby*). Poor academic performance meant that Fitzgerald was barred from extra-curricular activities; he was therefore unable to perform in *Fie! Fie! Fi-Fi!*, and took to the road with the production in an attendant capacity. Fitzgerald's progress at the Triangle and Cottage clubs stagnated (he made Secretary at Triangle nonetheless, but did not reach the heights he had imagined for himself), and his hopes of social dominance on campus were dashed.

The second half of the 1914–15 academic year saw a brief improvement and subsequent slipping of Fitzgerald's performance in classes, perhaps in response to a budding romance with Ginevra King, a sixteen-year-old socialite from Lake Forest, Illinois. Their courtship would continue until January 1917. King would become the model for a series of Fitzgerald's characters, including Judy Jones in the 1922 short story 'Winter Dreams', Isabelle Borgé in *This Side of Paradise* and, most famously, Daisy Buchanan in *The Great Gatsby*. In November 1915 Fitzgerald's academic career was once again held up when he was diagnosed with malaria (though it is likely that this was in fact the first appearance of the tuberculosis that would sporadically disrupt his health for the rest of his life) and left Princeton for the rest of the semester to recuperate. At the same time as all of this disruption, however, Fitzgerald was building a head of steam in terms of his literary production. Publications during this period included stories, reviews and poems for Princeton's *Nassau Literary Magazine*.

Ginevra King and Ill Health

The USA entered the Great War in May 1917 and a week later Fitzgerald joined up, at least partly motivated by the fact that his

Army Commission

uncompleted courses at Princeton would automatically receive credits as he signed up. Three weeks of intensive training and the infantry commission exam soon followed, though a commission itself did not immediately materialize. Through the summer he stayed in St Paul, undertaking important readings in William James, Henri Bergson and others, and in the autumn he returned to Princeton (though not to study) and took lodgings with John Biggs Jr, the editor of the *Tiger*. More contributions appeared in both the *Nassau Literary Magazine* and the *Tiger*, but the commission finally came and in November Fitzgerald was off to Fort Leavenworth, Kansas, where he was to report as a second lieutenant in the infantry. Convinced that he would die in the war, Fitzgerald began intense work on his first novel, *The Romantic Egoist*, the first draft of which would be finished while on leave from Kansas in February 1918. The publishing house Charles Scribner's Sons, despite offering an encouraging appreciation of the novel, rejected successive drafts in August and October 1918.

Zelda Sayre   As his military training progressed and the army readied Fitzgerald and his men for the fighting in Europe, he was relocated, first to Camp Gordon in Georgia, and then on to Camp Sheridan, near Montgomery, Alabama. There, at a dance at the Montgomery Country Club in July, he met Zelda Sayre, a beautiful eighteen-year-old socialite and daughter of a justice of the Alabama Supreme Court. An intense courtship began and Fitzgerald soon proposed marriage, though Zelda was nervous about marrying a man with so few apparent prospects.

As the armistice that ended the Great War was signed on 11th November 1918, Fitzgerald was waiting to embark for Europe, and had already been issued with his overseas uniform. The closeness by which he avoided action in the Great War stayed with Fitzgerald, and gave him another trope for his fiction, with many of his characters, Amory Blaine from *This Side of Paradise* and Jay Gatsby among them, attributed with abortive or ambiguous military careers. Father Fay, who had been involved, and had tried to involve Fitzgerald, in a series of mysterious intelligence operations during the war, died in January 1919, leaving Fitzgerald without a moral guide just as he entered the world free from the restrictions of Princeton and the army. Fay would be the dedicatee of *This Side of Paradise*.

Literary   Fitzgerald's first move after the war was to secure gainful
Endeavours   employment at Barron Collier, an advertising agency, producing copy for trolley-car advertisements. At night he continued to work hard at his fiction, collecting 112 rejection slips over this period. Relief was close at hand, however, with *The Smart Set* printing a revised version of 'Babes in the Wood' (a short story that had previous appeared in *Nassau Literary Magazine* and

that would soon be cannibalized for *This Side of Paradise*) in their September 1919 issue. *The Smart Set*, edited by this time by H.L. Mencken and George Jean Nathan, who would both become firm supporters of Fitzgerald's talent, was a respected literary magazine, but not a high payer; Fitzgerald received $30 for this first appearance. Buoyed by this, and frustrated by his job, Fitzgerald elected to leave work and New York and return to his parents' house in St Paul, where he would make a concerted effort to finish his novel. As none of the early drafts of *The Romantic Egoist* survive, it is impossible to say with complete certainty how much of that project was preserved in the draft of *This Side of Paradise* that emerged at St Paul. It was, at any rate, more attractive to Scribner in its new form, and the editor Maxwell Perkins, who would come to act as both editor and personal banker for Fitzgerald, wrote on 16th September to say that the novel had been accepted. Soon after he would hire Harold Ober to act as his agent, an arrangement that would continue throughout the greatest years of Fitzgerald's output and that would benefit the author greatly, despite sometimes causing Ober a great deal of difficulty and anxiety. Though Fitzgerald would consider his novels the artistically important part of his work, it would be his short stories, administered by Ober, which would provide the bulk of his income. Throughout his career a regular supply of short stories appeared between his novels, a supply that became more essential and more difficult to maintain as the author grew older.

Newly confident after the acceptance of *This Side of Paradise*, *Success* Fitzgerald set about revising a series of his previous stories, securing another four publications in *The Smart Set*, one in *Scribner's Magazine* and one in *The Saturday Evening Post*, an organ that would prove to be one of the author's most dependable sources of income for many years to come. By the end of 1919 Fitzgerald had made $879 from writing: not yet a living, but a start. His receipts would quickly increase. Thanks to Ober's skilful assistance *The Saturday Evening Post* had taken another six stories by February 1920, at $400 each. In March *This Side of Paradise* was published and proved to be a surprising success, selling 3,000 in its first three days and making instant celebrities of Fitzgerald and Zelda, who would marry the author on 3rd April, her earlier concerns about her suitor's solvency apparently eased by his sudden literary success. During the whirl of 1920, the couple's *annus mirabilis*, other miraculous portents of a future of plenty included the sale of a story, 'Head and Shoulders', to Metro Films for $2,500, the sale of four stories to *Metropolitan Magazine* for $900 each and the rapid appearance of *Flappers and Philosophers*, a volume of stories, published by Scribner in September. By the end of the year Fitzgerald, still in his mid-twenties, had moved into an apartment on New York's West 59th Street and was hard at work on his second novel.

Zelda discovered she was pregnant in February 1921, and in May the couple headed to Europe where they visited various heroes and attractions, including John Galsworthy. They returned in July to St Paul, where a daughter, Scottie, was born on 26th October. Fitzgerald was working consistently and well at this time, producing a prodigious amount of high-quality material. *The Beautiful and Damned*, his second novel, was soon ready and began to appear as a serialization in *Metropolitan Magazine* from September. Its publication in book form would have to wait until March 1922, at which point it received mixed reviews, though Scribner managed to sell 40,000 copies of it in its first year of publication. Once again it would be followed within a few months by a short-story collection, *Tales of the Jazz Age*, which contained such classics of twentieth-century American literature as 'May Day', 'The Diamond as Big as the Ritz' and 'The Curious Case of Benjamin Button'.

1923 saw continued successes and a first failure. Receipts were growing rapidly: the Hearst organization bought first option in Fitzgerald's stories for $1,500, he sold the film rights for *This Side of Paradise* for $10,000 and he began selling stories to *The Saturday Evening Post* for $1,250 each. *The Vegetable*, on the other hand, a play that he had been working on for some time, opened in Atlantic City and closed almost immediately following poor reviews, losing Fitzgerald money. By the end of the year his income had shot up to $28,759.78, but he had spent more than that on the play and fast living, and found himself in debt as a result.

The Fitzgeralds' high living was coming at an even higher price. In an attempt to finish his new project Fitzgerald set out for Europe with Zelda and landed up on the French Riviera, a situation that provided the author with the space and time to make some real progress on his novel. While there, however, Zelda met Édouard Jozan, a French pilot, and began a romantic entanglement that put a heavy strain on her marriage. This scenario has been read by some as influencing the final drafting of *The Great Gatsby*, notably Gatsby's disillusionment with Daisy. It would also provide one of the central threads of *Tender Is the Night*, while Gerald and Sara Murphy, two friends they made on the Riviera, would be models for that novel's central characters. Throughout 1924 their relations became more difficult, their volatility was expressed through increasingly erratic behaviour and by the end of the year Fitzgerald's drinking was developing into alcoholism.

Some progress was made on the novel, however, and a draft was sent to Scribner in October. A period of extensive and crucial revisions followed through January and February 1925, with the novel already at the galley-proof stage. After extensive negotiations with Max Perkins, the new novel also received its final title at about this time. Previous titles had included *Trimalchio* and *Trimalchio in West Egg*, both of which Scribner found too obscure for a mass readership, despite Fitzgerald's preference for them, while *Gold-Hatted Gatsby*, *On the Road to West Egg*, *The High-Bouncing Lover* and *Among Ash Heaps and Millionaires* were also suggestions. Shortly before the novel was due to be published, Fitzgerald telegrammed Scribner with the possible title *Under the Red, White and Blue*, but it was too late, and the work was published as *The Great Gatsby* on 10th April. The reception for the new work was impressive, and it quickly garnered some of Fitzgerald's most enthusiastic reviews, but its sales did not reach the best-seller levels the author and Scribner had hoped for.

Fitzgerald was keen to get on with his work and, rather misguidedly, set off to Paris with Zelda to begin his next novel. Paris at the heart of the Roaring Twenties was not a locale conducive to careful concentration, and little progress was made on the new project. There was much socializing, however, and Fitzgerald invested quite a lot of his time in cementing his reputation as one of the more prominent drunks of American letters. The couple's time was spent mostly with the American expatriate community, and among those he got to know there were Edith Wharton, Gertrude Stein, Robert McAlmon and Sylvia Beach of Shakespeare & Company. Perhaps the most significant relationship with another writer from this period was with Ernest Hemingway, with whom Fitzgerald spent much time (sparking jealousy in Zelda), and for whom he would become an important early supporter, helping to encourage Scribner to publish *The Torrents of Spring* and *The Sun Also Rises*, for which he also gave extensive editorial advice. The summer of 1925 was again spent on the Riviera, but this time with a rowdier crowd (which included John Dos Passos, Archibald MacLeish and Rudolph Valentino) and little progress was made on the new book. February 1926 saw publication of the inevitable follow-up short-story collection, this time *All the Sad Young Men*, of which the most significant pieces were 'The Rich Boy', 'Winter Dreams' and 'Absolution'. All three are closely associated with *The Great Gatsby*, and can be read as alternative routes into the Gatsby story.

With the new novel still effectively stalled, Fitzgerald decamped to Hollywood at the beginning of 1927, where he was engaged by United Artists to write a flapper comedy that was never produced in the end. These false starts were not, however, adversely affecting Fitzgerald's earnings, and 1927 would represent the highest annual earnings the author had achieved so far: $29,757.87, largely from

Paris

Hollywood

short-story sales. While in California Fitzgerald began a dalliance with Lois Moran, a seventeen-year-old aspiring actress – putting further strain on his relationship with Zelda. After the couple moved back east (to Delaware) Zelda began taking ballet lessons in an attempt to carve a niche for herself that might offer her a role beyond that of the wife of a famous author. She would also make various attempts to become an author in her own right. The lessons would continue under the tutelage of Lubov Egorova when the Fitzgeralds moved to Paris in the summer of 1928, with Zelda's obsessive commitment to dance practice worrying those around her and offering the signs of the mental illness that was soon to envelop her.

Looking for a steady income stream (in spite of very high earnings expenditure was still outstripping them), Fitzgerald set to work on the "Basil" stories in 1928, earning $31,500 for nine that appeared in *The Saturday Evening Post*, forcing novel-writing into the background. The next year his *Post* fee would rise to $4,000 a story. Throughout the next few years he would move between the USA and Europe, desperate to resuscitate that project, but make little inroads.

Zelda's Mental Illness   By 1930 Zelda's behaviour was becoming more and more erratic, and on 23rd April she was checked into the Malmaison clinic near Paris for rest and assistance with her mental problems. Deeply obsessed with her dancing lessons, and infatuated with Egorova, she discharged herself from the clinic on 11th May and attempted suicide a few days later. After this she was admitted to the care of Dr Oscar Forel in Switzerland, who diagnosed her as schizophrenic. Such care was expensive and placed a new financial strain on Fitzgerald, who responded by selling another series of stories to the *Post* and earning $32,000 for the year. The most significant story of this period was 'Babylon Revisited'. Zelda improved and moved back to Montgomery, Alabama, and the care of the Sayre family in September 1931. That autumn Fitzgerald would make another abortive attempt to break into Hollywood screenwriting.

At the beginning of 1932 Zelda suffered a relapse during a trip to Florida and was admitted to the Henry Phipps Psychiatric Clinic in Baltimore. While there she would finish work on a novel, *Save Me the Waltz*, that covered some of the same material her husband was using in his novel about the Riviera. Upon completion she sent the manuscript to Perkins at Scribner, without passing it to her husband, which caused much distress. Fitzgerald helped her to edit the book nonetheless, removing much of the material he intended to use, and Scribner accepted it and published it on 7th October. It received poor reviews and did not sell. Finally accepting that she had missed her chance to become a professional dancer, Zelda now poured her energies into painting. Fitzgerald would organize a show of these in New York in 1934, and a play, *Scandalabra*, that would be performed by the Junior Vagabonds, an amateur Baltimore drama group, in the spring of 1933.

His own health now beginning to fail, Fitzgerald returned to his own novel and rewrote extensively through 1933, finally submitting it in October. *Tender Is the Night* would appear in serialized form in *Scribner's Magazine* from January to April 1934 and would then be published, in amended form, on 12th April. It was generally received positively and sold well, though again not to the blockbusting extent that Fitzgerald had hoped for. This would be Fitzgerald's final completed novel. He was thirty-seven.

Final Novel

With the receipts for *Tender Is the Night* lower than had been hoped for and Zelda still erratic and requiring expensive medical supervision, Fitzgerald's finances were tight. From this point on he found it increasingly difficult to produce the kind of high-quality, extended pieces that could earn thousands of dollars in glossies like *The Saturday Evening Post*. From 1934 many of his stories were shorter and brought less money, while some of them were simply sub-standard. Of the outlets for this new kind of work, *Esquire* proved the most reliable, though it only paid $250 a piece, a large drop from his salad days at the *Post*.

Financial Problems and Artistic Decline

March 1935 saw the publication of *Taps at Reveille*, another collection of short stories from Scribner. It was a patchy collection, but included the important 'Babylon Revisited', while 'Crazy Sunday' saw his first sustained attempt at writing about Hollywood, a prediction of the tendency of much of his work to come. His next significant writing came, however, with three articles that appeared in the February, March and April 1936 numbers of *Esquire*: 'The Crack-up', 'Pasting It Together' and 'Handle with Care'. These essays were brutally confessional, and irritated many of those around Fitzgerald, who felt that he was airing his dirty laundry in public. His agent Harold Ober was concerned that by publicizing his own battles with depression and alcoholism he would give the high-paying glossies the impression that he was unreliable, making future magazine work harder to come by. The pieces have, however, come to be regarded as Fitzgerald's greatest non-fiction work and are an essential document in both the construction of his own legend and in the mythologizing of the Jazz Age.

Later in 1936, on the author's fortieth birthday in September, he gave an interview in *The New York Post* to Michael Mok. The article was a sensationalist hatchet job entitled 'Scott Fitzgerald, 40, Engulfed in Despair' and showed him as a

Suicide Attempt and Worsening Health

depressed dipsomaniac. The publication of the article wounded Fitzgerald further and he tried to take his own life through an overdose of morphine. After this his health continued to deteriorate and various spates in institutions followed, for influenza, for tuberculosis and, repeatedly, in attempts to treat his alcoholism.

His inability to rely on his own physical and literary powers meant a significant drop in his earning capabilities; by 1937 his debts exceeded $40,000, much of which was owed to his agent Ober and his editor Perkins, while Fitzgerald still had to pay Zelda's medical fees and support his daughter and himself. A solution to this desperate situation appeared in July: MGM would hire him as a screenwriter at $1,000 a week for six months. He went west, hired an apartment and set about his work. He contributed to various films, usually in collaboration with other writers, a system that irked him. Among these were *A Yank at Oxford* and various stillborn projects, including *Infidelity*, which was to have starred Joan Crawford, and an adaptation of 'Babylon Revisited'. He only received one screen credit from this time, for an adaptation of Erich Maria Remarque's novel *Three Comrades*, produced by Joseph Mankiewicz. His work on this picture led to a renewal of his contract, but no more credits followed.

Sheila Graham   While in Hollywood Fitzgerald met Sheila Graham, a twenty-eight-year-old English gossip columnist, with whom he began an affair. Graham, who initially attracted Fitzgerald because of her physical similarity to the youthful Zelda, became Fitzgerald's partner during the last years of his life, cohabiting with the author quite openly in Los Angeles. It seems unlikely that Zelda, still in medical care, ever knew about her. Graham had risen up from a rather murky background in England and Fitzgerald set about improving her with his "College of One", aiming to introduce her to his favoured writers and thinkers. She would be the model for Kathleen Moore in *The Last Tycoon*.

Among the film projects he worked on at this time were *Madame Curie* and *Gone with the Wind*, neither of which earned him a credit. The contract with MGM was terminated in 1939 and Fitzgerald became a freelance screenwriter. While engaged on the screenplay for *Winter Carnival* for United Artists, Fitzgerald went on a drinking spree at Dartmouth College, resulting in his getting fired. A final period of alcoholic excess followed, marring a trip to Cuba with Zelda in April and worsening his financial straits. At this time Ober finally pulled the plug and refused to lend Fitzgerald any more money, though he would continue to support Scottie, Fitzgerald's daughter, whom the Obers had effectively brought up. The writer, now his own agent, began working on a Hollywood novel based on the the life of the famous Hollywood producer Irving Thalberg.

Hollywood would also be the theme of the last fiction Fitzgerald would see published; the Pat Hobby stories. These appeared in *Esquire* beginning in January 1940 and continued till after the author's death, ending in July 1941 and appearing in each monthly number between those dates.

In November 1940 Fitzgerald suffered a heart attack and *Death* was told to rest, which he did at Graham's apartment. On 21st December he had another heart attack and died, aged just forty-four. Permission was refused to bury him in St Mary's Church in Rockville, Maryland, where his father had been buried, because Fitzgerald was not a practising Catholic. Instead he was buried at Rockville Union Cemetery on 27th December 1940. In 1975 Scottie Fitzgerald would successfully petition to have her mother and father moved to the family plot at St Mary's.

Following Fitzgerald's death his old college friend Edmund Wilson would edit Fitzgerald's incomplete final novel, shaping his drafts and notes into *The Last Tycoon*, which was published in 1941 by Scribner. Wilson also collected Fitzgerald's confessional *Esquire* pieces and published them with a selection of related short stories and essays as *The Crack-up and Other Pieces and Stories* in 1945.

Zelda lived on until 1948, in and out of mental hospitals. After reading *The Last Tycoon* she began work on *Caesar's Things*, a novel that was not finished when the Highland hospital caught fire and she died, locked in her room in preparation for electro-shock therapy.

F. Scott Fitzgerald's Works

Fitzgerald's first novel, *This Side of Paradise*, set the tone for his *This Side of* later classic works. The novel was published in 1920 and was a *Paradise* remarkable success, impressing critics and readers alike. Amory Blaine, the directionless and guilelessly dissolute protagonist, is an artistically semi-engaged innocent, and perilously, though charmingly unconsciously, déclassé. His long drift towards destruction (and implicit reincarnation as Fitzgerald himself) sees Blaine's various arrogances challenged one by one as he moves from a well-heeled life in the Midwest through private school and middling social successes at Princeton towards a life of vague and unrewarding artistic involvement. Beneath Fitzgerald's precise observations of American high society in the late 1910s can be witnessed the creation of a wholly new American type, and Blaine would become a somewhat seedy role model for his generation. Fast-living and nihilist tendencies would become the character traits of Fitzgerald's set and the

Lost Generation more generally. Indeed, by the novel's end, it has become clear that Blaine's experiences of lost love, a hostile society and the deaths of his mother and friends have imparted important life lessons upon him. Blaine, having returned to a Princeton that he has outgrown and poised before an unknowable future, ends the novel with his Jazz Age *cogito*: "'I know myself,' he cried, 'but that is all.'"

Flappers and Philosophers

Fitzgerald's next publication would continue this disquisition on his era and peers: *Flappers and Philosophers* (1920) is a collection of short stories, including such famous pieces as 'Bernice Bobs Her Hair' and 'The Ice Palace'. The first of these tells the tale of Bernice, who visits her cousin Marjorie only to find herself rejected for being a stop on Marjorie's social activities. Realizing that she can't rid herself of Bernice, Marjorie decides to coach her to become a young femme fatale like herself – and Bernice is quickly a hit with the town boys. Too much of a hit though, and Marjorie takes her revenge by persuading Bernice that it would be to her social advantage to bob her hair. It turns out not to be and Bernice leaves the town embarrassed, but not before cutting off Marjorie's pigtails in her sleep and taking them with her to the station.

The Beautiful and Damned

The Beautiful and Damned (1922) would follow, another novel that featured a thinly disguised portrait of Fitzgerald in the figure of the main character, Anthony Patch. He was joined by a fictionalized version of Fitzgerald's new wife Zelda, whom the author married as *This Side of Paradise* went to press. The couple are here depicted on a rapidly downward course that both mirrored and predicted the Fitzgeralds' own trajectory. Patch is the heir apparent of his reforming grandfather's sizable fortune but lives a life of dissolution in the city, promising that he'll find gainful employment. He marries Gloria Gilbert, a great but turbulent beauty, and they gradually descend into alcoholism, wasting what little capital Anthony has on high living and escapades. When his grandfather walks in on a scene of debauchery, Anthony is disinherited and the Patches' decline quickens. When the grandfather dies, Anthony embarks on a legal case to reclaim the money from the good causes to which it has been donated and wins their case, although not before Anthony has lost his mind and Gloria her beauty.

Tales of the Jazz Age

Another volume of short stories, *Tales of the Jazz Age*, was published later in the same year, in accordance with Scribner's policy of quickly following successful novels with moneymaking collections of short stories. Throughout this period Fitzgerald was gaining for himself a reputation as America's premier short-story writer, producing fiction for a selection of high-profile "glossy" magazines and earning unparalleled fees for his efforts. The opportunities and the pressures of this commercial work, coupled with Fitzgerald's continued profligacy, led to a certain unevenness in his short fiction. This unevenness is clearly present in *Tales of the Jazz Age*, with some of Fitzgerald's very best work appearing beside some fairly average pieces. Among the great works were 'The Diamond as Big as the Ritz' and the novella 'May Day'. The first of these tells the story of the Washingtons, a family that live in seclusion in the wilds of Montana on top of a mountain made of solid diamond. The necessity of keeping the source of their wealth hidden from all makes the Washingtons' lives a singular mixture of great privilege and isolation; friends that visit the children are briefly treated to luxury beyond their imagining and are then executed to secure the secrecy of the Washington diamond. When young Percy's friend John T. Unger makes a visit during the summer vacation their unusual lifestyle and their diamond are lost for ever. The novella 'May Day' is very different in style and execution, but deals with some of the same issues, in particular the exigencies of American capitalism in the aftermath of the Great War. It offers a panorama of Manhattan's post-war social order as the anti-communist May Day Riots of 1919 unfold. A group of privileged Yale alumni enjoy the May Day ball and bicker about their love interests, while ex-soldiers drift around the edges of their world.

In spite of the apparent success that Fitzgerald was experiencing by this time, his next novel came with greater difficulty than his first four volumes. *The Great Gatsby* is the story of Jay Gatsby, born poor as James Gatz, an *arriviste* of mysterious origins who sets himself up in high style on Long Island's north shore only to find disappointment and his demise there. Like Fitzgerald, and some of his other characters, including Anthony Patch, Gatsby falls in love during the war, this time with Daisy Fay. Following Gatsby's departure, however, Daisy marries the greatly wealthy Tom Buchanan, which convinces Gatsby that he lost her only because of his penuriousness. Following this, Gatsby builds himself a fortune comparable to Buchanan's through mysterious and proscribed means and, five years after Daisy broke off their relations, uses his new-found wealth to throw a series of parties from an enormous house across the water from Buchanan's Long Island pile. His intention is to impress his near neighbour Daisy with the lavishness of his entertainments, but he miscalculates and the "old money" Buchanans stay away, not attracted by Gatsby's *parvenu* antics. Instead Gatsby approaches Nick Carraway, the novel's narrator (who took that role in one of the masterstrokes of the late stages of the novel's revision), Daisy's cousin and

The Great Gatsby

Gatsby's neighbour. Daisy is initially affected by Gatsby's devotion, to the extent that she agrees to leave Buchanan, but once Buchanan reveals Gatsby's criminal source of income she has second thoughts. Daisy, shocked by this revelation, accidentally kills Buchanan's mistress Myrtle in a hit-and-run accident with Gatsby in the car and returns to Buchanan, leaving Gatsby waiting for her answer. Buchanan then lets Myrtle's husband believe that Gatsby was driving the car and the husband shoots him, leaving him floating in the unused swimming pool of his great estate.

All the Sad Young Men

Of *All the Sad Young Men* (1926) the most well-known pieces are 'The Rich Boy', 'Winter Dreams' and 'Absolution'. All three have much in common with *The Great Gatsby*, in terms of the themes dealt with and the characters developed. 'The Rich Boy' centres on the rich young bachelor Anson Hunter, who has romantic dalliances with women, but never marries and grows increasingly lonely. 'Winter Dreams' tells the tale of Dexter Green and Judy Jones, similar characters to Jay Gatsby and Daisy Buchanan. Much like Gatsby, Green raises himself from nothing with the intention of winning Jones's affections. And, like Gatsby, he finds the past lost. 'Absolution' is a rejected false start on *The Great Gatsby* and deals with a young boy's difficulties around the confessional and an encounter with a deranged priest.

'Babylon Revisited' is probably the greatest and most read story of the apparently fallow period between *The Great Gatsby* and *Tender Is the Night*. It deals with Charlie Wales, an American businessman who enacts some of Fitzgerald's guilt for his apparent abandonment of his daughter Scottie and wife Zelda. Wales returns to a Paris unknown to him since he gave up drinking. There he fights his dead wife's family for custody of his daughter, only to find that friends from his past undo his careful efforts.

Basil and Josephine

Between April 1928 and April 1929, Fitzgerald published eight stories in the *Saturday Evening Post* centring on Basil Duke Lee, an adolescent coming of age in the Midwest, loosely based on the author's own teenage years. A ninth story, 'That Kind of Party', which fits chronologically at the beginning of the Basil cycle, was rejected by the *Saturday Evening Post* because of its description of children's kissing games, and was only published posthumously in 1951. These stories were much admired by both Fitzgerald's editor and agent, who encouraged him to compile them in a book with some additional stories. Fitzgerald did not act on this advice, but between April 1930 and August 1931 he published, again in the *Saturday Evening Post*, five stories focusing on the development of Josephine Perry, a kind of female counterpart to Basil Duke Lee. In 1934 Fitzgerald then considered collecting the Basil and Josephine stories in a single volume and adding a final one in which the two would meet and which would transform the whole into a kind of novel, but he shelved the idea, as he had doubts about the overall quality of the outcome and its possible reception. He was still favourable to having them packaged as a straightforward short-story collection, but this would only happen in 1973, when Scribner published *The Basil and Josephine Stories*.

The next, and last completed, novel came even harder, and it would not be until 1934 that *Tender Is the Night* would appear. This novel was met by mixed reviews and low, but not disastrous sales. It has remained controversial among readers of Fitzgerald and is hailed by some as his masterpiece and others as an aesthetic failure. The plotting is less finely wrought than the far leaner *The Great Gatsby*, and apparent chronological inconsistencies and longueurs have put off some readers. The unremitting detail of Dick Diver's descent, however, is unmatched in Fitzgerald's oeuvre.

Tender Is the Night

It begins with an impressive set-piece description of life on the Riviera during the summer of 1925. There Rosemary Hoyt, modelled on the real-life actress Lois Moran, meets Dick and Nicole Driver, and becomes infatuated with Dick. It is then revealed that Dick had been a successful psychiatrist and had met Nicole when she was his patient, being treated in the aftermath of being raped by her father. Now Dick is finding it difficult to maintain his research interests in the social whirl that Nicole's money has thrust him into. Dick is forced out of a Swiss clinic for his unreliability and incipient alcoholism. Later Dick consummates his relationship with Rosemary on a trip to Rome, and gets beaten by police after drunkenly involving himself in a fight. When the Divers return to the Riviera Dick drinks more and Nicole leaves him for Tommy Barban, a French-American mercenary soldier (based on Zelda's Riviera beau Édouard Jozan). Dick returns to America, where he becomes a provincial doctor and disappears.

The "Pat Hobby" stories are the most remarkable product of Fitzgerald's time in Hollywood to see publication during the author's lifetime. Seventeen stories appeared in all, in consecutive issues of *Esquire* through 1940 and 1941. Hobby is a squalid Hollywood hack fallen upon hard times and with the days of his great success, measured by on-screen credits, some years behind him. He is a generally unsympathetic character and most of the stories depict him in unflattering situations, saving his own skin at the expense of those around him. It speaks to the hardiness of Fitzgerald's talent that even at this late stage he was able to make a character as amoral as Hobby vivid and engaging on the page. The Hobby stories are all short, evidencing Fitzgerald's skill in his later career at compressing storylines that would previously have been extrapolated far further.

Pat Hobby Stories

The Last Tycoon   Fitzgerald's final project was *The Last Tycoon*, a work which, in the partial and provisional version that was published after the author's death, has all the hallmarks of a quite remarkable work. The written portion of the novel, which it seems likely would have been rewritten extensively before publication (in accordance with Fitzgerald's previous practice), is a classic conjuring of the golden age of Hollywood through an ambiguous and suspenseful story of love and money. The notes that follow the completed portion of *The Last Tycoon* suggest that the story would have developed in a much more melodramatic direction, with Stahr embarking on transcontinental business trips, losing his edge, ordering a series of murders and dying in an aeroplane crash. If the rewrites around *Tender Is the Night* are anything to go by, it seems likely that Fitzgerald would have toned down Stahr's adventures before finishing the story: in the earlier novel stories of matricide and other violent moments had survived a number of early drafts, only to be cut before the book took its final form.

– Richard Parker

Select Bibliography

Biographies:
Bruccoli, Matthew J., *Some Sort of Epic Grandeur: The Life of F. Scott Fitzgerald*, 2nd edn. (Columbia, SC: University of South Carolina Press, 2002)
Mizener, Arthur, *The Far Side of Paradise: A Biography of F. Scott Fitzgerald*, (Boston, MS: Houghton Mifflin, 1951)
Turnbull, Andrew, *Scott Fitzgerald* (Harmondsworth: Penguin, 1970)

Additional Recommended Background Material:
Curnutt, Kirk, ed., *A Historical Guide to F. Scott Fitzgerald* (Oxford: Oxford University Press, 2004)
Prigozy, Ruth, ed., *The Cambridge Companion to F. Scott Fitzgerald* (Cambridge: Cambridge University Press, 2002)

ALMA CLASSICS

ALMA CLASSICS aims to publish mainstream and lesser-known European classics in an innovative and striking way, while employing the highest editorial and production standards. By way of a unique approach the range offers much more, both visually and textually, than readers have come to expect from contemporary classics publishing.

LATEST TITLES PUBLISHED BY ALMA CLASSICS

To order any of our titles and for up-to-date information about our current and forthcoming publications, please visit our website on:

www.almaclassics.com